Turn My World Upside Down:

Jo's Story

Maureen Child

St. Martin's Paperbacks

TURN MY WORLD UPSIDE DOWN: JO'S STORY

Copyright © 2005 by Maureen Child.

Cover photo © Gettyimages.

ISBN: 0-312-99754-X
EAN: 9780312-99754-0

Printed in the United States of America

St. Martin's Paperbacks edition / August 2005

St. Martin's Paperbacks are published by St. Martin's Press, 175 Fifth Avenue, New York, NY 10010.

10 9 8 7 6 5 4 3 2 1

"A touching story of friendship, deep love and scorching passion . . . A very good read."

—*Old Book Barn Gazette*

"A heartwarming read filled with a terrific cast of characters."

—*Rendezvous Review*

"Romance and sexual tension . . . charming, emotional."
—*RoadToRomance.com*

Loving You

"Packed with very strong characters and lots of emotion . . . an unforgettable story, and a romance to treasure."

—*A Romance Review*

"Maureen Child always writes a guaranteed winner, and this is no exception. Heartwarming, sexy, and impossible to put down."
—Susan Mallery, bestselling author of *The Sparkling One*

Finding You/Knowing You

"An absolutely wonderful contemporary romance. A delightful blend of humor and emotion, this sexy love story will definitely keep readers turning the pages."

—Kristin Hannah, author of *Distant Shores*

"The Candellano family is warm and wonderful . . . you'll get swept up in the lives and loves of these passionate and fascinating individuals."

—*Romantic Times*

ST. MARTIN'S PAPERBACKS TITLES
BY MAUREEN CHILD

Finding You

Knowing You

Loving You

Some Kind of Wonderful

And Then Came You

A Crazy Kind of Love

Turn My World Upside Down:

♡

Jo's Story

One

Cash Hunter made Hugh Hefner look like a blushing virgin.

He'd been in Chandler more than a year now and the talk still hadn't died down. In fact, he'd earned a catchy little nickname. People called him "the Woman Whisperer." A title not unearned.

Josefina "Jo" Marconi remained immune, though.

Well, mostly.

"Ignoring me won't make me go away." Cash, in all his male gorgeousness, leaned one shoulder against the wall and crossed his booted feet. He moved slowly, lazily, as if he had all the time in the world.

Oh, Jo *so* wished he was wrong about that. He'd just walked into the Barclay house, instead of staying outside, where he was supposed to be finishing up the trim work. As annoying as Cash might be on a personal level, when it came to woodworking, the man was as talented as he was gorgeous. And that was plenty talented. Still, Jo'd managed to go all morning without actually having to talk to him. Figured it wouldn't last.

She never should have hired him to help repair and repaint the Barclay house. The man was determined to seduce her for some reason and saying no all the damn time was really tiring. But damn it, she was too short-handed to ignore experienced help.

She reluctantly lifted her gaze to meet his. The man was just too good-looking for any woman's self-control. Even *hers*. Of course, there was no way she'd let *him* know that.

Tall, with broad shoulders and long legs, Cash had black hair that was slightly too long, his dark eyes were too piercing, his wide grin too knowing, and to top it all off, he even smelled too good.

A serious irritation.

"What *will* make you go away, then?" Jo asked, her patient tone sugary sweet despite the annoyance pumping inside. Usually the soul of patience—despite what her sisters might think—Jo couldn't seem to help the spurt of temper. There was just something about this man that made her want to tear at her own hair.

Never taking his gaze from hers, Cash shifted and dropped into a crouch beside her. Resting his forearm across his knee, he grinned at her, and tiny lines at the corners of his eyes fanned out. "You agreeing to have dinner with me."

Jo's fingers tightened around the handle of her favorite hammer. "Like that's gonna happen."

He'd been playing this game for months. Didn't seem to bother him that she blew him off regularly. He didn't care that she never encouraged him—in fact, went out of her way to avoid him.

For whatever reason, she had become Cash Hunter's Mount Everest. Didn't matter how many other women had fallen at his feet. He was bound and determined to conquer *her*.

Well, he was doomed to disappointment. Jo Marconi wasn't about to be conquered. She wasn't interested in a man at the moment—hell, at *any* moment. Especially one with Cash's track record.

Cash was to women what kryptonite was to Superman. One night in the man's bed was apparently enough to convince even the most sane, reasonable, *intelligent* woman to give up her ordinary life and go do good deeds. One had gone off to join Habitat for Humanity, one was now in Chechnya, working with foreign adoptions, and still another was off volunteering with the Literacy Foundation.

Of course the talk around town now was that Cash had become a *monk.* According to the truly excellent grapevine in Chandler, he hadn't been out with *any* female in months.

Which, to Jo's mind, just meant he was getting desperate enough to keep bothering *her.*

"You know," she said tightly, "you're just one more straw tossed onto a camel who's already thinking about having a breakdown—when she can find a few extra minutes."

He lifted one shoulder in a shrug. "I could help."

"Is that right?" she asked, and slammed her hammer against a small finishing nail before she looked at him again. Just like a guy to think he could step right in and handle any situation better than a woman. "And just what kind of help would that be?" she asked, glaring at him with enough heat to sizzle his skin. "I've got one sister so pregnant she can't stand up, let alone work. Another sister just pregnant enough to hurl every fifteen minutes. My father and his girlfriend are off on a cruise, and I'm playing temporary mommy to a ten-year-old brother who hates my guts."

Cash laughed. "Jack doesn't hate you."

"I'm not so sure about that," she muttered, and thought about how the kid had looked at her just that morning when he'd headed off to school. It was the look that she used to give her biology teacher.

"I am. He's just a kid."

"I know," Jo muttered, shooting him a quick look, then shifting her gaze again. "And I wasn't fishing for sympathy."

Even though, God, saying it all out loud made her want to hop in her truck and hit the nearest freeway ramp. In three days, she could be *anywhere.* But almost as soon as the idle fantasy erupted in her brain, she shut it down again. She wasn't leaving, despite how tempting the thought was at the moment. If she left, who the hell would hold everything together?

Nope. She was going to keep doing what she *had* been doing.

Being the oldest Marconi sister.

Being the responsible one.

Being in charge. Even if that meant working double shifts to pick up the slack on their construction jobs— or dealing with a brother she hadn't even known existed this time last year.

Man, it really sucked being her.

And it really pissed her off to have Cash Hunter try to swoop in on a white charger and slay all of her dragons. For God's sake. Hadn't she made it plain enough that she just wasn't interested in being the next bouncee on Cash's bed? Hadn't she insulted him? Baited him? Ignored him at every opportunity? What did it take to get through to a guy like this?

Her hand fisted around her hammer again, and

briefly, she gave in to the indulgent daydream of giving him a good thump with the business end. But then he'd be unconscious and she'd have to drag his body to a clinic. And who had time for that?

"So, Mr. Wonderful," she said tightly, when he only continued to stare at her through those dark, liquid chocolate eyes. "If you really want to help, how about you go finish up the trim work? You know . . . *outside*?"

He smiled at her. "Mr. Wonderful. I like that."

"You would." Wouldn't you know that would be the only part of her statement that he paid attention to? Honestly, the man was a walking hormone.

"How's Jack doing, anyway?"

Good question. Her little brother hardly spoke to her. But then, he hadn't exactly had a great year, either. At ten years old, he'd lost his mother three months before in a car accident, then been uprooted from his home in San Francisco to live with his father in Chandler. Not to mention, he had three sisters who were still walking a little warily around him.

It wasn't Jack's fault that Papa had had an affair with the kid's mother while Jo's mother, Papa's *wife,* lay dying. God. Just remembering it made Jo furious all over again. No one had ever guessed that Papa had been anything but a loving, faithful husband.

Until his minor heart attack a few months ago. For a few terrifying hours, they'd all felt the whisper of Death hovering close. So close that Grace Van Horn, Papa's sixtyish ladyfriend, had shattered the Marconi sisters' nice little world by insisting on calling the mother of Papa's *son*. Jo was the first one to admit she hadn't taken it well.

But then, finding out that the one man in the world

you trusted above everyone else had actual feet of clay was a real eye-opener. She'd just recently been able to look into Papa's eyes when she talked to him. And even now, the pain of betrayal was still there.

And so was Jack.

The unwitting reminder of her father's fall from grace.

As if they needed a reminder. Things were still . . . *uneasy* in the Marconi family. Oh, Jo's sisters, Sam and Mike, had made their peace with their father. But Jo . . . she hadn't been able to let go of the pain yet. The numbing sense of betrayal.

But she so didn't have time to think about all of this now. So didn't have the luxury to indulge in a good old-fashioned pity party with hats and balloons.

"Jack's fine," she said grimly, determined to believe it.

"Yeah," he said. "I'm convinced."

She gritted her teeth and tried to swallow down another flash of irritation. "What do you care anyway?"

He shrugged and Jo determined to not notice the ripple of muscle beneath the black T-shirt he wore. He so didn't need any more female fans.

"He's a good kid." Cash shifted position slightly as if he were suddenly uncomfortable. "A little lost, maybe. But good."

"I know." Jo sighed and hated to admit that the man had a point. Since moving to Chandler, Jack Marconi had wandered around the family home like . . . well, like a kid who'd had his world pulled out from under him. And she didn't have a clue how to help him through it.

Frowning at Cash, because she couldn't very well

frown at herself, she asked, "Don't you have an else-where to be?"

"Not at the moment."

"Lucky me." Okay, if he wouldn't leave, then she'd just go back to ignoring him. Not so easy, though, when he was right beside her, and she could feel his gaze pinned on her. Besides, his scent kept wrapping itself around her like some damn unwanted blanket.

Leather, spice, *male*.

Damn it.

"You know what your problem is?" Cash asked, his voice a lazy drawl.

"At the moment?" she asked. *"You."*

"Wrong."

She blew out a breath, slammed the head of her hammer against the finishing nail jutting up from the baseboard she was trying to attach. The heavy smack of metal on wood zinged up her arm and Jo enjoyed it. No matter what the rest of her world was like, she could always at least find pleasure in the work.

And when all else failed, she could use her hammer to beat the crap out of something. Always cathartic.

"Don't you want to know?" he prodded and inched back as she pressed ever onward.

"Do I get a choice?"

"Not really."

"Oh, then please," she said, looking up at him and fluttering her eyelashes until she was nearly blind. "Tell me so you can go about your merry way."

He grinned again, and Jo swallowed hard. The man was as attractive as he was annoying and God knew that was *damned* attractive.

"You're afraid of me."

She snorted and sat back. "You're a piece of work, you know that?"

"I like to think so."

She shook her head so hard, her dark brown pony-tail whipped around and slapped her in the eye. "You're incredible. I didn't mean that in a *good* way."

Sunlight poured in through the windows behind her and spotlighted Cash as if he were the only player on a stage. His dark eyes, filled with secrets and promises and all kinds of tempting things, were locked on her and there was a knowing smile on his handsome face.

That was his problem, she thought. Too many women over the years had thrown themselves at him. He'd come to think of himself as God's gift to womankind and every female he met had agreed with him. Until her.

Sure, she was attracted.

There was a nice little hum of electricity whenever he got near her.

But she was in construction. She knew damn well how much damage electricity could cause, so she wasn't about to go sticking her fingers—*or anything else*—in Cash Hunter's socket.

"So am I really that scary to you, Josefina?"

She winced. "I've told you like a million times I hate that name."

"Yeah, but I told you a million times I really do," he teased, that smile deepening. "So, how about it? You going to admit that I scare the crap out of you?"

"You really think you can *dare* me into your bed?" she asked and lifted the hammer. Not that she'd actually hit him with it or anything. Well . . . not unless he pushed her into it.

A damn dimple appeared in his left cheek. "Hey,

you're the one talking about *beds*. I said dinner."

A shriek sounded in her head and it was only through sheer determination and stubbornness that she was able to keep it from exploding out her mouth. "I don't have time for you," she snapped instead.

"One of these days, Josefina," he said, leaning forward until they were practically nose to nose. "You're going to have to *make* time."

Her teeth ground together as he pushed himself to his feet with a lazy motion. Then brushing his hands together, he hitched his tool belt a little higher on narrow hips. "Guess I'll go and finish packing up. Finished the trim already."

"Thanks for the news flash," she muttered. God, that she had come to this. Actually *hiring* Cash Hunter. But with her sisters Mike and Sam both too pregnant to be any help whatsoever, she'd had to hire on extra hands. Even if they were attached to the one man in the world who pushed all her buttons the wrong way.

"I really think you're starting to like me, Josefina," he said, his boot heels thumping on the hardwood floor as he headed for the kitchen door.

"And I think you're delusional," she said. "Wonder which one of us is right."

His laughter floated back to her as he stepped out of the room and it took Jo an extra minute or two to convince herself that she was *not* affected by that low, rich sound.

She wasn't.

She was almost sure of it.

Michaela "Mike" Marconi Gallagher pushed herself into a sitting position, then scooted her heavily pregnant bulk to the edge of the sofa. Bracing her hands on the highly polished coffee table, she gave a mighty heave and . . . *nothing*.

She glared at her belly and muttered, "You know, before you guys settled in down there, I could actually get up off a couch anytime I wanted to."

"What're you doing?"

"Apparently," she snapped, lifting her gaze to her husband, "not a damn thing."

Lucas Gallagher scowled at her, set down the tray of cookies he was carrying on the table and then loomed over his wife. "The doctor said bed rest. I compromised with the damn couch. But you *said* you wouldn't get up."

Mike tried smiling at him, but her husband was no pushover these days. He watched her like a mother hen chasing its last chick. And while she appreciated the loving concern, the lack of mobility was making her *nuts*. Which, for her, translated into crabby.

"Damn it, Lucas," she blurted, when his features remained stony, "I can't just *sit* here."

"You're right," he said, stepping around the table. Lifting her legs, he swung them back up onto the couch, then dropped a colorful crocheted afghan over her. "You're going to just *lie* there."

"Like a beached whale," she muttered, looking down at her huge belly.

He dropped one long-fingered hand onto the mound of their children and gave her skin a slow stroke. "The mother of my kids is *not* a whale." He paused, said, "A hippo, maybe."

Her eyes narrowed.

"Kidding, kidding," he said, laughing.

"You're either very brave or very dumb, Rocket Man," Mike muttered, willing herself not to chuckle as she covered his hand with hers. "Teasing a cranky woman with access to power tools is perhaps not your best move."

"I'm not worried," he said, and gave her that crooked smile that had first attracted her. "My wife loves me."

"Yeah?" Mike asked. "And why's that?"

"Because," he said, leaning down to stroke one hand across her swollen belly, "I happen to think my very pregnant wife is the most beautiful, the sexiest, the most incredible female on the face of the planet."

God, he could turn her to goo in no time at all. "Well, you're right. There is *that*."

"You're doing great, Mike," he said, and grinned again when one of the twins kicked at his hand.

"Oh yeah, great. I haven't been out of the house in *weeks*." She waved one hand at the high, arched window behind her. "Look. It's April. It's beautiful out there."

"If you're a good girl," Lucas said, straightening up again, "maybe I'll carry you out to the patio later."

Oh, Mike really hated it that he was being so nice. Took all the fun out of whining. "You gonna have Jo bring the crane over?"

"Just a dolly," he said, and bent down to plant another kiss on her forehead.

"Oh, that makes me feel *way* better."

The front door opened and her sisters' voices piped into the stillness.

"I don't know what you're complaining about,"

Samantha—"Sam"—was saying. "*You're* not the one tossing your cookies every twenty minutes."

"Yeah," Jo countered, "I'm just the one left holding the bag while you and Mike gestate."

"Okay," Lucas said, as the two women stalked into the room. "I'm out of here. You guys have a good meeting."

Then he disappeared. Like any smart man, he knew when to make himself scarce.

Jo carried a cardboard tray holding three cups of coffee and Sam held a bag with the Leaf and Bean logo on the front of it at arm's distance.

"Oh, at last. My daily dose of caffeine," Mike moaned.

"Thank God Shelly didn't pull you off the stuff cold turkey," Jo said as she handed over one of the tall cups. "As it is, you're a pain in the ass. Without caffeine, you'd be—well, unimaginable."

"I'd be insulted at that if it weren't true," Mike said, taking her first, glorious sip. "The good doctor said she didn't want to be responsible for all the resulting dead bodies that would no doubt surround me if she cut me off," Mike said, then asked, "Are those muffins?" as she reached for the bag.

"Blueberry," Sam said, through gritted teeth.

"Gimme."

Jo shook her head. "You keep eating like this and you're going to weigh three hundred pounds by the time you deliver."

"What do you mean, *going to*?" Mike asked, opening the bag and grabbing one of the still warm muffins. Greedily, she ripped off a chunk of the crunchy top and popped it into her mouth. She sighed as she chewed. "God, Stevie's the best."

Stevie Ryan Candellano, wizard of espresso machines and baker extraordinaire, owned the Leaf and Bean, and as far as Mike was concerned, the woman should be president.

"How can you eat like that?" Sam whispered, her face going pale as paper.

"Hey, the kids're hungry," Mike whined. When she'd first found out she was pregnant, she'd laughingly teased Lucas by saying she was going to have twins. As it turned out, she was right. Now she was just eight weeks from delivery and felt as big around as she was tall.

"Just last night I forced Lucas to call Terrino's and get me a large pizza with double anchovies." Mike shook her head in fond memory as she chewed. "I swear, even now, I can still taste the little fishies."

"Oooh, God . . ." Sam clapped one hand to her mouth and bolted for the guest bathroom off the kitchen.

Mike shrugged and took another bite.

"You don't even feel guilty, do you?" Jo asked, shaking her head at her youngest sister.

"Why should I? I already survived the pukey thing."

"Yeah," Jo said, leaning forward and glancing over her shoulder to make sure Sam was still out of hearing. "But she's like five months into it now. Shouldn't the hurling be over?"

"What am I?" Mike asked with a shrug. "The baby expert? Sam's the one who's done this before."

"Man," Jo said, grabbing her coffee and leaning back into the dark green sofa opposite the one Mike lay stretched out on like the Queen of Sheba. "Can't see why anyone would want to do it more than once."

"I can," Mike said, rubbing her belly. "It's great. Well, except for the whole 'lie down and shut up' thing." She paused for a minute, then, delighting in a fresh audience, she launched into a whine about feeling like a prisoner.

While her sister complained, Jo tuned her out and glanced around the living room of the Gallagher house. It was a great place, she had to admit. Shining tile floor, arched windows and doorways, and a kiva-shaped fireplace on one wall.

Less than a year ago, Lucas Gallagher had moved to Chandler to build this house exactly where Mike had planned to build her own dream house. Mike, being Mike, had driven the poor guy nuts, hanging around, changing things, reworking his plans to fit her vision. And instead of strangling her, which Jo had been half expecting, Lucas had fallen for the youngest Marconi.

Apparently, true love could bloom in even the rockiest ground.

Though she had to hand it to Mike. The woman had great taste. The house was beautiful, and because a Marconi had been involved in the building of it, Jo knew the place was built to last.

She and her sisters had been working in the family construction business since they were old enough to swing a hammer and hit the target. Their father had trained them, taught them, and together, they'd built Marconi construction into one of the top outfits in Northern California.

"So how's Cash working out?" Mike asked.

Speak of the rocky ground.

"Fine," Jo snapped, studying the lid of her coffee cup as if trying to figure out how it was made. That's what she got for having warm fuzzy thoughts about her sisters.

"Oooh," Mike said, gleeful. "Nerve touched and I wasn't even trying."

Jo glared at her.

Mike ignored her.

"Thinking about giving Cash a whirl?"

Her insides lit up, but she dismissed that as just hormonal. After all, the man was really built. And really sure of himself. "Please. Cash Hunter is a cautionary tale to women everywhere."

"Are we talking about Cash again?" Sam asked as she came back into the room, looking a little paler than before, if that were possible.

"Not me," Jo said, pointing at Mike. "Her."

"Hey, I'm not the one who goes all defensive the minute the man's name comes up."

"Who's defensive?" Jo winced at the screech in her own voice.

"Right. Nothing to worry about there," Sam said, and filled with regret, reached for her cup of tea. Coffee just wouldn't stay down.

"Does pregnancy short out brains?" Jo wondered, glancing from one sister to another. "I'm *so* not interested in Cash." She shifted on the couch. "Hell, I don't even want him around. But with the two of you letting me down—"

"Pardon the hell out of us for getting pregnant," Mike said.

"You know, there are other carpenters in town," Sam pointed out, grimly taking a swallow of her tea.

"Yeah, but most of them are lined up to work at Grace's place this year."

"Thank God that's not our problem," Mike said solemnly.

"Amen," Jo said.

Every year, Grace Van Horn ran the construction crews in and around Chandler nuts. She had more money than sense and the decision-making abilities of a three-year-old. And every summer, the construction companies took turns being at her disposal. The Marconis had been up to bat the summer before, which meant they were in the clear this year. And with most of the crews working for Grace, Marconi Construction would be picking up all the other available jobs.

Great for business.

If she only had her sisters to help.

"So, the Dailys want us to paint the interior of their house," Jo said, reaching for the binder she'd brought into the house with her. "Seems the Money Fairy showed up last week."

"Ah, he strikes again!" Mike crowed.

The Money Fairy was legendary in Chandler. Always popping up with anonymous gifts of cash when it was needed most. Whoever it was had excellent sources, because the money that showed up was always just the right amount at just the right time. For more than a year now, people had been trying to unmask the mysterious benefactor—so far, with no luck. It was a nice little mystery that kept everybody guessing.

"I figure I'll get Kyle Hinckey and Fred Soames for the painting," Jo said. "They're good and pretty fast."

Sam winced. "Wish I could do it," she said, frowning at her tea before setting it aside. "I've always wanted to get my hands on their family room."

Jo frowned. Sam was the best painter/faux finisher in the business. Hurt like hell to farm jobs out and only claim a commission, but there just wasn't any choice. "Maybe when you're back up to it, you can talk 'em into a mural or something."

Sam smiled.

"The Caseys' roof needs replacing and we've almost finished the Barclay kitchen and porch."

"That was fast," Mike said. "Who handled the repair of the gingerbread trim on that porch?"

Jo scowled. "Cash."

"Hmmm . . ." Mike slid the tip of one finger around the rim of her coffee cup. "And was he good?"

"Does everything that comes out of your mouth have to sound sexual?"

"Only to the cranky and horny," Mike said, grinning.

"What about the Santoses' new bathroom?" Sam asked, reaching for the binder that Jo had color-coded and cross-referenced.

Jo snatched it away. "We start that next week. We'll need to use a different plumber since *ours*"—she looked at Mike pointedly—"wouldn't fit into the bathroom itself, let alone under the sink."

"No need to get nasty." Mike pouted.

"That's what you think," Jo said.

"You could call Andy Bremer," Sam suggested, making another grab for the folder. "His wife's expecting number four. He's looking for extra work."

Jo shook her head. "What is up with this town? It's like a major population explosion all at once."

"Hey," Mike said, "cold winter nights equals cuddling equals sex equals babies."

She wouldn't know about that.

"Will you hand over that binder for a damn minute?" Sam snapped, and made a lunge for it, prying it out of Jo's determined grip.

Jo frowned at her. "Don't mess it all up. I've got everything lined up according to dates and cross-referenced by customer names."

"Of course you do," Sam muttered, shaking her head as she glanced over the first of the job orders. "Why are you so damn territorial about our files, anyway?" she demanded, leaning back in the cushions to study the work orders that were neatly tucked into their own manila envelopes.

Mike laughed. "You know how she is with paperwork. Like foreplay or something."

"True," Sam agreed solemnly.

"Is *everything* about sex to you?" Jo demanded, glaring at Mike while taking a slug of her still hot coffee. Inevitably, talks with her sisters turned to the glories and wonders of sex. And since Jo couldn't really identify, she usually just changed the subject.

"Better than *nothing* being about sex." Mike shook her head sadly and reached for another muffin, dropping crumbs onto the floor as she shifted her girth. "God, Jo, do everybody a favor and take Cash out for a test-drive, will ya?"

"Not gonna happen," she said firmly, despite the flash of heat that swamped her in a quick and thorough wave.

"Then stop torturing yourself and *tell* him that."

She looked at Sam. "Don't you think I *have*?"

"Not clearly enough, apparently."

"Yeah," Mike said. "You've never had trouble getting your point across—even if it meant using a hammer! So if you're *not* being clear, maybe you're not as disinterested as you think you are."

Oh crap.

That was a helluva thought.

Two

Cash Hunter focused his frustration and funneled it into his work. Hell, no wonder people called him a master craftsman. With this kind of energy pumping through him, he could probably tear down and rebuild the Louvre inside a week.

A tall man, with black hair that always needed a good trimming, he had shoulders broad enough to carry the chip that had been lodged there since he was a kid. His dark eyes promised pleasure and guarded secrets. His smile charmed, but didn't necessarily welcome.

He liked his privacy, and there was nothing wrong with that. He preferred keeping a distance between himself and the rest of the world and figured that it saved a lot of trouble—both for him and everyone else.

But then he'd gone and shattered his nice, easy life by running into Josefina Marconi.

No matter how many times he told himself to steer clear of her, he somehow ended up wandering back into range. The woman had a temper that could melt steel at a hundred yards and a disposition better suited to a pit bull.

And, she had blue eyes that looked like a cloudless summer sky and lips full enough to tempt a man to taste them, despite the danger involved.

"Damn it."

Shaking thoughts of her out of his mind, Cash gathered his focus again and concentrated on the work in front of him. His hands gripped the planer tightly, until his knuckles stood out white against his darkly tanned skin. He regulated his breathing, steady, even, fighting for control over the roar of aggravation within. But he'd had years to practice. Years to refine his technique for mentally compartmentalizing whatever happened to be bugging him. This he knew. This he was good at.

Over and over again, he stroked the precision tool over the edges of the rich teak wood. Inch by painstaking inch, he shaved away the excess, smoothed the rough edges. Small curls of wood rose up and dropped away, littering the workshop floor and the toes of his battered boots.

Aerosmith pumped from the radio, the clashing instruments jangling along his nerve endings, soothing in a weird sort of way. Afternoon light slid through the open double doors and lay in a long rectangle of gold across the brick-colored concrete floor of the massive workshop behind his house.

Immune to the beauty around him, Cash centered his mind and tried to tuck all thoughts of Josefina Marconi into the tidy little compartment he'd reserved for her in his brain. Unfortunately, though, thoughts of Josefina just wouldn't be contained.

The woman irritated him on every possible level and

attracted him on even more. Hardheaded and funny, generous and loyal, she snarled at him every time they crossed paths and had a body that kept him locked in sweaty dreams night after night.

The woman was wound so tight, she practically gave off sparks. She vibrated with energy even when she was still—which wasn't that often. She kept her long, thick dark brown hair tied back in a ponytail that never failed to capture his attention.

He'd even been watching that fall of hair to judge her moods. It measured her emotions like a damn metronome did music. When she was angry, it flew around her head in vicious swings. When she was thoughtful, she tipped her head to one side, letting that fall of hair hang there, like string dangling over a playful kitten.

He wanted to know what that hair felt like. What it looked like, spread across his pillow. What it smelled like when he buried his face in it.

"Great. Good job." Muttering darkly, he shifted uncomfortably, trying to adjust his jeans to ease the ache in his suddenly hard, uncomfortable body.

There was no relief in sight and he knew it.

He wanted her and he couldn't have her.

That was the plain, simple truth of it.

Lifting his head, he inhaled sharply, deeply, in and out, several times until he felt control sliding back into place.

It wouldn't last.

He knew that.

Accepted it.

Since the moment he'd first seen Jo Marconi, she'd

been able to tap into something in him that Cash really didn't want to encourage. She made him *want*. And damned if he was going to go that route again.

He'd had his hard lesson a few years ago. He'd learned that as much as he wanted to be a part of a town like Chandler, the safest way was to remain an outsider. Someone who lived on the fringes.

Trouble was, the fringes weren't as comfortable as they used to be.

Turning around, he stalked across the workshop floor, the heels of his worn cowboy boots clacking loudly, toward the full-sized refrigerator on the back wall. Yanking open the door, he grabbed a beer, twisted off the top, and took a long drink, hoping the icy froth would help with the tangle of hot knots inside him. When he closed the door and turned around again, he wasn't alone.

"What're you workin' on?"

Startled, Cash told himself he was losing his touch if a ten-year-old could sneak up on him. He shifted a look at the boy standing in the long rectangle of light at the mouth of the shop. "You're too quiet, kid."

Jack Marconi straddled his bike, ratty sneakers planted on either side of the cross bar. His fists were curled around the handlebars and his hair hung down into the pale blue eyes so much like his sisters'. The boy shrugged and twisted the front wheel of his bike back and forth, making the rubber squeak against the concrete.

Cash sighed, walked to the radio on the workbench and silenced Steven Tyler mid-howl. "What's going on, Jack?" he asked, leaning back against the edge of the waist-high worktable.

"Nothin'," the kid said, and swung his right leg over the bike before letting it drop with a clatter.

There was a lot of *something* in that "nothin'," Cash thought and frowned as he watched the boy stroll around the workshop. He never had people here. This was his own personal space. A private retreat where he could go to avoid the rest of the world.

But how in the hell he could toss the kid out, he didn't know. Cash saw himself in the boy and it wasn't really something he liked to admit, even to himself. No point in clinging to memories that weren't worth a damn. Better to focus on the *now*.

"You said I could come over sometime," Jack was saying as he zeroed in on Cash's work-in-progress and ran one finger along the still rough sides.

"So I did." His own damn fault, Cash thought and took another swig of beer. Say something polite to an adult, and they almost never took you up on it. Say it to a kid, and pretty soon that kid was showing up on your doorstep, whether you wanted him to or not.

The kid was only ten, but his feet were big enough to trip him up constantly. His jeans were baggy, his shirt stained. His hair, the color of Jo's, was long enough that the boy had to keep jerking his head to one side just to keep from being blinded. He was too quiet for his age, but then, having your world turned upside down on you could do that.

"Your sister know you're here?"

Jack shot him a look and shrugged again. "She's not home. At a meeting with Sam and Mike at Mike's house."

"So she doesn't know." Cash winced as he imagined Jo's reaction to her little brother's riding his bike the two miles to Cash's place. But it was too late now to avoid the storm that would descend when she found out.

"She won't care," Jack said softly, picking up the heavy planer to study it.

"That's sharp," Cash said before the kid could cut himself. "And she *will* care. Trust me."

"Only 'cause you make her mad."

"Well, yeah," he said, remembering their conversation earlier that day. "I do."

"Besides, she's just my sister, she's not my *mom*," Jack muttered, and if possible, his narrow shoulders drooped even farther.

Cash sighed, and took another sip of his beer before setting it down on the workbench. Looked like he was going to have company for a while. Josefina was going to be royally pissed, but damned if he'd shoo the kid off just to keep his sister from erupting.

Walking across the room, he took the planer away from Jack and said, "You have to lay this evenly against the edge of the wood. Then you push it slowly forward. It shaves off a little bit of wood at a time."

Jack shuffled his feet through the curls of wood on the floor. "Like that?"

"Yeah. You want to try it?"

"Really?" Blue eyes lit up with eagerness, and Cash told himself that he'd deal with Jo when he had to. A part of him was already looking forward to watching her fury and that was enough to convince him that he was a sick, sick man.

"Yeah. Go ahead." When the boy had hold of the tool, Cash dropped his big hands on top of Jack's and guided him through the first stroke. "Think you can handle that?"

"Yeah," the boy said, chewing determinedly on his bottom lip. "I can do it."

"Okay." Cash turned for the workbench, picked up his favorite planer, and then walked around the project that would eventually become a hand-carved, one-of-a-kind chest of drawers. "You do that side, I'll do this one. And if you need help, *ask.*"

"Right. Okay." The boy kept his gaze on the task at hand and concentrated on making each stroke of the planer exactly like the first one.

Cash kept one eye on the kid while he settled into a patient silence. Something had brought the boy all the way out here, and he figured if he waited long enough, the kid would eventually spill it.

Didn't mean he *cared.* Didn't mean he was letting the boy *in.* He was just . . . getting a little free labor. He only hoped Jack would talk before Josefina showed up and skewered both of them.

"So how's Jack doing?" Mike finished off the last of the muffins, licked her fingers, and turned a look on Jo.

"Okay, I guess," Jo said, closing the binder and leaning back on the sofa.

Truth to tell, she and her new brother weren't exactly hitting it off real well. Probably her fault, she acknowledged. But then, she hadn't *asked* to be a temporary mom, had she?

Just a week ago, her father had come to see her at her condo.

Things were still a little strained between her and

Papa and they both knew it, though neither one of them mentioned it. Jo hadn't been able to get past her father—the one man in the world she'd trusted above all others—having an affair while his wife lay dying. And Papa was so busy walking on eggs around her that it only made the situation more uncomfortable.

"I don't like to ask, Josefina," he'd said, rocking nervously on his heels.

"I know, but—"

"Michaela, she can't watch Jack for me right now with the babies so close, and Sam, she's too sick all the time, plus she has Emma and . . ."

"I know," Jo said, trying to find just the right argument and coming up empty. She knew darn well she was going to lose. "But Papa, the business . . ."

He sensed her weakening and moved in for the big finish. "It's just a couple of weeks, Josefina. I know I shouldn't go, but Grace made the reservations and I don't want to disappoint her."

Grace Van Horn, Papa's lady friend, was worried about him. But then, they all were. He'd had a heart attack several months ago. A minor one, but it was enough to rub mortality in everyone's faces. Now, Grace had arranged for the two of them to take a romantic cruise around the Greek Islands and Jo, though she really hated to think of her father in a "romantic" situation, couldn't really tell him no.

"Fine," she murmured and let herself enjoy the hard, brief hug from Papa. God, she'd missed him. Missed the easy way they'd always had together.

And she didn't know how to get it back.

"Good. Good. This will be a good thing for you and

Jack, too. Give you a chance to know each other. To find your way to—"

"Papa, don't," Jo said, stepping back from his embrace. "I'm fine with Jack. I don't blame him."

"No," Papa said softly. "You blame me."

"Papa—"

"It's all right," he said gruffly, rubbing his eyes viciously. "I said I would give you time."

Pain slapped at her and she felt, not for the first time, like an ungrateful child. Like a spoiled-rotten daughter. Why couldn't she forgive her father for the mistake that still haunted him? Why couldn't she see past her own pain, her own disappointment, like her sisters had?

But she knew why, Jo thought, coming out of her memories with a jolt. Because she carried her own secrets. Secrets that she'd never shared with anyone because she'd been too ashamed. Too afraid to tell her father because she hadn't wanted *him* to be disappointed in *her.*

Ironic.

"What do you mean, you *guess* he's all right?" Sam repeated, staring at her wide-eyed. "You're living in the same house with him. How's he doing?"

Jo shifted uncomfortably in her seat. She sure as hell didn't want to admit to her sisters that she and their little brother weren't exactly becoming best friends. Mike and Sam would assume that it was Jo's fault. That, somehow, she was punishing the boy for being the result of their father's affair.

And that so wasn't true.

She wasn't an idiot. She knew none of this was

Jack's fault. But that just didn't make it any easier to relate to the kid.

"He never *talks*," Jo blurted, as if that would explain everything.

"You're kidding," Sam said.

"Wow. A *quiet* Marconi," Mike muttered, astonished. "Who would have thought?"

"Not *you*, that's for damn sure," Jo said tightly.

"So you complain because I talk too much and Jack talks too little," Mike said, looking around for something else to eat. "Yeah, you're stable."

"Oh, for God's sake," Sam demanded, "is it really so surprising? The boy's mother just died a few months ago, for heaven's sake. He's moved in with Papa and now Papa and Grace are gone and he's forced to live with—"

"What?" Jo stiffened and sat up straight. She was the first one to admit she wasn't the easiest person in the world to live with, but she wasn't exactly the Wicked Witch of the East, either.

"Oh, look who's Ms. Sensitive all of a sudden," Mike said on a laugh.

"All I'm saying," Sam said, shutting Mike up with a quick glare, "is that the kid's a little on edge."

"Who isn't?" Jo muttered. Hell, she had the boy to look after, a business to run, and oh, hey, how about taking final exams so she could finally graduate from college?

But no one in the family knew about the night classes she'd been taking at UC Chandler for the last three years. In fact, the only person who *did* know was Cash Hunter, of all people.

She did a mental head slap and swallowed a groan.

She'd spilled her guts to him last year, when she'd discovered she was flunking astronomy. He'd caught her at a bad moment—when she was at the end of her rope and frantic. And he'd kept at her until she'd told him everything. Maybe she'd been able to talk to him because they *weren't* close. Anyway, she'd worried about him keeping her secret, but she needn't have. Not only had Cash given her a book that had actually helped her through the course, he'd also kept his mouth shut about her going back to college.

She hadn't wanted to tell anyone until she knew she'd succeeded. And within the next week or so, she'd know.

"Okay," Sam said, swallowing hard and covering her mouth with her fingertips. "But he's ten and you're . . . almost *thirty*."

"Thanks so much. And if it's so damn easy . . ." Jo countered, fixing her gaze on Sam, the middle sister. The peacemaker. The innocent bystander who was about to get flattened. "Why don't you get him to open up to *you*? You're the only one of us who actually *has* a kid."

"So far," Mike put in.

Jo ignored her, as usual. Keeping her gaze fixed on Sam, she said, "He goes to your house after school three days a week to play with Emma. So why don't *you* tell *me* how he's doing?"

Jo folded her arms across her chest, knowing she had her sister there. Sam's daughter, Emma, was a year or so younger than Jack, but the two of them had formed a bond over the last year. "What'd he have to say today? Tell me, O great one with all the answers."

"Today?" Sam said, swallowing again and rubbing her mouth uneasily. "He didn't come over today."

"What do you mean?" A trickle of unease rolled down Jo's spine. "He was supposed to."

"He wasn't there by the time I left. I figured—" She jumped to her feet, one hand clapped tightly to her mouth. "Oooh . . ." Then she bolted for the bathroom.

"Swear to God, I'm *never* getting pregnant," Jo said, shifting a look at Mike.

"No problem there," her youngest sister said. "You actually have to have *sex* to get pregnant."

"Not anymore."

"Are you *sure* you're Italian?"

Jo scowled at her and reached across the coffee table for the phone. "Never mind about my sex life—"

"Or lack thereof—" Mike finished for her.

"—the question now is, where's Jack?"

"Relax, Jo," Mike said, "this is Chandler, not downtown L.A. He probably stopped at a friend's house before going to Sam's."

"Yeah. Probably." But as far as Jo knew, their little brother hadn't made any friends yet. He was quiet and sad and too damn alone all the time. And whether she wanted it or not, she felt fear begin to creep through her bloodstream.

Punching in Sam's phone number, she listened to it ring for what seemed like forever before a man answered.

"Jeff?" Jo said quickly. "Is Jack there yet?"

Mike watched her from across the table.

"Okay. Okay," Jo said, nodding as she listened to her brother-in-law's calm voice. But despite Jeff's reassurances, her insides started jumping ferociously. "Just—call Mike or call me at Papa's house when he shows up, okay?"

"Not there?" Sam asked as she came back into the room.

"No." Jo frowned down at the silent phone and tried to tell herself there was no reason to worry. But how the hell was she supposed to *not* worry?

Mike pushed herself up onto her elbows. "Like I said, he's probably at a friend's house, you guys."

"He doesn't *have* any friends," Jo snapped, and jumped to her feet. Pacing wildly, she muttered, "He plays video games. Or reads. Or watches TV. Or studies."

"Jo . . ." Sam reached out for her, but Jo dodged her sister's hand.

"No," she said, "I've gotta go. Gotta—" Reaching down, she grabbed up her binder and her dark brown leather purse.

"Where're you going?" Sam asked.

"To look for him." Jo was already planning her search route. She knew all the fun spots in Chandler. Having grown up here gave her a huge advantage. First and foremost was the beach, of course, and then there was the lake. God. Did Jack know how to swim? Oh God, put that worry away. Pick it up later.

"You're worried."

She looked at Sam and lied. "Not yet."

"He's fine," Mike said, dropping both hands to her belly and stroking her own children in protective reflex. "You know he's fine, *right*?"

"Sure." Jo nodded. "I'll call you la—"

Her cell phone rang and she reached into her purse to grab it. Flipping the top up, she noted the caller's number and felt a flash of irritation rush through her. Radar, she thought. The man had radar.

"What?" she snarled into the phone.

He talked fast, not giving her a chance to say anything, which was probably just as well. Because at the moment, what she wanted to say would be better said in person.

While holding something heavy.

When he stopped talking, she hung up and looked at her sisters.

"Speak," Mike demanded. "Who was that?"

Jo took one deep breath after another until she felt control slip back into her system. She banked her inner fury until it was a nice, contained blaze. When she was sure she could speak without shrieking, she looked at first Sam, then Mike. "Seems like our little brother does have one friend after all."

"Yeah?" Sam asked. "Who?"

Fisting her hand around her cell phone in a grip tight enough to turn charcoal into a diamond, Jo only whispered, "Cash Hunter."

Three

The so-called road to Cash Hunter's house was so narrow and rocky, it was little more than a trail.

Jo's teeth rattled as she stubbornly steered her black truck between the overhanging branches of trees, bushes, and God knew what else. Her hands fisted on the steering wheel, she clenched her jaw and braced for impact as the truck jounced along this stupid track. "Couldn't the man take care of the damn road? Is he really so busy out seducing women that he can't take a day off to hack a way through this jungle?"

Okay, she told herself, maybe she ought to try to calm down a little before meeting up with Cash. Sure. No problem. All it should take is about thirty years and way more patience than *she* was known for. No matter how she tried to keep the man at a distance, he kept finding a way back in. What was that about?

"It's not like I'm falling at his feet or something," she muttered, and grunted when her right front tire dropped into a pothole the size of Kansas. "Damn it!"

The toolbox in the back of her truck jostled and clanged from the lockup box directly behind the cab. In fact, the whole damn truck was shaking as if it were at the epicenter of an 8.1 earthquake. Which did nothing to improve her mood.

The trees were thick here, their branches stretched out across the road, thick and leafy, and just filling out as winter slid into spring. Sunlight stabbed its way through the overhanging tree limbs to lie in tiny, bright splotches of gold on the dirt road.

It felt as if every plant in the world were deliberately trying to hold her back. Keep her from reaching her destination. And if she were a big believer in signs, like her sister Sam, Jo would have turned the truck around and headed back to the house.

Unfortunately, *she* was the logical one. The organized one. She believed that people made their own destinies. Their own luck. Their own problems.

She winced as an old memory darted through her brain, dragging pain and shame behind it. Took her a minute or two, but Jo pushed that memory back into the dark recesses of her mind. She'd survived. That was all that mattered.

And memories could only hurt you if you actually gave them that power.

Well, Jo was never going to give away her power again. Not to anyone.

"Okay, focus," she muttered thickly, concentrating on what Cash Hunter laughingly referred to as a "road." A minute or two farther along the rutted lane, she passed the turnoff for the little guest cottage she and her sisters had renovated several months ago.

That had been a long couple of months, she remembered. Every time she turned around, there was Cash. Closing in on her personal space. Insinuating himself into her day. Smelling good and looking even better.

Reminding her that he was all male—as if any woman with two good eyes would need reminding—and in general making himself a pain in the ass.

Of course, her sisters hadn't seen it. Oh no. All he'd had to do was bring a newly pregnant Mike a glass of water, or help Sam down from the roof, and they were charmed. But then, they were both married and he hadn't been using his big guns on them.

He saved *that* ammunition for Jo.

And why, for God's sake?

He could plainly see that she wasn't interested—okay, that was a lie. She *was* interested, she was just not going to do anything about it. She couldn't. She'd come up against a man like Cash once before. A man who was all charm and smiles. A man she trusted. A man she thought she knew.

A man who—

"Just *stop it*." She slapped her hand against the steering wheel. Cash wasn't that guy and, logically, she knew it.

He didn't *scare* her, for pity's sake.

He just . . . *bothered* her.

The man was a menace.

A menace who was, at the moment, holding her little brother hostage. "And that has to be a new high in low for the tricky bastard." Her fists tightened on the wheel and her temper spiked until she was nearly blinded by the red haze coloring her vision. "Imagine using a kid to get to me." She shook her head and her ponytail whipped from side to side. "Must be losing his touch. Can't get a woman through charm, so then try kidnapping."

But even as she thought it, she was already half dis-

missing the notion. Just wasn't Cash Hunter's style.
And while she steered her car through the Amazon jungle of his property, she thought back to his brief phone
call.

"Before you get all snarly," he'd said quickly, *"I'm
just calling to let you know Jack's here. At my house.
You can come and get him anytime."*

Snarly.

She'd show him snarly.

Then the tricky bastard had hung up before she
could tell him what she thought of him. What she
thought of driving out to his house. Or even ask him
why the hell Jack was *there* in the first place. She and
her little brother were going to have to have a long talk.
And she wasn't looking forward to it.

How was she supposed to know how to deal with a
little boy? *She'd* never been a boy. She didn't know
how they thought, or what they wanted or needed.
She'd never been around kids much, except for her sisters, and even then, *she'd* mostly been a kid herself.

Oh, she so wasn't cut out for the "mother" thing.

She'd known all along that taking care of Jack while
Papa was gone was going to be trouble. She'd just had
no idea how *much* trouble was headed her way.

"And speaking of trouble . . ." The truck lurched out
of the woods and into the bright, late-afternoon sun,
and for a second or two her eyes were dazzled by the
brightness. Which was probably why Cash Hunter
looked so damn good to her as he took long, lazy
strides toward the truck.

There couldn't be any other reason, because
frankly, Jo refused to be one of the thundering herd of
women who were constantly coming and going from

the man's life. She didn't really like being one of a crowd. And besides, any man who'd been around the block as many times as *he* had, was bound to be bad news.

Still, he was really easy on the eyes.

His black hair was just long enough to be sexy and the sharp planes and angles of his face were softened when he smiled. Which he was doing at the moment. Damn it.

He wore a black T-shirt tucked into faded jeans and worn, beat-up cowboy boots that fed into every woman's fantasy of a "tall, dark stranger." Well, Jo told herself firmly, despite the fact that her pulse skipped a little unsteadily, not *every* woman's fantasy.

He walked up to the truck, leaned on the open driver's side window and looked in at her. Jo could have sworn she felt heat radiating from the man and wondered if he'd somehow found out how to do that purposely. She wouldn't have put it past him.

"Heard your truck," he said with a shrug. "Came out to meet you."

"Where's Jack?" she asked tightly.

"Good to see you, too, Josefina." He smiled and she refused to notice how good it looked on him.

She gritted her teeth and folded her lips back to give him a grimace. "The name's Jo."

"Doesn't suit you."

"Gee, thanks very much. Back off." When he did, slowly enough to make her hum in frustration, she opened the truck door, hopped down, and slammed it shut after her. She didn't much like having to look up at him. Tall herself, she was used to meeting men more or less eyeball to eyeball. Cash, though, wouldn't you know it, was a good three or four inches taller than her own five feet nine.

He'd probably done *that* on purpose, too.

"Besides," she added. "How would you know what suits me or not? You don't even *know* me."

"I know you better than you might think," he said, and one corner of his mouth lifted, then fell again. "And all I meant was—Jo's a very . . . *plain* name and you're too beautiful to—"

Something inside Jo leaped up and growled. "Okay, let's just get this out on the table. I'm not one of your 'babes.' " She poked a stiff index finger into his chest and watched as his eyes narrowed. Good. Finally, she was getting through to him. "I'm not going to throw myself at your feet and beg you to whisk me off to bed."

In a heartbeat, the flash of temper she'd noticed was gone, replaced by amusement that sparked in his black eyes. "Now I'm hurt."

She blew out a breath and threw her hands wide. "I couldn't hurt you with a hammer."

He laughed. "Damn, I like you, Josefina."

"Color me happy." Man. Ten seconds with Cash Hunter and she was a raving loon. She stomped past him, farther up the drive, following the curve around a huge stand of trees that blocked her vision of the rest of the road. Glancing back at him, she demanded, "Where's Jack?"

"In a hurry?"

"You have no idea."

She wanted away from him. Not that she didn't trust herself around him, but hey, why take chances? He was too practiced. Too smooth.

Too irritating.

"Beautiful," my ass, she thought. Here she stood in her work clothes—faded blue jeans, polished, steel-toed work boots, and her favorite MARCONI CONSTRUCTION T-shirt, in dark green. Yeah, she was the picture of elegance.

Not exactly the fairy-princess type.

Nope, no one had ever called Jo beautiful. Striking, sure, even pretty at times. But Sam was the beautiful sister and Mike was damn near gorgeous. It was as if the Marconi genes had just gotten better and better, until with the last child they'd come together just right.

Although, she thought, Mike was no longer the youngest Marconi. Now there was Jack. A little boy who hadn't yet found his spot in the family. A boy she was responsible for. Which brought her right back to the reason for standing here talking to a man she ought to be avoiding like the plague.

Narrowing her eyes at Cash, she asked, "Where is my brother and why is he here?"

"In the backyard. And why don't you ask him?"

"I plan to," she said, and started walking. She took only a couple of steps before she stopped and looked back at him again. Lifting both hands before letting them fall to her sides again, she asked, "And this backyard is *where*?"

Jo turned in a circle and saw only trees, bushes, and at the edges of the road, wildflowers beginning to burst through the rocky ground to dot the area with blue and purple.

Shaking his head, Cash walked to her, took her arm and steered her around the curve in the road.

"You know," Jo snapped, yanking her arm free of his

grasp before she could get too used to the sizzle of heat spreading up her arm from the spot his fingertips had touched. "I've been walking all on my own for several years now."

Staring down at her, he studied her for what felt like way too long before he finally blurted, "You want to tell me why I bug you so much?"

Something inside her fisted, then released again. Oh, there was a reason. But she wasn't about to tell him what she'd never told *anyone*. Still, maybe she should dial down her temper a little. Stop making every moment she spent with Cash a battleground. Otherwise, he'd just get too curious, start prodding her, and then she *would* have to get out her hammer and let him have it.

She gave him a tight smile. "Love to. But neither one of us has that much time at the moment."

"You've got a tongue on you that could slice the flesh right off a man."

"You're still standing," she pointed out.

He shook his head and folded his tanned, muscular arms across his chest. "Can't figure out why I find such a nasty disposition so intriguing."

She folded her own arms across her own chest, matching his stance deliberately. "Maybe it's the refreshing change from your legion of drooling fans."

One corner of his mouth quirked. "I don't think so."

Inhaling sharply, Jo blew the breath out again before trying a different tactic. If she kept goading him—no matter how much she enjoyed it—she'd never find Jack and get home. "Look. I don't want to play games. I'm too tired for one of our typical 'conversations.' So why don't you just show me where Jack is and we'll both get out of your hair?"

Nodding, he unfolded his arms and said, "Okay, we'll play it your way for now. But sooner or later, you're going to talk to me, Josefina."

"Don't put money on it," she muttered.

"There's that prize-winning personality again. Can't understand why I enjoy that so much."

Before she could tell him what he could do with his "enjoyment," Cash shoved his hands into his jeans pockets and started walking. "The house is just around the bend there."

They came around the edge of the stand of trees and Jo stopped dead in the middle of the road. She *felt* her jaw drop, but was simply too stunned to snap it closed again.

The house was *breathtaking.*

Tucked into the trees, it was a palace of wood and glass. Sharp angles slid into curved walls and back into a slice of terrace that dropped nearly to the surface of the lake crouched at the foot of the building. The forest reflected in the windows until it looked as though the house itself were a part of the woods that surrounded it.

Jo took one slow step, then another, unable to tear her gaze from the structure. It was . . . *magic.*

"You like it?"

Pride hummed in his tone and she couldn't even be irritated by how close he stood beside her. "It's wonderful," she said softly, her voice trailing away as she studied his home.

Everywhere she looked, she found something new to admire. The curve of a window box at a tiny dormer window. The wide expanse of glass that swept around the far edge of the house like a clear shawl the building had wrapped around itself. Two river-rock chimneys sprouted from the multilevel roofline and a second-story balcony zigzagged down the side of the house in a series of ramps that reminded Jo of an old-fashioned fire escape—but this one was built for sheer beauty.

A soft wind danced across the lake and swatted at them as it passed. Blinking, Jo finally forced her gaze from the amazing house and turned to look at him. "Grace always said you lived in a 'cabin.' "

And actually, Jo thought, even that wasn't accurate. Grace Van Horn had told Jo that Cash lived in a shack on the back edge of her property.

Shack.

Only Grace, queen of the mini-mansions, would think of this place as a shack.

Still stunned, Jo realized that all the time she and her sisters had spent working on the tiny guest cottage for Cash, they'd never seen his house. Never known that this incredible place was here, just a few hundred yards farther along that beaten track.

If the man wanted privacy, he'd sure gotten it.

Cash shrugged and started walking again. "It started out a cabin. I've made some changes."

"*You* did this?" she asked, stopping again because shock does tend to immobilize a person. "*You* built this house?"

His lips quirked. "Don't sound so surprised."

She couldn't help it. She *was* surprised. Oh, she knew Cash was a good carpenter. But she never would have guessed that a man like him would have so much *artistry* inside him.

And damn it, she didn't like the flush of admiration she felt for his skills. His vision. Jo didn't want to think of Cash as having *depth*.

It would be so much easier on her if she could keep considering him as just a shallow womanizer.

"Sorry," she said, shifting her gaze back to the wood and glass glory spread out in front of her. "I just never would have guessed that you could do something like this."

"Maybe it's you who doesn't know me as well as you think you do," Cash said, his dark gaze fixed on her with a heat that seemed to sear the very air separating them.

Her heartbeat jittered and her mouth went dry. For just a moment or two, Jo felt . . . *possibilities* fluttering around her like drunken butterflies. And that was more than enough to bring her to her senses.

"Maybe not," she said firmly, whether to convince herself or Cash that she meant business, she wasn't really sure. "But I know you as well as I'm *going* to."

He shook his head at her as if even he were amazed at her stubbornness. "You might want to ask yourself sometime, Josefina, why you're so determined to keep me at a safe distance."

Oh, she *knew* why. Knew it all too well. And that reason reached up from the pit of her stomach and grabbed at the base of her throat, just to give it a good squeeze. Air pumped thinly into her lungs and she had to swallow hard to be able to talk past that tight throat.

"I don't owe you a reason, Cash," she said, lifting her chin until their gazes locked. "But if you're in the mood for some soul-searching, maybe you should ask yourself why you keep beating your head against a brick wall. Why you're so damn eager to break down my defenses instead of moving on to someone more . . . *willing*."

She stalked off then, headed for the house and the backyard beyond, leaving her words hanging in the air like a challenging banner.

"She's got a point," Cash muttered when he was sure she couldn't hear him.

If he had any sense at all, he'd back away from her. But somehow or other, she kept drawing him in. In the year or so he'd known her, he'd seen the many different sides of Jo Marconi—and every damn one of them fascinated him. He'd seen her furious, watched her laugh with her family, and seen her so vulnerable and hurt after the blowup about her father's affair that it had torn at him.

She held nothing back. A man always knew where he stood with Josefina. He watched her throw herself into life, giving everything she had. He'd seen her heart.

What he couldn't see, was him ignoring her anytime soon. And that was just something both of them were going to have to live with.

"You're *here*!" Jack Marconi raced up to his older sister, excitement blistering in his eyes and dancing across his features. She hadn't seen him that happy in well . . . *ever*. "You have to see. Come on." He grabbed her hand and Jo let herself be dragged across the neatly tended backyard.

She refused to be impressed any further.

She absolutely would *not* look at the incredible flower beds, in rioting colors, ringing the sweep of manicured grass. She would *not* admire the length of deck spearing off the back of the house, or its hand-carved railings.

But damn it, she was forced to notice the difference in her little brother.

For the first time in days, Jack was *grinning*. Gone were the drooping shoulders, the scowl, and the slouching walk. He was laughing, happy. And somehow or other, *Cash Hunter* had pulled off another miracle.

Damn it, what was it about the man? Not just women responded to him, but little boys and probably dogs and cats, too. What ability did he have that she so clearly lacked?

Ouch.

She winced as that thought trotted through her brain, but how could she avoid thinking it? She'd been in charge of Jack for three days and the kid hadn't cracked a smile. He spends a couple hours in Cash's company and he's practically *dancing* across the lawn.

And it didn't help any to have Cash walking along just behind her, probably enjoying the hell out of this whole situation.

Trying to take back control, Jo said, "You shouldn't have come here without telling us, Jack."

"Yeah, I know, but—"

Jo stopped, digging in her heels and bringing Jack to a sharp halt along with her. "No buts. You worried everybody."

"Didn't mean to." He dipped his head, and his hair, the same brown color as her own, fell across his eyes. Probably would have blinded him if he hadn't suddenly jerked his head to one side to blink up at her. The frown was back. "But you wouldn't understand and Cash did."

Ouch again.

She glanced over her shoulder at Cash and noticed that he was practically whistling and rocking on his heels, trying to pretend that he wasn't listening to the conversation. Fine. She'd do the same.

"Wouldn't understand what?" she asked, dropping to one knee on the sun-warmed grass.

Jack blew out a breath that ruffled his hair, then rubbed the back of his hand under his nose. "The kids at school say I throw like a girl."

"What?"

Jack rushed on. "Justin Shepard says I can't throw cuz my dad is old and all I got is sisters."

Temper flickered inside her. "Justin Shepard."

"Yeah," Jack said, and glanced at Cash before looking back at his sister. "And he wouldn't pick me to be on the baseball team at school and I had to stand there like a girl and do nothing while everybody else played and stuff and I just thought that maybe Cash could show me how to throw like a guy because I have to know how, all the guys know how and . . ."

He was still talking, showing absolutely no sign of stopping or even, hell, slowing down. Regret bubbled through Jo. She should have been able to figure out what was bothering the kid. Should have *made* him tell her.

Threw like a girl because he only had *sisters*?

Poor kid had come to Cash out of desperation. Because his own sister hadn't known what to do. Or maybe because she hadn't cared enough to look closer. To really listen to what Jack needed.

And that stung.

Shame rippled through her as she acknowledged, at

least silently, that "taking care" of a kid required more than just making sure he showed up at school and brushed his teeth after dinner. She should have been paying closer attention. Should have gotten past her own discomfort with the fact of Jack's existence to understand that the little boy was really lost.

And somehow, Jo pledged, she'd make that up to him.

When Jack finally ran out of breath, she stood up and winked. "Justin's father went to school with *me*," she told him. "And Tom Shepard couldn't catch a ball if someone had handed it to him and stitched it into his glove."

Jack laughed.

Cash moved up closer.

But she focused on her little brother. "You know, the guys are right, you do only have sisters." She wouldn't touch that "old father" thing at all. "But every one of your sisters plays ball better than Justin's father ever did."

"Really?"

"Really. I could have helped you. I played shortstop on every school team and I still play softball."

"Yeah," he said, swiping the toe of his shoe across the grass and watching as every blade went down, then sprang back up again. "But it's still not the same. You're not a *guy*, Jo."

"Ah." And that was the real problem. He hadn't just needed to know how to throw, he'd needed a *guy* to teach him. She really tried not to mind that the guy he'd chosen was *Cash*.

"Now watch," Jack said eagerly, and sprinted for one corner of the yard, where a sheet of plywood with a hole cut dead center of it was propped against a tree. "I'll show you."

"The Testosterone Club is very exclusive," Cash whispered from just behind her.

"So says its president," she murmured, keeping her gaze locked on the boy who was winding up and letting a baseball fly.

"We all have our strengths."

"And shortcomings," she pointed out.

"Are we really going to talk about size before our first date?"

Jo snorted, amused in spite of herself.

"Did you see?" Jack called, crowing and doing a silly little step-dance in celebration of the pitch that had gone straight through the hole in the plywood.

"I saw," Jo yelled back. "Way to go!"

"You didn't answer me," Cash said.

"Ignoring you *was* my answer," Jo said.

"Haven't you figured out yet," he asked, "that ignoring me just isn't working?"

"What will?" she countered, turning around to look at him.

His mouth curved. "Kiss me."

Her stomach did a slow dip, but she managed to keep sarcasm in her tone as she answered, "In your dreams."

"Every night, Josefina," he whispered, his gaze locked with hers. "Every night."

Four

When her cell phone rang, Jo grabbed for it gratefully. Stepping away from Cash, she flipped it open, checked who the caller was, and then said, "What is it, Mike?"

"Jack okay?"

She shifted a glance at the boy, who was throwing another pitch at the target Cash had provided. Burned her butt to have to admit even to herself that Cash had done a good thing for her brother. But true was true.

"Yeah," she said, through gritted teeth. "He's fine."

"Good. One problem down, one to go."

"Huh?"

But her sister was already talking again. "I figured out why Papa suddenly agreed to go on that cruise with Grace."

A yawning hole opened up in the pit of Jo's stomach. She closed her eyes against that sinking sensation as she said, "That sounds ominous."

"Oh yeah." Mike paused and snapped at someone else, "I'm getting to it. Jesus, Sam, why don't you go puke some more and let me handle this? Jo? You still there?"

She gritted her teeth. "And waiting."

"You're not gonna believe this."

Jo's gaze shifted from her little brother, playing in a splash of sunshine, to the dark-eyed man standing way too close to her. "Just spit it out, will you?"

"Guess who just called like five minutes ago?" Mike asked, then didn't wait for her to answer. *"Nana."*

"What?"

"You heard me," Mike said, then spoke to Sam again. "If you give me five lousy minutes, I will tell her. God, how does Weasel Dog live with you, anyway? Aren't you supposed to be the calm one?"

Her sisters' arguing did nothing to close that gaping chasm in the pit of her stomach. In fact, she was pretty sure sharks were now swimming down there. She could almost hear that foreboding music from *Jaws*.

Da-dum. Da-dum. Dum-dum-dum-dum . . .

Jo's nerves jittered and she sucked in a deep breath. She shifted her gaze from Cash to something less dangerous. Less distracting. She stared blindly at a wall of trees and absently watched as a slight breeze ruffled the new leaves, brushing them against each other in a quiet little dance.

It should have been relaxing.

It wasn't.

"Will you talk to *me,* not Sam?" she muttered darkly, trying to keep her voice down, despite the sudden, almost overpowering urge to shriek.

"Fine, fine," Mike snapped. "I get chewed on by both of you. That's fair."

"Mike," Jo grumbled, "if you make me hunt you down like a dog I'm going to—"

"Nana's already on her way here."

"What?"

"You heard me. Honest to God, does nobody *listen*

in this family?" She huffed out an impatient breath and said, "No, I'm not giving you the phone, this is my phone, if you want to talk to her, call Jo on your own damn—"

"Jo?"

"Sam," she muttered, sighing. "Sanity. Thank God. What's going on?"

"Just what Mike said—hold on—"

In the background, Mike was shouting and Sam was telling her to be quiet and not get upset, that it wasn't good for the babies.

Jo counted to ten.

Then twenty.

Before she hit thirty, Sam was back on the line again.

"What the hell is going on over there?" Jo demanded.

"Mike tried to take the phone back, so I had to get up and move out of her reach. No way can she lever herself off the couch without Lucas to pull her up."

"Oh," Mike shouted, "that's *really* nice."

Jo felt a headache blossom between her eyes. And she also felt Cash's gaze pinned on her. Strangling the impulse to shout and throw the cell phone through the target he'd made for Jack, she finally asked, "Will one of you guys tell me about Nana?"

"She just called. Apparently," Sam was saying, "Nana talked to Papa three weeks ago. Told him she was coming for a visit. She wants to see her newest great-grandchildren born."

"And make Papa's life miserable," Jo added.

"Always a plus from her point of view," Sam conceded.

"Trouble?" Cash asked.

Her head snapped up and her gaze locked with his. Oh yeah. Trouble. Capital *T* kind of trouble. But nothing anyone outside the family would understand. *Or* know about. She shook her head and forced a smile.

Turning her back on him, she whispered, "When's she arriving?"

"That's the thing," Sam said. "Tomorrow morning. She said, and I quote, 'Tell Josefina I will make calzones for supper.' Unquote."

"Oh man . . ."

"Exactly. Lucas already volunteered to pick her up at the airport and—"

"Is he crazy?" Jo asked as little black dots danced in her suddenly swimming vision. "Did Mike finally make that poor man suicidal?"

"He's never met Nana."

"Good point."

"She didn't say how long she's staying, but my guess is she's here for a *looooonnnngggg* visit."

"Oh crap."

"Pretty much covers the situation," Sam said, then added, "She said 'Oh crap,' Mike. Happy now?"

"He knew about this three weeks ago," Jo said, furious to realize that Papa hadn't said a word about it to anyone. He hadn't told *her.* And he'd *known* that his mother-in-law was on her way to town.

"Yep. Makes it easy to understand how Grace talked him into that cruise, doesn't it?"

Yeah, it really did. No wonder the man who'd never been interested in long vacations had run like a rabbit for the Greek islands.

Nana Coletti had *never* been a big fan of Henry

Marconi's. She'd always been convinced that her daughter Sylvia could have done much better in the husband market. And, since finding out about little Jack Marconi, and how Papa had been off with another woman while his wife lay dying . . . well . . .

Jo had to admit, she really couldn't blame her father at all for wanting to get out of the country before Nana hit town. That little reunion, when it finally *did* happen, wouldn't be pretty.

But oh man. "Wish Grace could take me on a cruise right about now," Jo muttered.

Not that she and her sisters didn't love Nana. They did. When they were kids, summer visits to Nana's house in Omaha were always special. They'd camp out in the backyard and catch fireflies at dusk. Nana always had ice cream in the freezer and hot dogs on the barbecue.

But having your grandmother running your life when you were ten was a lot easier than having the same thing happen when you're thirty.

"I hear that," Sam said, then muffled a groan.

"What's wrong?" Jo asked her.

"Gotta go throw up. Talk to Mike."

"Oh, for God's sake—"

"Hi," Mike said, "me again!"

"Good-bye, Mike," Jo snapped and hung up while her youngest sister was still talking about how no one ever listened to her.

Stuffing her phone back into her pocket, she took a deep breath and pushed thoughts of Nana to the back of her mind. Of course, her grandmother wouldn't stay there, but for now, she'd give it a shot. Bracing herself, she turned around and faced Cash. He was still watching her, a question that wouldn't be answered shining in his dark eyes.

"Everything all right?" he finally asked.

"Oh, terrific."

"Anything I can do to help?"

She tipped her head to one side and studied him. "Why would you want to?"

"I'm a nice guy?"

Jo laughed shortly.

Cash grinned and Jo's stomach did a fast little two-step. Oh boy.

"Okay, so maybe I just want to help so you'll be indebted to me."

Her eyebrows shot straight up. "That's honest, anyway."

"No it's not," he said softly, taking a step toward her. "But it's what you were thinking."

"Ooh. You read minds, too."

"I'm a man of many talents," he said, one corner of his mouth quirking.

"So I've heard." She blew out a breath. "Look, Cash," she started and then paused, searching for the right words, the right—oh, the hell with it. "I appreciate the offer. Seriously. But it's a family thing and, really, there's nothing you can do."

"You sure?"

"Yeah." She nodded and suddenly admitted, at least to herself, that she wished there *were* something he could do. Was she weakening toward him? Oh, good God. She *was*. Damn, he really was good.

She took a step back and said what had to be said so she could leave. "Look, I, uh . . . *thanks*. For helping Jack out—"

"Bet that hurt," he commented wryly.

She shrugged and smiled. "Not as much as I thought it would."

"Progress," he said, smiling back at her.

"Why don't you tell me what's wrong? What your sister said that made you go pale?"

"You know?" she said, backing up to keep that distance between them. She needed it now more than ever, since there was a part of her that really wanted to step right up and let him hold her. She could use a little comforting right at the moment. But that path was a bit too dangerous. "I really don't think so."

Then she turned to look at the boy, still happily pitching baseballs through a target. "Jack! We gotta go! Get your bike and put it in the truck."

While Jack, shoulders slumped, dragged his feet across the lawn as if they were blocks of concrete, Jo stalked to the truck and flung open the driver's-side door. Didn't even surprise her when Cash followed her.

He grabbed hold of the door's edge when she would have slammed it shut and leaned in toward her.

"I'll see you tomorrow."

Jo pushed a strand of hair out of her eyes and tucked it back behind her ear. "What?"

"At the job site. The Santiagos' new deck?"

"Oh." Damn it. She'd forgotten about that. Forgotten about having to hire Cash because neither of her sisters was up to the work at the moment. When did her life become an amusement park ride? "Right." She tugged at the car door.

He let it go and it slammed shut with a metallic clang that echoed over and over again inside her head.

"Yeah," he said, stepping back from the truck, his

dark eyes damn near sizzling as they fixed on her. "I'm looking forward to it, too."

Her stomach jumped, her blood pumped, and she told herself to back off the caffeine for a while. No way was Cash Hunter getting to her. Oh please, God, he wasn't getting to her.

Jack clambered into the truck and slammed his own door before leaning down to peek out at Cash. "Thanks a lot, Cash."

"Anytime, Jack," he said, then shifted his dark, damn near smoldering gaze to Jo. "See you, Josefina," he said in a low voice designed to rattle a woman's defenses.

"Oh, for God's sake . . ."

She threw the truck into reverse, and as soon as Jack had buckled himself in, Jo stepped on the gas and peeled out, spinning dirt into the air and never once looking back at the man who watched her go.

His smile slowly fading, Cash walked back to his workshop, trying unsuccessfully to put Jo Marconi out of his mind. But try as he might, she just wouldn't go.

He knew damn well that the safest thing for him to do was to stay away from her. And yet, she pulled at him. She was a mixture of temper and gentleness that appealed to him on too many levels.

Maybe she was right. Maybe he was attracted to her because she didn't coo and flirt with him. Maybe a part of him was intrigued by the fact that she didn't seem to want him.

But it was more than just that.

Something about Josefina resonated with him in a way that he'd never experienced before. And while a part of him wanted to enjoy it, wanted to bury his hands in her thick hair and *himself* in her damp heat, he knew damn well that if he ever *did* get her into his bed, he'd lose her.

He kicked at a rock on the road and sent it skittering into the high grass and wildflowers. Stopping dead, he lifted his head and stared up at the sky, already streaked with color as the sun slowly slid out of view. Clouds drifted, the wind kicked up, and the scent of the nearby lake filled him.

He should be happy. This house was everything he'd once dreamed of. All he'd wanted as a kid was somewhere to belong. Now he had it and it wasn't enough.

He was a part of Chandler and yet separate. Still on the outside looking in, and there was no way past the invisible barriers that shielded him from the rest of the world.

Of course, he'd erected those barriers himself so he had no one but himself to blame.

"Small consolation," he muttered. Reaching up, he pushed both hands through his hair, scraping his fingertips along his scalp, then let his arms drop as he headed for the workshop again. He'd lose himself in work. It was the one refuge he could still count on.

STEVE SMITH FOR STATE SENATE.

Jo winced as she looked at the poster tacked up outside Jackson Wyatt's law office. She studied the face of the man in the picture and fought down the chill snaking along her spine. Her mouth went dry and her palms went damp as her gaze locked on Steve's image.

It was as if he were looking right into her soul.

Smirking at her.

God, ten years and it was just like yesterday. She could almost smell the stale odor of beer—hear the music pumping through the frat house—feel the wood floor beneath her back—

"Jo?"

She heard Jack's voice as if it were floating up from the bottom of a well. Today drifted into a thick mist as yesterday came sharper, clearer.

Her breath quickened.

Her heart pounded.

The little boy at her side grabbed her hand and shook it. "Jo!"

As if it were a life rope tossed to a drowning woman, she latched on to the feel of Jack's hand in hers and used it to pull herself out of her nightmare memories. Blinking, breathing, she looked down into his worried eyes.

"Are you okay?"

"Yeah," she said, trying to convince herself as well as the boy. She'd survived ten years. Ten years of squelching memories, shattering dreams. She wasn't about to let that man come back and take another bite out of her life at this late date.

Deliberately not looking at the poster again, she reassured her little brother as she tugged him toward Terrino's pizza parlor. "I'm fine, Jack."

Or she would be, she thought, if she could just pass her final exams next week, stop seeing posters of Steve Smith, keep Nana appeased while she was in town, survive her sisters' pregnancies, keep herself from falling for Cash Hunter, and find a way to make her little brother happy.

Sure.

No problem.

Nana Coletti was eighty-six years old, four feet nine inches tall, and a whirring buzz saw of activity. The woman never slowed down and didn't see a reason why anyone else should, either.

She still lived on her own in the tiny house in Omaha where she'd spent her entire adult life. She knew everyone for blocks around and she was the only person the grocery store would make home deliveries for. She baked on Sunday, did laundry on Monday, washed floors on Tuesday, windows on Wednesday. She volunteered at the local nursing home because she felt "sorry for those poor old people," and she swore that red wine and olive oil were the secrets to longevity.

And maybe, Jo thought, she had a point. After all, the tiny woman had outlived most of her friends and still showed no signs of slowing down. Or of mellowing, for that matter.

"Josefina," Nana said, sitting in Papa's favorite chair and smoothing the skirt of her black dress across her knobby knees. "When isa your papa home again?"

"A couple of weeks, he said."

"He should be here. With his *son.*"

Jo blew out a breath and wished to hell Lucas had stuck around for a while. But she couldn't really blame her brother-in-law for heading for the high country. He'd had Nana all to himself for the ride in from the airport, and she knew from past experience, it couldn't have been a pleasant journey.

Nana had never learned how to drive, but that didn't stop her from telling everyone else how to. In a mixture of Italian and English, she cursed the other drivers and shouted instructions to her own. Not to mention the fact that she had an opinion on everything and felt that, at eighty-six, she had the right to tell everyone exactly what she was thinking.

Whether they wanted to hear it or not.

As kids, Jo and her sisters had been crazy about Nana. She baked cookies and always had ice cream in her freezer. Whenever they went to Omaha to visit, it was an adventure. Nana's friends indulged them and Nana herself made every visit special. She had a way with kids. It was adults she wasn't very fond of.

But Jo knew that Jack's very existence had to be a sore point for the old woman. Her daughter, Jo's mom, had been dying of a cancer that had swept her away on a tidal wave of pain and misery when her husband had made his only marital slip.

Lonely and afraid, Papa had looked for comfort somewhere else and Jack was the result. It had taken Jo a long time to get past her own anger and, if truth be told, she still wasn't past the sting of disappointment in her father. But none of that was Jack's fault. He was a Marconi.

And Marconis stuck together.

Against all comers.

Which was why she had to have this little talk with Nana before heading off to the Santiago job.

"A cruise," Nana said with a sniff. "He lives inna sin. He will pay," she said, pointing an index finger at the ceiling as if signaling to God it was time He took control of this situation.

Jo winced. She really didn't want to think about her father "living in sin" with Grace Van Horn. There were just some things daughters shouldn't know about their fathers.

"Nana," Jo said, leaning forward and bracing her elbows on her knees. "You know I love you . . ."

The old woman smiled, her papery skin crinkling at the corners of her dark brown eyes. "You're a gooda girl, Josefina. Not like your papa. Like your mama. A saint, my Sylvia, God rest her soul."

She crossed herself automatically, whispering a little prayer for her late daughter.

Jo nodded, thinking it was probably best to just go with the flow. No point in antagonizing her by trying to defend Papa. Especially, she reasoned, since she still wasn't feeling all that happy with him herself.

"About Jack . . ."

"My grandson." Nana's narrow chin lifted and her eyes narrowed. "Where issa he?"

"School."

"Ah." She nodded. "Good. I will have cookies for him when he comes home." She snapped a look at Jo. "What time he gets home?"

"He's out at three, but he usually goes to Sam's house. Plays with Emma until I'm off work."

"No more," Nana decreed, pushing herself up from the chair and reaching back to replump the pillow. Then she bent, straightened a stack of magazines on the coffee table, and dragged her index finger across the dusty surface. Frowning, she held the evidence of laziness up for Jo to see.

She winced guiltily, but hey, there hadn't been a lot of time for dusting. Since moving back into the Marconi family home to take care of Jack, she'd been a little busy. You know, running the business single-handedly, looking after her brother . . . No excuse would be good enough and she knew it.

Nana clucked her tongue, shook her head, then brushed her hands together, ridding herself of the dust while simultaneously glaring at Jo. "They should come here. Be with their Nana."

Sunlight speared through the living room window, highlighting the streaks on the glass. Nana was sure to notice that, too, any minute now. And to hear her tell it, dirty windows were the *real* path to hell.

"Um . . ." Jo stood up too and tried not to hover over the much smaller woman. She suddenly felt like an Amazon at a leprechaun convention. "Weasel D—" She caught herself when Nana's eyes narrowed. Okay, note to self: Don't use the family nickname for Jeff in front of Nana. "I mean, Sam's husband, Jeff, usually watches the kids and he—"

Nana held up one hand, cutting off the rest of that speech. "Tell him to bringa the children here. They will want to be with their Nana. Is only right."

"You don't have to babysit."

"Is why I came. To see the children. To be with Michaela when her bambinos are born."

Ooh. And she was sure Mike was delighted at *that* prospect.

"Yeah," Jo said, following her grandmother as she started across the living room for the kitchen. "But Nana, about Jack—"

She whirled around, her black skirt flapping around her knees. "He is sick? Something issa wrong?"

"No, he's just—"

"Speak up, Josefina," her grandmother said, folding

her gnarled hands at her waist. "What issa wrong? You think I maybe will not love this Jack? You think that I am foolish enough to blame the child for what his father has done?"

Jo cringed. Okay, yes, she had been worried. After all, ever since the family had found out about Jack, Nana had made it a point to let everyone know just what she thought of a man who would cheat on a dying wife. Was it so hard to understand that she'd been afraid Nana would take out her anger on the child, too? But she should have had more faith in a woman who was a born mother. A nurturer from way back.

God, she did feel like an idiot. But in her own defense, it had been a full week so far. "Of course not, Nana."

"This boy is my grandson. The son of the *bastardo*, yes, but still, my grandson."

Well, as long as there were no hard feelings.

And technically, Jack wasn't really her grandson. But apparently, Nana wasn't looking at it like that.

"You're right, Nana, but—" Jo said, then stopped when the old woman's eyes narrowed on her. "Fine. Forget it. I'll call Jeff. Tell him to bring the kids here after school."

"Good." She turned for the kitchen again, a spring in her step. Nothing like stomping your way through a conversation to give you that little extra zip. "Be home at six. Supper will be ready."

"Yes, Nana." Jo sighed, surrendering to the woman who could make a four-star general look like a shy Cub Scout.

Leaving the house, she stomped down the front

steps and headed for her truck, parked in the tree-shaded driveway. Somehow or other, she was losing control of her life.

The hell of it was, she was starting to like the wild ride.

Five

Chandler, California, had the best of everything.

Almost perfectly situated in the middle of the state, Chandler was just far enough north to avoid most of the summer heat and just far enough south to escape snow in winter. Sitting right on the coast, the little town was nestled between the sea on one side and a forest that stretched out at the feet of the mountains on the other.

Decades ago, Chandler had survived on the strength of its natural harbor and the fishing boats that plied the waters—not to mention its closeness to the vineyards that crowded central and northern California. Now, though, tourists were the backbone of the economy and there were festivals planned for every season to make sure they kept coming. The town was big enough to keep neighbors from living in each other's pockets and small enough to retain the cozy feel of a fishing village.

Shops crowded the main street, where old-fashioned street lamps stood proudly with bright splashes of flowers jumbled at their feet. Tourists and locals alike crowded the sidewalks, bustling in and out of the shops and restaurants.

In another week or so, the Flower Fantasy would open and buses filled with eager shoppers would descend on Chandler to buy up the local growers' supply of cut flowers, plants, bulbs and seeds. Then it would be summer, and the beaches would be packed with people determined to get a summer's worth of tan in one weekend. In the fall the Autumn Festival brought out the local artisans, selling their wares in the open meadow outside town. By late October, streets would clog with people coming in to see the brilliant gold and scarlet foliage, and in winter, there would be the Victorian Christmas festival, when street vendors sold everything from hot apple cider to actual roasted chestnuts, and period-garbed carolers wandered the street, serenading tourists and locals alike.

Contrary to popular opinion, something was *always* happening in small towns.

But for now, Jo mused as she parked her car outside the Leaf and Bean, things were relatively quiet in Chandler. She stepped out of the truck and lifted her face into the wind sweeping in off the ocean. Smiling to herself, she listened to the distant bark of the seals angling for a handout, the conversations bubbling up around her, and underneath it all, the rhythmic sigh and hush of the ocean itself, like the heartbeat of Chandler.

She slammed the truck door and headed for the sidewalk, waving absently to Gloria Harding as she dragged her tantrum-throwing three-year-old behind her.

Jo shook her head, tugged her sweatshirt tighter around her, and stalked up to the Leaf and Bean. Maybe she was stalling a little before going out to the work site. But she'd already dealt with Nana and she figured she owed herself a latte before facing Cash.

The minute she opened the door and was slapped by the combined scents of coffee and freshly baked pastries, Jo felt every cell in her body stand up and shout "hurray."

A dozen or so round tables were scattered across the gleaming wood floor and the people huddled around those tables sent up a muted roar of conversation that drew newcomers in. The walls were cream colored, with dark wooden beams as accents. Sunlight sliced in through the wide front windows facing onto Main Street and glanced off fern- and flower-filled copper pots hanging from heavy silver chains. Across the far wall, a long glass case was filled with the pastries Stevie Ryan Candellano baked fresh daily, and the hiss and sputter of the espresso machine drew Jo forward like metal shavings to a magnet.

Her gaze swept the room as she headed toward paradise. At this time of year, most of Stevie's customers were locals. In another couple of months, tourists would be battling for the seats and Stevie's cash register would be singing. Jo waved to Trish Donovan, sitting in the corner, with a spread of tarot cards laid out across her table. Then she stopped when Phillip Howell called to her.

"Jo! Going to need you and your sisters before summer," he said loudly. "My roof sprang a leak in the last storm."

"I'll call," she said, smiling, and in her mind, she tucked Phil's name into her file folder marked "pending." "And," she added, turning back to look at him again. "Don't try to fix it yourself this time, okay?"

"I remember," he said with a grimace as his friends laughed.

Last time Phil had tried a little roofing on the weekend, he'd put his foot right through the overhang and damn near broke his leg.

Nothing like a weekend handyman to make a construction worker's life happy, Jo thought.

By the time she reached the counter, she was feeling a lot more cheerful. A latte was in her immediate future and she already had another job lined up.

"The usual?" Stevie asked, grinning.

"Oh God, yes," Jo said, then stood back to admire the pastries lined up in the case in front of her. "And I think a cinnamon roll, too."

Stevie's blond eyebrows lifted as she wielded the buttons and levers on the espresso machine she ran like a magician. Steam rose, hot milk bubbled, as Stevie bent to snatch up a pastry and tuck it into a small paper bag. Sliding it across the counter, she asked, "Nothing for Mike or Sam?"

"Not today," Jo muttered, reaching into the bag to break off a corner of the roll. Popping it into her mouth, she closed her eyes and sighed at the glorious taste. "Mike's on bed rest, making Lucas nuts, and Sam can't even smell coffee without turning green."

"Poor thing," Stevie said as she wiped down the metal tubes and clicked a plastic lid atop Jo's coffee cup. "Thank God I don't have *that* worry. Don't know what I'd do if I couldn't at least *make* coffee while pregnant."

Hard to keep up, Jo thought. Not just her sisters were in the middle of a population explosion. It seemed that all of her friends were also on the mommy train. Pretty soon, she'd be the only woman in town without a gang of kids hanging off her body.

She took a sip of coffee and even the glorious taste of the perfectly done latte couldn't completely wipe away the bitterness blooming inside. But what did she really have to be miserable about, anyway? It wasn't as though she were interested in having a man in her life.

Shaking her head, Jo pushed the stray thoughts out of her mind and focused on Stevie instead. "So when're you due again?"

The blonde stepped out from behind the espresso machine, put one hand on the small of her back and shrugged as she glanced down at the mound of her belly. "A couple of months still," she admitted, then added, "And Carla's not letting me forget it that she beat me to the baby finish line."

Carla Candellano Wyatt. Another old friend. Now a married mom to a newborn boy and stepmother to a darling little girl. "How's she doing, anyway?"

"She's fine, the bitch," Stevie said wryly. "Already getting her figure back and making sure she tells me at least once a day that I'm still fat and she's not."

"Oh, evil," Jo agreed, "but on the bright side, neither one of you is as big as Mike."

"Good point!" Stevie crowed. "I feel better."

"Happy to help."

"So, how's Cash working out?"

"Huh?" The abrupt shift in subject had Jo's mind rattling.

"Cash. He's been working for you a lot lately since Sam and Mike have been out of the picture."

"Get that gleam out of your eye," Jo warned, leaning in across the glass counter and lowering her voice so that the people behind them couldn't hear her. "There is *nothing,* repeat, *nothing* going on between me and Cash."

Stevie chuckled. "Who said there was?"

Jo stiffened. "Cute. Very cute."

"So my husband tells me."

Jo sagged a little and tapped her fingertips against the top of the cool glass case. "He's being . . . *helpful.*"

"Well, God," Stevie said, in mock horror, "call Tony and have him arrested."

She took another sip of her latte and let the heat sweep through her, as the caffeine gave her system a much-needed kick. "I just don't get *why* he's being helpful," she said, choosing to ignore Stevie's limp attempt at humor.

"Maybe he likes you."

"He likes *all* women." And that was exactly why she was so determined to keep her distance. She'd fallen for a smooth-talking guy once before and all it had gotten her was years' worth of nightmares.

"Used to," Stevie said, then glanced to a corner of the room and shouted to a customer wanting a refill, "Coming!" Turning back to Jo, she said, "Word is, Cash has been living like a monk for months."

Jo'd heard that, too. She just didn't know if she believed it. Or if she believed it, what it might mean—if anything.

"Doesn't matter," she said firmly a second later. Because she wouldn't *let* it matter. She picked up her coffee and cinnamon roll and said, "You're busy and I've gotta run anyway."

"Sure," Stevie said, lifting a coffeepot and heading

around the edge of the counter. "But, um, let me know if there's anything *to* know."

"There won't be," Jo said, and wasn't really sure if she was promising Stevie . . . or herself.

The Marconi kitchen was bright and warm and smelled as if Italian angels had been at work. Papa's big golden retriever, Bear, snored under the table, his wide head resting on the toe of Jack's shoe in a comforting weight.

Jack swung his hair out of his eyes, then reached for a cold glass of milk sitting in front of him on the kitchen table. While he took a long drink, he let his gaze slide to the old lady walking around the room. She stopped at the stove and stirred a big pot of something that sent steam and really good smells into the air.

His *grandmother*.

He'd never had a grandma before. Or a grandpa, either.

So far, he kind of liked it.

After school, he'd gone to his sister Sam's house like always. But then instead of staying to play video games with his niece Emma—which he still thought was pretty weird, that he could be an uncle and only be ten years old—Emma's dad had brought them both here.

To meet Nana Coletti.

He'd been a little worried about it. But since his mom died, he'd been a little worried about everything. Chandler was nice and everything, but it was all so new and stuff, and he still missed his best friend, Dennis Ferris, a lot.

Jack broke his cookie in half and watched the melted chocolate stretch out.

Everything was different now and he didn't want it to be different anymore. Oh, he had sisters now, and mostly, Jo was okay, and there was Emma to play with, and sometimes Jonas Candellano came over, but most of the time he just wished he could go back to the way it used to be.

Just his mom and him, living in their house in San Francisco. He used to like it when his dad came to visit. But living here was hard. He still didn't feel like this was his place. Like he belonged here.

His heart ached at the thought and he frowned as he bit into another warm cookie. The chocolate chips got all gooey, which was really cool, and he licked the strings of chocolate off his fingers and Nana didn't even yell at him, so that was okay, too.

She was nice.

She was also *really* old.

And, she kept looking at him a little funny. Like she was trying to see inside him, and Jack wondered if old people could really do that. Maybe when you got old, you got superpowers—and wouldn't that be cool?

"My mommy's having a brother for me, he's in her tummy and she says he'll be really, really nice and love me a lot." Emma Hendricks took a bite of her hot chocolate chip cookie, and while she chewed she kept talking, as her sneaker-clad feet beat against the rungs of her chair. "And I told Mommy that I wanted a sister but she says I'll like a brother too and I like Jack"—she shrugged—"so maybe I will."

Jack sighed with the patience of a ten-year-old for a *much* younger nine-year-old. Emma was okay mostly, but she was always talking about the baby. He didn't care about babies. He wanted to talk about baseball or about how Cash had taught him how to throw. And how maybe now the kids at school would let him play on the team and then maybe things wouldn't be so hard here anymore.

"Jack," Nana said, stroking one hand along the back of his head. "You want some more cookies?"

He liked the feel of Nana petting him. It was nice. As nice as warm cookies.

"I can have more?" he asked, lifting his gaze to hers.

She smiled, and her eyes smiled too as she clucked her tongue and pushed his hair out of his eyes. "Growing boys need cookies. Issa good for you." She shook her head. "Also haircuts issa good."

"Aunt Mike says haircuts can make you stupid." Emma nodded solemnly.

Jack snorted a laugh. "That's dumb."

"Yeah, I think she was kidding." Emma shrugged and grabbed another cookie. "Are you gonna stay here for a long time, Nana?"

Jack stiffened and under the table Bear snorted. He wasn't sure what kind of answer he wanted Nana to give. Before, it had been just him and Jo living in his father's house while Papa was gone. But people kept coming and going out of his life so much that he'd really like *somebody* to stay.

The old lady sat down in a chair at the head of the table and reached out to lay her hands atop one of theirs. "Long enough," she said, giving each of them a pat. "Now. You wanna help make calzones for supper?"

. . .

Jo took her frustrations out on the Santiagos' new deck. Thankfully, there were plenty of nails that needed pounding into the soft redwood planks. The zing of the hammer jolted up her arm, and with every strike, she felt a little bit better.

What kind of personality was it, she wondered, when hitting something was comfort food? Italian? She smiled, set another nail into place and held it with her thumb and forefinger as she swung the hammer again. Two even strokes and the nail was home and she was moving on to the next one.

The growl of a saw hummed in the background, and to Jo it was like music. It soothed her as thoroughly as a lullaby did a cranky baby. And damned if she wasn't feeling a little cranky at the moment.

Jack was alone with Nana and who knew how that was going. Plus, now she knew that Stevie—and who knew how many other people in town—was wondering about her and Cash.

"So, Jo." Eva Santiago walked across the lawn and stopped just below the edge of the new deck. "The weatherman's promising rain by the weekend."

Pausing in her work, Jo rested the hammer on her lap and turned her face up. Clouds scuttled across the deep blue sky, pushed by a wind racing in from the nearby ocean. Rain. Well, April in Chandler usually meant plenty of rain.

"It'll be all right," she said, smiling at the woman, who had been one of her mother's best friends. "We should be finished in a couple of days, but if we're not, we'll cover it all with a tarp." Pain in the ass, but part of the job.

"Oh good." Eva rocked back on her heels, swept one

hand across her neatly styled salt-and-pepper hair, then sighed in pleasure. "I can't believe the Money Fairy is making this deck possible just in time for Jamie's big birthday party."

"Handy," Jo agreed. The Money Fairy was back at it in Chandler. After taking a month or so off last winter, the anonymous benefactor was back in full swing.

Talk around town was that the Money Fairy was slipping cash into mailboxes all over town. But strange thing was, the fairy left only what was needed—at just the right time. A discriminating fairy to say the least. Take the Santiagos. Not that they were desperate for money, but there wasn't a lot extra. And somehow, the Money Fairy had found out that Eva wanted to build a deck with a wheelchair ramp in her backyard. Jamie Santiago, sixteen, brilliant, and just recently confined to a wheelchair, thanks to a car accident, would now have the run of the yard.

"Marsha Fielding found two hundred dollars yesterday. Just what she needed to buy some new part or other for her car—" Eva paused to take a breath. "You know how that junker of hers is always breaking down."

"True." Marsha's car was older than Jo. The fairy should have left her enough to buy a new car so the town could hold a tasteful memorial for the old clunker.

But the Money Fairy had been busy lately. Jimmy Harris had found just enough money to pay for summer camp, so he could go with his friends this year. Vicky Fletcher had received the three hundred dollars she needed to pay a vet bill for her ancient cat. And just last week, Terry Summers opened her mailbox to find the eighty-five bucks she'd wanted to buy a fancy pair of shoes for the high school dance.

Whoever the fairy was, he was well informed.

Eva sighed and glanced over her shoulder at the
sawhorses set up in the corner of the yard. Cash was
there, running the table saw through long planks of
redwood. When the older woman turned back to Jo,
she smiled and winked.

Jo stiffened. "What?"

Eva leaned in closer and kept her voice to a whisper
that could only be heard next door rather than down the
street. "I like your young man."

"You *what* my *who*?"

"Now, Jo," she said, laying a hand on Jo's forearm.
"No need to pretend with me. Your mother and I were
like this." She held up two fingers, overlapped. "Remember?"

"Yeah, I do but—" Well, that answered her earlier
question. It wasn't just Stevie doing some wondering
about Cash and Jo. If Eva Santiago was talking, you
could bet that there were plenty of others doing the
same damn thing.

Oh man.

"Isn't he a handsome one, though?" She stole a look
at Cash again and Jo followed her gaze. "All that thick
black hair and, oh my goodness, cowboy boots on a
man are really hot, aren't they?"

"*Hot?*" Jo blinked up at the woman, both fascinated
and appalled. Mrs. Santiago thought Cash was *hot*. So
wrong in so many ways.

"My Jamie, she's sixteen now, you know," Eva said,
nodding briskly. "Well, she took one look at your
young man and told me he was the definition of hot."

Jamie obviously needed a cold shower, but that
wasn't really the point here.

"He's *not* my young man." And oh God, she really hoped he couldn't hear this weird conversation over the whine of the saw.

Eva smiled and shook her head. "Oh, you go ahead and keep your secrets, and heaven knows I won't say a word . . ." She made a motion of zipping her lips closed, locking them, then throwing away the key.

Which didn't mean a thing. In the gossip chain of Chandler, Eva Santiago was right near the top. What she didn't know wasn't worth knowing. And what she hadn't told, hadn't happened yet.

"Now, don't you worry about a thing, dear," Eva said, "I'll just go see if your young man would like something cold to drink."

Kill me now, Jo thought.

The day went downhill from there.

She and Cash had finished up the work at the Santiagos in time for Jo to get home and be put to work by Nana. They'd scrubbed the kitchen and both bathrooms before the old woman had given in to jet lag and gone to bed.

Now, with both Nana and Jack sound asleep, Jo finally had the chance to relax a little. Sitting on the darkened front porch of her parents' house, Jo leaned her head against the newel post and stared up at the stars. A clear night, the sky was black and the sweep of stars shone like, well, like diamonds. Funny. A few months ago, she'd looked up at those same stars and cursed them because of the stupid astronomy class she'd been flunking at the time.

Then Cash had sent her a book, *Astronomy for Dummies.* Now she knew more about the stars and less about Cash. For so long, she'd been sure she knew just what he was about. Fast talker, smooth lines, women falling at his feet.

Now, though, she just didn't know.

Oh, he was still irritating. That she could depend on. But he was also being . . . helpful. And . . . God help her, *nice*.

Why?

Cash's reputation had become legend in Chandler as every woman he slept with up and left town immediately after. They'd all "seen the light" or whatever and had trotted off to do good works. Now, whether that was just a strange coincidence, or Cash was some sort of hypnotist or—

"Right. A hypnotist." Shaking her head she focused her gaze on the Big Dipper and tried to line her thoughts up again in an orderly manner.

But they just wouldn't fall into line.

No surprise there.

Cash was slippery. And probably devious. And definitely sexy as hell. So why was she thinking about him at all?

Because it had been too long since she'd been with a man.

That's all it was.

And she'd get over it.

As she shifted uncomfortably on the hard wooden steps, a distant movement in the shadows caught her eye. Wind rustled the leaves on the trees and draped a long strand of brown hair across her eyes. Carefully, she pushed it back and turned her gaze to the house across the street.

Mrs. Sanchez, a widow approximately a hundred and eighty years old, lived alone and went to bed as soon as the sun set. Her house was dark. Quiet.

Another shadowy movement from the hedges at the edge of Mrs. Sanchez's yard caught and held Jo's attention. She held her breath and waited. Yes. Someone was moving around the yard. Someone who didn't want to be seen.

Who the hell would be sneaking around an old lady's house in the middle of the night? Fear rippled through her, but she moved on instinct. Mrs. Sanchez was alone. She was a neighbor. A friend. Jo didn't need to think beyond that.

Moving as quietly as the shadow across the street, she slipped up to her truck, parked in the driveway. Shadows within shadows. No moonlight, just the quiet night and a sky filled with stars.

Wincing, she reached over the edge of the truck bed and quietly, carefully, lifted a heavy pipe wrench. Clutching it tight in her right fist, she started across the yard, stepping carefully, silently.

Her gaze locked on the intruder across the street and her mind raced. She should have called the police. Tony Candellano, the sheriff, could have been there in five minutes. Maybe ten. But by then, she reasoned, whoever was sneaking around the Sanchez house could be long gone.

Nope.

She gritted her teeth and crossed the street as quietly as a tall woman in work boots could.

The shadow was close to the porch now, slipping out of the darkness to climb the short flight of steps to the house. Fury rushed through her and Jo let it surge as she charged the last few feet separating her from whoever was sneaking around Mrs. Sanchez's house.

Raising the pipe wrench high, she warned the man in a low-pitched growl, "Whoever the hell you are, you'd better get gone fast."

"Jesus Christ!" The shadow's voice came low and rough and was way too familiar.

"Cash?"

Six

"I'd just as soon you kill me with that pipe wrench as *scare* me to death," Cash muttered, scraping one hand across his face and glaring at Jo.

In his black jeans, black T-shirt, and black leather jacket, he'd convinced himself he was damn near invisible. Apparently not. He'd never even heard her come up behind him. In the stealth contest, she was a winner.

God, she looked like an avenging angel. Stepping out of the dark, one shadow among many. Her pale eyes were wide, astonishment clear on her features. And as his thudding heart dropped from his throat back into his chest where it belonged, he could enjoy the sight of her.

He'd known going in that taking money to Mrs. Sanchez would be risky. With the Marconi house right across the wide street, he was taking the chance of being seen. Recognized. But there wasn't much choice in the matter. The old woman needed this money to pay her property taxes. She'd been in the house for fifty years, and while Cash had never known continuity like that, he could appreciate it. And not want to see it end.

"What the hell are you doing?" Jo demanded, keeping her voice to an urgent whisper, as if she too realized the need for quiet. Then, before he could come up with some clever lie to explain why he'd been sneaking around an old woman's house in the middle of the night, Jo's jaw dropped open and she stared at him, amazed.

"It's *you*," she said finally, her voice strained with incredulity. "*You're* the Money Fairy."

Cash scowled at her, but as long as she already knew what he was up to, he went ahead and finished his task for the night. Turning his back on her, he stepped onto the porch, opened the mailbox, tucked an envelope inside, then closed the lid quietly.

Shaking his head in disgust, he left the porch as silently as he'd arrived. He couldn't believe this. He'd been delivering money anonymously—and damn successfully—around Chandler for more than a year and who was it who finally caught him?

"Come on," he whispered, and grabbed her arm, dragging her farther down the flower-lined walk.

She pulled away from him. No surprise there, though he had to admit he was still a little stung. She was always yanking free of his touch. He rubbed his fingertips together as if savoring that brief contact before shoving his hands into his jeans pockets.

"I can't believe this," she was saying. "*You?* The Money Fairy?"

Cash winced at the title the town had bestowed on him so many months ago. "Will you *not* call me that?"

Her fabulous mouth quirked a bit. "Object to the word 'fairy,' do you?"

He shrugged and gave her a quick smile. "Let's just say it doesn't fit my self-image. Most men wouldn't be comfortable being called a good fairy."

"Nobody said anything about your being 'good.'"

He glanced back at the still darkened house behind him, then back to her. "Hey, everybody in town loves me."

Her mouth dropped open again. "Is that what this is about? You wanting to be a hero?"

A spurt of anger shot through him, but he throttled it back until it fizzled harmlessly. "For chrissake, if that's what I was after, why would I be sneaking around town at night? Why am I hiding from those damn Stevenson kids with their motion-sensor video camera traps?"

Unexpectedly, Jo snorted out a laugh. "Those kids are way too clever."

"Tell me about it," Cash muttered, but smiled back at her, until she realized they were sharing a moment and squelched her smile. Cash, though, found that he missed it and was willing to work to see it again. "They almost had me a couple months ago."

She tipped her head to one side and he watched that ponytail dip as she waited.

He cleared his throat. "They, uh, set up surveillance at the edge of their lawn and got me on tape taking some money to the Hardwick house next door."

"I would have heard about that and—"

Cash shook his head and winked. "I saw the light flash from the camera. When I was finished, I walked over and erased the tape."

"Clever."

"Yeah, real smart," he said with a groan, remembering that night and how . . . *impressed* he'd been by the kids' setup. "I just barely managed to outmaneuver a pair of genius thirteen-year-old twins."

Her mouth twitched again, but she fought it back valiantly. "Don't take it personal," she said. "They drive their own parents insane."

"That's something, at least," he admitted, and glanced around the darkened neighborhood. The streetlights shone with a yellow glow, the fog lamps making misty circles of gold in the darkness. A soft wind raced down the street, carrying the scent of the sea.

"So if you're not looking to be a hero, then why?" she asked.

He sighed and shifted his gaze back to her. "You're really not letting this go, are you?"

"Nope."

He brightened. "What if I leave *you* some money?"

"A bribe?" she asked, one eyebrow lifting as she shook her head and that ponytail of hers whipped back and forth. "That's pitiful."

"Yeah, probably." Jo wouldn't be bought off. He knew her well enough for that, anyway. The woman was like a terrier, once she had her eye on a prize. If she decided to have the whole story, he wouldn't escape until she'd gotten it. Stubborn. He actually liked that about her. Which was just wrong, he supposed.

He gave another glance at the still dark house behind them and winced slightly. By standing around here, he was risking being caught by someone other than "the Great Marconi" and he didn't want his identity being broadcast all over town. If it got out, he'd have to stop helping. Stop connecting. And this was the only way he knew.

"We should be going," he said firmly.

"Not a chance," she countered, now swinging the

pipe wrench in a lazy motion at her side. "Not until you explain."

Amazing woman. She swung that wrench, which had to weigh thirty pounds, as another woman would have dangled her purse. Tall and toned and way too gorgeous for his own good, Josefina Marconi was the most woman he'd ever known.

And she wasn't going to move from that spot without either an argument or a long discussion. "Now's probably not the best time," he said, jerking his thumb at the quiet house behind him.

"Oh please. Mrs. Sanchez sleeps like the dead." Jo shook her head and smiled again. "Start talking, Cash."

A shame she didn't smile more often, Cash told himself. Then realized that if she did, he'd be in worse shape than he was already.

And who the hell needed that?

"What's to explain?" he demanded, keeping his voice low. "You caught me. Congratulations. Now go away."

"Why are you doing this?"

He scrubbed one hand across the back of his neck and stalled. It was a long story. One he hadn't planned on sharing with anybody. But even in the dim starlight, he could see the stubborn glint in Jo's pale blue eyes and knew he wasn't going to ease out of this one.

"Fine," he said shortly, feeling just a little trapped. "But can we go somewhere else?"

"I don't know what you're so—" She stopped, cocked her head and listened. "Did you hear something?"

"I can only hear you," he snapped, but then shut up himself to strain his ears for whatever sound she'd caught.

"I'm sure I heard . . . *there*."

Cash went completely still and, a moment later, he heard it, too. Just below the rustle of the wind through the trees. It sounded like . . .

Growling.

"What . . . ?"

"Oh crap." Jo sucked in a breath and blew it out again hurriedly. Her voice rushed and colored with desperation, she whispered, "It's Precious!"

An instant later, she turned and bolted for the street and the safety of her own lawn. Apparently giving up on the whole secrecy thing, she shouted, "Run for it!" as she sprinted.

It wasn't until then that Cash noticed the doggy door cut into the bottom of Mrs. Sanchez's front door. As he backed up, that door slapped open and a tiny brown ball of fur shot through it like a bullet, aimed right at Cash.

Instinctively, he backed up, then caught himself and laughed at Jo's panic. A damn *Yorkie* made her run?

But his laughter died as the tiny brown dog lunged at him, all fangs and snarls. It buried its needle-sharp teeth in the leg of his jeans and tore at them as if Cash were a giant milk bone.

The little bastard meant business.

"Cut it out," he said, trying to keep his voice low as he shook his left leg and hopped on his right.

"Head for the street," Jo urged from across the way. "He won't go into the road."

"Great," he shouted, forgetting all about covert maneuvers himself. What was the point with the world's angriest rat attached to his left leg? "Just great. Get off me, you rotten little . . ." He swung one hand at the mutt, trying to dislodge it, and missed.

The little dog hopped and jumped around him, rearing back, snarling, biting through the jeans and trying to work its way down to flesh. It shook its head hard enough to send the little pink bow in its hair flying.

"Don't hit him!" Jo warned.

"Him?" He glared down at the little monster still shredding his jeans, then lifted his gaze to see that a light had snapped on in the Sanchez house. "Perfect," he muttered thickly, still shaking his left leg, despite the little dog dangling from him like some weird Christmas tree ornament. "Just perfect. Damn it, let go, you little fleabag . . ."

From down the street, a chorus of dogs picked up on Precious's concert. Howls and barks filled the quiet night and lights flashed on behind closed curtains up and down the block.

"Precious?" A high, wavering voice called out in the night and the hairs on the back of Cash's neck lifted straight up. Mrs. Sanchez could do voice-overs for horror movies.

He kept hopping, headed for the promised land—determined now to escape with what little dignity he had left.

This had all started out so well, too.

A simple job.

Leave the money, slip away.

Nothing to it. He'd been doing it for almost a year now and everything was fine. He had a system. He had a plan. He had . . . reached the curb. He hopped off and

Precious instantly released him. Sniffing, snorting, the little dog lifted its hairy chin and then victoriously trotted back up the neat sidewalk to its house.

The porch light snapped on.

And Cash had to make a run for it. Still cursing the dog, he sprinted for Jo's house. He joined her on the lawn and together they hid in the dark behind her truck while Mrs. Sanchez flashed her porch light on and off as if she were signaling ships at sea.

A few minutes passed as they huddled together, listening to the street settle down again. One by one, the other dogs quieted and lights clicked off, welcoming the darkness.

"Well," he said finally, leaning back against the cold steel bumper. "That was humiliating."

She grinned at him in the dark and Cash had to fight down a rush of something hot and ridiculously needy pulsing inside him. The woman had no idea what she did to him. Or maybe she did and she was just enjoying the torturous aspect of their relationship.

"I told you to run," she said, still chuckling over the picture he and the little dog had made.

"So you did," he admitted, raising his knees to rest his forearms on top of them. "But I wasn't expecting that clump of hair to be so damn mean. He wrecked my jeans."

"Poor baby," Jo said, then gave his arm a friendly pat. "Maybe the Money Fairy will visit you so you can get a new pair."

He ignored that. "And what kind of name is Precious for a male dog? And a *pink* bow? Hell. No wonder he's vicious. He's fighting for his manhood every time he steps outside."

Jo leaned her head against the back of the truck, set the wrench down on the cold concrete and laughed again, a low, warm rumble of sound that seemed *intimate* in the shadows. "The male ego is a fragile thing, it's true."

"Speaking for my gender . . . *hey*."

"Sorry," she said, lifting both hands in mock surrender. "Didn't mean to hit a nerve."

"No nerves hit. Just . . . bruised." He shrugged. "You're not exactly catching me at my best."

"Is that right?" She tipped her head to one side to look at him and he tried not to notice how that thick brown ponytail lay against her shoulder.

Swallowing hard, he pointed out, "I've been doing this nearly a year. Tonight's the first time I was caught."

"Which," she pointed out, "brings us back to the 'why' portion of our evening. You said you'd explain."

Yeah, he had. And he should have known Jo wouldn't let it go. The woman was like Precious in that. Once she had hold of something, she just dug in her heels and hung on for all she was worth. So, he surrendered to the inevitable and started talking.

Staring up at the starlit sky, he focused on the brightest spot of light he could find. "Chandler's the only place I've ever thought of as 'home.' "

"It's my home too, but I don't run around at night playing Santa."

He shook his head. "You don't get it. This place." He waved a hand at the big old house with its shutters and wide front porch and overgrown flower beds. "—This place was always yours. You never had to doubt it. Never wondered if you could stay. It just . . . *was*."

He shook his head, glanced at her, then turned his

gaze back on the heavens. It was easier to talk if he wasn't looking at her. If he looked at her, he wanted her, and then all thinking went right out the window.

"Every summer, I came here with my mom and her friends and we'd stay at Aunt Grace's and—"

She grabbed his upper arm and Cash felt the flash of heat jolt through him like a summer-fueled brush fire. "Aunt? *Grace?* Grace Van Horn is your *aunt?*"

He nodded. "My mom's older sister."

"Grace never said anything."

"Any reason why she should?"

"No . . ."

"I live on her property," he reminded her.

"Yes, but I just thought—hell. Don't know what I thought." Jo released her grip on his arm and eased back against the truck. A night for surprises, she thought, studying his profile as he studied the night sky.

She'd thought he was finished surprising her. When she'd seen the house he'd created, she'd taken a new look at him and admitted the possibility that there was more to Cash than she'd thought. Tonight, she discovered that Cash was the Money Fairy. Still more depths to the man she'd have been willing to bet money was as deep as a cookie sheet.

Now she'd found out he was related to Grace? Instantly, she cringed to think of all the snide comments she'd made about the fluttery, sometimes nutcase older woman. Not that she didn't have reason. Grace was enough to drive any contractor right out of his mind. But she felt bad now, knowing that Cash had heard plenty of her tirades. Just went to show, her mother had been right. Better to not say anything at all, if you couldn't say something nice.

But then, Jo mused, if she and her sisters lived by that rule, they might as well be mute.

As her mind raced, one thought flashed through, demanding to be noticed. "You said you used to come with your mom and her friends. You mean the gypsies?"

He winced and nodded. "You know they're not really gypsies, right?"

"Sure." It's just what the town called them. A small group of women who traveled the country together. They'd been coming to Chandler since before Jo could remember—and now she knew at least part of the reason why. "So your mom's one of them."

"Kate."

The beautiful one, Jo thought now, remembering last summer and how she'd seen Cash walking with the woman with long, inky black hair. She'd been disgusted with him at the time, thinking that he was hitting on a woman old enough to be his mother—now, she was chagrined to find it really *was* his mother.

"I'm an idiot," she murmured, shaking her head and smiling.

"Care to tell me why you think so?" he asked, his voice a whisper of sound, barely louder than the gentle wind dancing around them.

"Not particularly," she admitted as she remembered the stinging slap of jealousy she'd felt at the time, watching Cash and Kate together. *Idiot.*

Nodding, he said, "Anyway, a few years ago, I decided to move here. Started building my house . . ."

God, that amazing, incredible house, she thought.

"When it was ready, I moved in."

She shook away the memory of that house and her

hunger to get a look at the inside. "Still doesn't explain the Money Fairy thing."

He shrugged and rubbed his palms over his knees. "Just . . . looking to belong, I guess."

"By *buying* your way in?" Jo stretched her legs out in front of her, folded her arms over her chest, and shook her head. "That's not belonging," she said.

"Good enough for me," he insisted, and pushing to his feet, he stood up and held out one hand to help her up, too. "I can help people out and—nobody has to know it's me." When she was standing, he released her hand and shoved both of his into his pockets. Glaring at her defensively, he asked, "What's it hurt?"

She wished for more light.

She wished she could see his dark eyes more clearly. Try to read what he was thinking. Feeling. But in the heavy shadows, she could only guess, judging by the tone of his voice—and that told her plenty. He was embarrassed and defensive and a little on edge. So not like the Cash she'd thought she knew.

"It doesn't hurt, I guess," she admitted. "And you've helped a lot of people. It's just—"

"Look." He interrupted her and pulled both hands free of his pockets to drop them on her shoulders. Jo felt the heat of his touch right down to the soles of her feet. Wow. Hadn't really expected that.

"Josefina, I'm not hurting anybody. I can afford it. So what's the harm?"

"None, but—" She wondered how a carpenter made enough money to play Mr. Benevolent all over town, but she wouldn't be getting the answers to that question tonight.

"Glad you agree. So, the question is, are you going to squeal on me?" he asked, his grip on her shoulders tightening reflexively.

"Squeal?" she repeated, smiling in spite of the situation—in spite of the growing heat blossoming under the spot where his hands held her. "What're we? In the mob?"

His answering grin flashed white in the shadows, then disappeared again quickly. She found she missed it.

"Are you going to keep my secret?"

A few seconds ticked past while she considered it. After all, did it really matter who the Money Fairy was? Lots of people had been helped when they most needed it. And weren't most people in town enjoying the mystery? The sense of expectation? And hey, best of all, wasn't it great to know something neither one of her sisters had a clue about?

"Okay," she said, stepping out from under his hands, because having him touch her didn't help the whole "thinking" thing. She moved farther out into the yard, needing a little distance from him, a little space from the heat he engendered with a single touch. "For now, I'll keep quiet."

"For now?"

She shrugged and looked up at him. Here, in the open starlight, the darkness was lifted just enough for her to see the whisker stubble on his jaws. To notice how his dark hair fell across his forehead. To see his equally dark eyes narrow on her thoughtfully.

"For now's the best I can do," she said, reserving the right to spill the beans at some later date.

"I guess that'll have to be good enough," he said, less worried now about keeping his voice low. A moment passed, then two. "Well, it's been nice being attacked with you."

She smiled again, remembering Precious attached to Cash's leg. "Yeah," she said. "We'll have to do it again sometime."

Something flashed across his features, brightening his eyes, tightening his mouth. Reaction jittered through Jo, but she really didn't want to think about it. Didn't want to consider that she was actually starting to feel something for the one man who could be a real danger to her.

Then the moment was gone again and he was taking a step closer. "I think I'm going to have to hold you to that, Josefina."

For the very first time, a ripple of something delicious stole through her when he said her full name.

Oh boy.

Behind them, a bedroom window on the second floor of the Marconi home opened and a loud, clear voice rolled out into the quiet. "Basta, Josefina! Enough! Is late. Who issa that man?"

Jo muttered a curse, but Cash was already shouting, "Cash Hunter, ma'am."

"Ah." Nana leaned on the window sash. "Bring your young man inside. Issa too cold for making romance outside. I make him some soup."

"Ohmigod." Jo closed her eyes, groaned, and prayed that the ground would open up beneath her.

Cash laughed and called out, "Another time, ma'am. Thank you!"

"Call me Nana," the older woman shouted back.

"Josefina! Kiss your Cash good night and come inside!"

Jo glared at the man still grinning at her. "One move, Cash Hunter, and you're a *dead* Money Fairy."

Seven

Jo looked across the bed of the truck at her little brother. Sunlight danced in his eyes, and though he tried to control his grin, his mouth just wouldn't cooperate.

Forced to swallow a smile of her own as she remembered the excitement of going out on jobs with her father, Jo narrowed her eyes on the boy. "Remember. You're going to do everything I tell you to do. And you're *not* going to get into trouble."

"Right." He nodded so hard, his hair dipped into his eyes and he whipped his head back to clear his vision.

"Really got to get you a haircut," Jo murmured as she reached into the lockbox for her battered, red steel toolbox.

"Mike says haircuts make you stupid."

Jo stopped, looked at him and shook her head. "You start listening to your sister Mike, and that's a bad sign."

He grinned and shrugged. "Emma told me she said it."

Jo sighed. "Sam had better tell her daughter not to listen to Mike too much."

"Why not? She's funny."

"Yeah, she is." Then she winked at him. "But don't tell her I said so."

He laughed and Jo felt a small rush of pleasure. Funny, but since Nana had arrived, she and Jack were getting closer. Probably, she thought, from banding together in self-defense.

Nana hadn't stopped cleaning since she hit town.

For the last five days, the only rest Jo got was when she was on a job site. And Jack was in no better shape. Their grandmother had cut off his video-game and TV time in favor of reading aloud and telling her how he had spent every minute of his day.

Hell, no wonder the kid was so delighted at her invitation to come along with her after school.

"Is Cash even here?" Jack asked, turning to look around the wooded area as if expecting the man to pop out from behind a bush.

"He'd better be," Jo murmured, hefting the heavy toolbox over the edge of the truck. The solid weight of it jerked her arm as she headed toward the main house.

It had been two days since she'd caught him in the act at the Sanchez house. Two days of listening to Nana talk about "that nicea Cash. So polite. Issa he *italiano*? *Cattolico*?" Two days of listening to her sisters and the rest of the town speculate on the Money Fairy's identity. Two days she'd spent remembering sitting beside him in the night, hearing the soft rumble of his voice.

She was really slipping.

Lifting one hand, she rubbed at the spot between her eyes and told herself that a headache was just punishment. She had no business thinking about Cash—the way she'd been thinking about him. Hadn't she learned firsthand just how bad things could get when you fell for a smooth line?

"Jo?"

She glanced at her brother, pushed her thoughts to one side, and concentrated instead on *him*. This time with Jack was a chance for her to connect. To find a relationship with a little brother she'd never expected to have. And all in all, he was a good kid. "Right. Let's go get him so we can finish up the work on that guest house of his."

She'd only taken a few steps when Cash walked out the double front doors and headed down the walk toward them. A long, slow breath slid from her lungs. She didn't know which was more impressive, Cash— or the house he'd built.

Clearing her throat, she spoke, her voice coming out a little louder, a little harsher than she'd intended. "Haven't seen you in a couple of days."

He pushed one hand through his thick, black hair and shrugged. "Been busy."

Doing what? she wondered, but squelched that thought fast.

"How's Nana?" he asked, one corner of his mouth lifting just enough to tantalize her.

She lifted one hand and pointed at him. "Don't start with me, Cash."

He only grinned and said, "Hi, Jack. You here to work with us?"

"Uh-huh. Jo says you want to add some more stuff to your cottage," Jack said, then glanced at his sister before adding, "But first can we show her what you're making over there?"

Jo's gaze followed the boy's pointing finger and she

noticed an outbuilding tucked some fifty feet behind the main house. Sheltered by trees, one long wall of the huge structure was windows and the wide, barn-style double doors were closed. She shifted her gaze back to Cash and noticed his hesitation. And since he clearly didn't want her to see inside, her curiosity raged.

"More secrets?" she challenged.

He shot a look at the boy, as if reminding her that she'd promised to keep quiet about the whole Money Fairy thing, before narrowing his gaze on her. "No."

"C'mon, Cash. Let's show her." Jack turned to his older sister. "It's really cool. He's got all these neat tools and he let me use a planner."

"Planer," she corrected automatically, still watching Cash. He looked uncomfortable. Interesting. The man was usually smooth and confident enough for three healthy men. What was it that could make him seem so . . . *vulnerable*?

A soft wind kicked up out of nowhere and lifted dirt from the road to twirl it into a mini-tornado. It blew it-self out again a moment later when it bumped into the tree line. Sunlight dappled the area, and from a dis-tance, a barking dog did its best to keep the quiet at bay.

"Fine," Cash finally muttered, as if surrendering to a fate worse than death. "You can show her. Go open it up," he said, with a nod for Jack.

The boy didn't need to be asked twice. He took off at a dead run down the road and across the sun-splashed backyard. But Jo wasn't really watching her brother.

"A gracious invitation," she said, lifting her toolbox to set it down on the hood of the truck.

He scowled, then shrugged, and the black T-shirt he wore rippled over the muscles hidden beneath the soft, worn fabric. "It's not like I'm trying to hide anything."

"Uh-huh. So why're you looking like you really wish I were somewhere that was *away*?"

At that, he gave her a half-smile. Just a minor quirk of his full mouth and something inside Jo took a nose-dive. Weird, but she felt as if every nerve in her body were doing somersaults all at once. Which was so not what she was looking for.

"Trust me, I like having you around."

He might like having her around, but she *didn't* trust him, and that was the whole problem, wasn't it? With that thought firmly rooted in her mind, she started walking, and when she passed him, he fell into line beside her. The wind off the ocean sighed around them, carrying the scent of the sea and the promise of the coming summer.

"So what am I about to see?"

He matched his steps to hers and the crunch of rocks and leaves beneath their feet was a friendly sound.

"Another well-kept secret, I guess."

She tipped her head up to look at him. "You're a real man of mystery, aren't you?"

"Never thought so before," he muttered.

Up ahead, from inside the building, the sounds of Jack rattling around drifted out to them. God knew what he was getting into. But before they joined her brother, Jo said what she'd wanted to say for two days.

"Mrs. Sanchez has been telling everyone who'll listen about how wonderful the Money Fairy was. How he'd saved her house and now she wouldn't lose it."

He stopped in the road and with the sunlight dropping over them like a warm blanket, he looked at her. "I don't do it to get the applause."

She studied his features, his dark, fathomless eyes, the tight set of his jaw, the nearly *embarrassed* expression on his face. "Yeah, I get that."

He nodded. "Good. Good."

"But . . ." She reached out and grabbed his upper arm when he took a step forward again. Instantly, she released him, before she could get used to the feel of all that tightly coiled strength beneath her hand. "If you don't mind my asking, one thing's been making me nuts."

Black eyebrows lifted. "Just one?"

Her mouth twitched. "Lately."

"Shoot."

"Okay. How does a carpenter, even a *talented* carpenter, get enough money to play benefactor to a whole town?"

Cash frowned and scrubbed one hand across his jaw. He'd been sort of hoping to avoid that question. Should have known that Jo would want to confront it.

She picked up on his hesitation in a heartbeat, and when she spoke again, her voice was filled with suspicion. "What're you into?"

Irritation snapped like a whip inside him. "Get that 'I'm gonna call the cops' look off your face. Do you really think I'm some kind of criminal or something? And if I *was*, I'd invite the kid into it?"

She scowled right back at him. "Well, none of us knows much about you, do we?" she countered. "Hell, for all I know you're some mob guy hiding out from the feds."

Astonished, he simply goggled at her. "Your mind is a *very* interesting place to visit. Living there must be a nightmare."

"You're not answering the question."

"Wasn't a question. *Was* an accusation."

Jo blew out a breath and held up one hand. "Okay, you're right. Fine. Fine. I don't think you're a mob guy."

"Hey," he drawled. *"Thanks."*

"Come on, look at it from my point of view, okay?" she said, poking him in the chest with the tip of her index finger. "You blow into town a year ago, start seducing women right and left, sending them off to be Mother Teresas all over the damn world."

He shifted position uncomfortably, scraping his boots against the rocky ground.

"Then this Money Fairy starts making itself known, dropping cash all over town—and now I find out it's *you.*"

He glanced at the workshop, to make sure Jack was still inside where he couldn't overhear. "Keep it down, will ya?"

"So pardon the hell outta *me* for being just a tiny bit suspicious."

Her pale blue eyes were lit with a kind of fire that could singe a man right down to his bones. He knew she had no idea just how amazing she looked when her temper was kicking and her body all but vibrating. Dangerous, but amazing.

And what kind of weirdo did it make him that he actually *liked* fighting with her?

He reached up, shoved both hands through his hair,

scraping it back from his face and stalling to figure out just how to tell her. "In college," he finally said, deciding to simply blurt out the truth, "my roommate was always tinkering with shit. Mechanical stuff. Wires, chips, whatever." Smiling to himself, Cash remembered their dorm room. "I was always stepping on some stray piece of metal or the clipped ends of wires."

"So . . ."

"There's that legendary patience of yours," he said, with a shake of his head. "The guy didn't have *any* extra cash. He was always hungry, always scrounging for a little extra money to buy parts for the computers he built in our room."

"He *built* computers."

"Oh yeah," Cash said, grinning now at the memories flashing through his brain. "He was brilliant—couldn't remember to tie his own shoes but he could probably have built a working spaceship if he'd wanted to. Anyway, he eventually started selling some of them to the other students, so his cash flow improved a little. But I kept him in pizzas and spare parts for three years."

Jo shook her head and threw her hands wide before letting them fall back against her sides. "And this has *what* to do with you being the Money Fairy?"

He winced. Seriously, he hated being called that. "At the end of our third year, Jimmy dropped out of college. Wanted to make a go of his computer business."

"Risky."

"Oh yeah, but like I said, he was brilliant." Shrugging his shoulders, Cash continued, "I introduced him to some former associates of my mother's. They backed him and he went into business. He gave me a million shares of the company as a thank-you."

"This is going to have a happy ending, isn't it?"

He nodded. "Ever hear of Holt Computers?"

She staggered. Eyes wide, mouth open, she breathed, "Are you kidding me?"

"Nope." He grinned at her reaction. You never had to wonder too long what Josefina was thinking. Usually it was right there on her gorgeous face. "Jimmy Holt started the business in our dorm room. Now, he's making Bill Gates sweat."

"And you got a million shares."

"Well, there's more now," he mused, and started walking again, not surprised when Jo fell into step beside him. "They've split and split again a few times."

"Right." She blew out a breath. "And you don't want anyone to know this because . . ."

He stopped again. He could hear the radio playing in the workshop and figured Jack was making himself at home. He only hoped the kid wasn't trying the planer again without supervision. They needed to get in there, but first he wanted to make his point. "Because when people find out about the money—they act different. Treat me differently."

"Poor little rich man?"

"Funny." He reached out, grabbed her shoulders, and dragged her close. Looking down into her eyes, he realized that this was one of the few times he *couldn't* read her expression. Perfect. Was she going to be like all the rest? Was Jo going to start acting weird around him? "I don't tell people because I don't want them to know. Okay?"

"Dial it down, geez," she muttered, clearly over her shocked surprise. She stepped out from beneath his hands, shoved her own into her jeans pockets, and looked him up and down dismissively. "I don't care if you've got more money than God. You still bug the hell out of me."

Relief shot through him at a blistering rate. But he took a deep breath and blew it out anyway, just to steady himself. He should have known that piles of money wouldn't impress Josefina. Strange how pleased that made him. "Good to know."

"Good. Now. You want to show me your other little secret so we can finish up the *latest* additions to the cottage?"

Marconi Construction had been working on the guest cottage at Cash's place off and on for the last eight months. Every time she thought they were finished, Cash came up with something new to do. Expand the kitchen. Add a built-in Murphy bed to the living room. A river rock fireplace. You name it, Cash wanted it.

And now that Jo knew he was Grace Van Horn's nephew, she wondered if compulsive construction was hereditary.

He laughed, took her elbow and steered her toward the workshop. They stepped into the wide, sunlit area and Jo stopped dead beside him. When he told her about the money, she'd been surprised, but clearly unmoved. But this was different, he thought, watching her as she stepped into the part of his life that was the most important to him.

Her pale blue eyes went soft and dewy and she

moved forward slowly, carefully, as if she were entering a church. She turned in a slow circle, letting her gaze linger over the finished furniture and the projects he was still working on. He followed her gaze himself and felt a swell of pride as he looked at the handcrafted armoires, beds, and tables crowding the hangarlike building.

The rich smell of freshly sawn wood filled the air and classic Stones pumped from the radio.

"Isn't it *awesome*?" Jack shouted over the music. "Cash *made* all this stuff!"

Jo ignored her brother and let her gaze sweep over the collection of furniture stacked in Cash's workshop. She hadn't given a damn about his money. Hadn't cared that he was sneaking around town being Santa, the Tooth Fairy, and the Easter Bunny rolled into one. But this.

This was different.

Shaken, she stared at the exquisite craftsmanship of the pieces surrounding her. This was the kind of thing she appreciated. The kind of work she loved to do herself—when she could find the time to indulge herself.

To find the hidden beauty in a block of wood and coax it to the surface. To show it to those who would never have seen it on their own. The detailed carving, the painstaking care involved in true craftsmanship took patience, she knew. But it also required sheer talent to create such beauty.

The wide windows lining one side of the building allowed plenty of sunlight to enter the room, and it dazzled off polished wood surfaces, spotlighted works in progress, and showcased some amazing completed pieces.

She recognized the style. The artistry. Now she knew who had made the special "one of a kind" furniture that was sold at a specialty store right outside of Chandler. Now she knew who had carved the magnificent bed her sister Mike and her husband, Lucas, had bought there.

And one more time, she was forced to admit that there was a lot more to Cash Hunter than she'd first imagined. How did he manage to keep surprising her?

Shaking her head, licking dry lips, she looked up at him and whispered, "Okay, *now* I'm impressed."

"Nana," Mike said, inching back into the sofa as far as her nearly eight-months-pregnant body would let her. "I just don't think olive oil on my stomach is the look I'm going for."

"*Silenzio*, Michaela, quiet," the old woman translated just in case Mike had missed the order given.

But she was used to listening to half Italian, half English. Nana was still more at home with her first language than with the English she'd learned as a young woman. Just as she was more at home with herbal remedies than aspirin, or olive oil instead of expensive body creams and lotions.

Mike was already a woman on the edge. Hadn't she just that morning practically chased her own husband out the door? She felt like an overfilled balloon and wished to hell someone would pop her already. It had been years since that moment when she'd so giddily announced her pregnancy. *Years.*

She couldn't even remember a time when she could bend over to pull her own boots on. Hell, she hadn't seen her *feet* in two weeks!

"What's going on?" Sam asked as she came back from the bathroom.

"Michaela issa making a fuss," Nana said primly, clasping the bottle of olive oil at her waist as though it were a sword in the hands of a skilled fighter.

"Ooh. News flash," Sam said, swallowing hard and easing down onto the soft green couch opposite its twin, where Mike lay like a beached whale. "What's wrong now?"

Nana straightened up to her full four feet nine inches—used to be five feet even, but she was shrinking—and lifted her chin. In a slice of sunlight, she was silhouetted. A short, thin woman still wearing black for the husband who'd died more than thirty years before. Her snow-white hair lay close to her head in a series of tightly wound curls that looked like sausages snuggled together in a package.

Her face was lined, but her dark brown eyes snapped with life and energy. Her voice was quiet but steely, and her stubbornness was the stuff of legend.

"Michaela issa *arguing* with me."

"Impressive," Sam whispered, "but a losing proposition." She propped her feet up and dropped her head back onto a pillow. Taking deep breaths, she cupped her palms over her slightly rounded belly.

"Drink your tea," Nana said.

Mike smirked as she looked at her sister. "Nana doesn't think you should still be so sick. So she made you a special tea. To *help*."

Sam's eyes widened as she finally noticed the steaming mug set near her on the low coffee table. Her nose wrinkled at the flowery yet stinky smell drifting toward her. "Oh." She swallowed hard. "Thanks, but—"

"Drink your tea, Samantha. Issa good for you. Good for the bambino."

"The bambino doesn't like *anything* I eat, Nana."

"He will like this." She narrowed her eyes on Sam until the younger woman surrendered and picked up the mug.

Taking one slow, cautious sip, Sam swallowed and waited. When nothing disastrous happened, she took another and began to breathe a little easier.

"What's in this?" she asked.

Nana smiled. "Issa secret recipe. I tell you another time."

"Cool." Sam cradled the mug between her palms and took another sip.

"Now you, Michaela."

"Seriously, Nana," Mike said, tugging at her shirt to hold it down even as Nana pulled up on it. "I'm glad the tea worked for Sam, but I'm good. Really."

"Michaela, I come to take care of you and your bambinos."

"I know." She sighed out a breath and gave up the fight as Nana's gnarled fingers won the tugging war on her shirt. Incredible, really, just how much strength remained in her hands. "But I don't want to smell like a Caesar salad."

Sam snorted and Mike glared at her.

"Issa good, you see." The older woman leaned over

Mike, lifted the hem of her shirt and exposed her full belly. "Olive oil issa good for the skin," she said, pouring a big puddle of extra virgin oil into the hollow of her hand. "And the babies will like the rubbing."

Mike stared at the beamed ceiling as her grandmother massaged her huge stomach and the slow slide of gentle hands began to work some of the tension from her body. She sighed and let herself enjoy the moment, not really thinking about how she was going to get olive oil out of her clothes or, God help her, the fabric of the couch.

"Ah," Nana said, her voice as comforting as her touch, "this issa a good time for us. Your papa, the *bastardo,* is gone—"

"Nana," Mike warned.

She waved one bony hand. "Issa fine. I no talk about the *bastardo*. This is not about him. This is about the boy. Jack. He is a good boy. Smart. Handsome. And you girls." She smiled and her wrinkled face shifted, falling into comfortable, familiar lines. "All of you. You and Samantha with the babies, Josefina with her young man—"

"What?" A single word shot from both Mike's and Sam's mouths and together they stared at their still smiling grandmother in stunned shock.

For one brief moment, there was perfect understanding between Jo and Cash. It hung in the air, and sizzled in the undercurrent of electricity humming all around them.

Jo felt it. Wasn't sure what to *do* about it, but she felt it.

"Did you see the chair back there?" Jack called out, shattering the moment and giving Jo time to reel in the emotions stuttering to life inside her.

She wanted to kiss the kid for it.

"Which chair?" she asked, tearing her gaze from Cash's.

"That one." He pointed. "There's a dragon carved into the top of it."

Even as Jo moved in for a closer look, Jack took off, exploring, leaving the two of them alone. "Hey," she shouted, "don't run around in here, it's—"

"It's okay." Cash spoke up quickly. "He's been by here a few times after school. He knows his way around. He can't hurt anything."

"So the baseball visit wasn't the only time he's come here then."

Cash grinned. "He's come back a few times to practice. He's getting pretty good."

Irritation fluttered inside her, but she fought it down. Wasn't *Cash's* fault she hadn't had time—or, to be honest, hadn't *made* the time—to play catch with Jack. She was just so damn busy all the time. It was as if the Marconi house of cards were tumbling down around her and she was the only one left who could support the last pillars standing.

Papa was gone, Mike was down for the count, and Sam spent most of her free time hurling. Which left *Jo* to pick up all the slack.

Pity party, aisle three.

She blew out a breath, promised herself to spend more time with her brother, and then turned her gaze on the chair the boy had wanted her to see. "Oh my . . ."

Cash folded his arms across his chest and said only, "It started out a simple Mission style. But the burl of the wood looked—"

"Like a dragon," Jo finished for him as she walked closer to the chair and ran her fingertips over the detail work. Smooth. Every inch of it was smooth as glass and intricately carved. The tiny dragon with its tail furled looked as though it could leap out of the wood and spring into life with a roar and a blast of fire. "It's beautiful."

"Thanks."

She looked up at him. "I think we're having a moment."

He grinned. "First time we've talked without you threatening to hit me."

Jo felt the smile on her lips and couldn't seem to stop it. "First time you haven't pushed me into wanting to."

That indefinable *something* was back, stretching between them like a slender, tenuous thread. The slightest movement could break it.

Something crashed in the back of the room and Jack yelled, "Sorry," his voice drifting just under the clash of classic rock still pumping from the radio.

She practically *heard* that thread snap.

"I'd better go see if I can afford whatever he just broke," Jo mused.

"Don't worry about it," Cash said, reaching out to lay one hand on her arm. "Jo, I—"

The music died and in its place came a commercial with a too enthusiastic announcer urging them to vote for Steve Smith for State Senate. A moment later, the voice of the man himself could be heard, promising to fight for *all* the people of California.

A yawning chasm opened up inside her and Jo felt all the blood in her head drain down into it. Her stomach did one wild, lurching spin and tiny black dots danced festively at the corners of her vision.

"Hey. Are you okay?" Cash's hand on her arm tightened.

"Fine." She swallowed hard and repeated the single word, for her own sake if not his. Valiantly, she tried to block the sound of Steve Smith's voice, but it seemed to storm her defenses and sink right into her bloodstream like some toxic oil leak. "Fine."

"You don't look fine. You look sick." He lifted one hand and cupped her chin, turning her face up to his. "You have that reaction to all commercials or just to political crap?"

His touch was too comforting. His voice too filled with concern—especially when she was feeling a little rocky.

"It's nothing," she said, stepping back and away from him, drawing air into her too tight chest, forcing the frantic gallop of her heart to ease into a trot. "That guy—Steve Smith? He's just . . . *icky.*"

"Not going to be voting for him, I guess," he said.

"That's a safe bet," she murmured, and walked toward the back of the building and the little brother she sorely needed for a distraction—to get Cash off this subject, *fast.*

"So what about him bugs you?"

She felt the crawl of cold memories inching down her spine and did what she could to cover the shiver. This was not something she was going to get into.

Not now.

Not ever.

"It's a long story."

"Do I look busy?"

She stopped, looked up at him, and tried not to notice the flash of curiosity mingled with *compassion* in his eyes. "No, but *I* am."

"Jo, there's something there."

"It's none of your business," she said, closing the door firmly on whatever friendly moments they'd had. "Besides, you wouldn't understand."

"Never know if you don't try."

She felt crowded. Silly. Standing in the middle of the huge workshop, she felt as though the walls were sneaking up on her. "Fine. You say you'd understand. Have you ever been in love?"

"Yes."

Another little ripple of shock rocked through her and Jo could have kicked her own ass for saying anything. She'd thought, being the Woman Whisperer that he was, he'd say no and she'd be able to tell him he'd never understand what he hadn't experienced. Love. Betrayal. Pain.

Now, she was stuck. No way out.

"Me, too," she said simply, and started walking again, distancing herself from not only Cash, but the conversation.

Naturally, his long legs made up the distance between them in a heartbeat.

"With Steve Smith?" he asked, his voice tight and low.

Jo stopped dead, half turned her head to look back at him over her shoulder. She met his gaze briefly, but

long enough to fry him with a look that would have
warned off an armed warrior. "I don't want to talk
about it."

She'd managed to avoid talking about it for nearly
ten years.

No reason to change things now.

Eight

A few hours later, Cash wandered through his empty house and tried to find the satisfaction he kept expecting to feel. He'd built the house of his dreams, lived in the town that had seemed almost magical to him as a child, and yet . . . "Nothing."

He stalked across the gleaming, light oak floor, his boot heels clacking loudly in the silence that seemed, now that Jo and her brother had gone home, too loud. His gaze drifted around the room as he crossed to the wall of windows overlooking the tiny lake on the outskirts of Chandler.

The walls, like the floor, were pale oak, and looked almost golden in the soft, late afternoon light spearing through the glass. The walls were crowded with art, an eclectic mix of modern and traditional that suited his personality—a man haunted by his past and determined to never think about the future.

Maybe if things had been different, he thought, then shut that line of thinking down. Regrets were useless. He'd made his choices and now he would live with them.

Talking to Jo had stirred things up in his mind again. The stunned surprise in her eyes when he'd admitted to once being in love. The shaken hurt in her eyes when he'd said the name Steve Smith.

What was that about?

What was tearing at her?

And why the hell was he letting himself care?

Even a *stupid* man would have learned better by now and Cash was no idiot. He knew what everyone in Chandler called him—the Woman Whisperer. He supposed most men would be pleased to have such a "gift" with women. But Cash knew it wasn't so much a gift as a curse.

It had started in college.

Cash liked women. *All* women. Tall and short, fat and thin. They were all beautiful to him. He liked the way they laughed, the way they thought, and the way they smelled. And women loved him back.

Which, taken by itself, was a good thing. But he'd noticed that the women he took to his bed never stayed. They spent the night with him, and in the morning, they invariably left his bed and went off to save the world or some damn thing.

The first couple of times it happened to him, Cash just figured it was a coincidence. And when he fell in love, he never for a moment believed that she too would go.

But she had.

He slapped one hand against an oak beam and peered out through the glass at the streaked colors of the sunset reflected on the surface of the lake. In that cool blue mirror, clouds sailed and colors blended and the water rippled lazily in a soft wind.

But he hardly noticed. His mind was lost in memory. Again, he saw the woman he loved toss his ring back at him and walk out of his life, taking her child—the child that had become almost as important to him as she herself had been—with her.

Now history, it seemed, was repeating itself. Not only was he thinking way too often about Jo—but her little brother was etching out a place of his own in Cash's heart. Another danger. Another chance for pain.

He shook his head, tapped his fingers against the cold glass, and lost today in the memories of the past he usually ignored.

Cash'd discovered much later that his own father had had this "gift" with women. Cash's mother had once been a rising young executive at a prestigious ad agency in New York City. Then she'd married Cash's father and changed. She'd lasted a few months with him before resigning from the real world and going off with a group of friends. They traveled the country, working when they had to, exploring all the little roads people so seldom saw.

A hundred years ago, they would have been called gypsies. In the sixties, they would have been hippies. Now, he supposed, they were just . . . odd.

Cash traveled with them until he was thirteen and old enough to tell his mother he wasn't interested in being a wanderer for the rest of his life. That he wanted a home. School.

She'd said she couldn't give that to him, but she did take him to his father. But the old man didn't want him, either, though he was willing to pay for boarding school.

Every September, his mother Kate dropped Cash off for the school year and every year he begged her to stay. She never did, though, and Cash was alone again.

By the time he won a scholarship to college, he'd stopped asking her to stay.

Then, when the woman he'd loved left him, he'd vowed to never ask *anyone* to stay again. Because he was tired of being the one left behind.

He'd made a choice years ago. He'd decided back when his heart was still aching that he would only sleep with women he didn't love. Or better yet, women who were unhappy with their own lives.

That way no one got hurt.

No one expected more than they got.

"And nothing's changed," he muttered, and the sound of his own whispered voice sounded like a shout in the stillness.

But even though he'd like to tell himself otherwise, Jo Marconi didn't fit his "rules." She didn't slide easily into any little compartment in his mind. She was . . . *different*.

Damn it.

He enjoyed her. Liked being around her. Dreamed about the feel of her skin against his, the taste of her mouth, the sigh of her breath. And he didn't *want* to care. Didn't *want* to want her.

Sleeping with her was the answer, of course. Then she'd be out of his life. She'd move on and he could go back to doing what he did best.

Alone.

"But the hell of it is," he said, shifting his gaze to the deepening blue of the sky, "I don't want to lose her yet, either."

And that bugged the hell out of him.

When the doorbell rang, he jumped, startled at the intrusion. He was far enough out of town that you had to make a real effort to "drop by." And since he knew damn well that Jo was probably still steaming over the way they'd left things that afternoon, it wouldn't be *her* ringing his bell.

He left the great room and moved down the long hall to the double doors, his boot heels beating a loud rhythm against the wood floor. Grabbing hold of the antique brass knob, he gave it a turn and yanked the door open.

And his day finished its trip to hell in an instant.

The sun was down by the time they got home, but Jo thought it was worth it. Once they left Cash's place, she'd decided that it was time for a little Marconi bonding. Hell, Jack deserved better from his oldest sister than having his homework checked. Besides, she'd needed the extra time to cool down after having her past jump up and slug her in the stomach.

"This is great," the boy said from the passenger seat. He spooned up another mouthful of hot fudge sundae and Jo felt as if she'd won a medal. Stopping on the way home for ice cream had made her a hero.

Wasn't as hard as she'd thought, she realized. Only a year ago, she'd wondered if she'd ever find a way to be close to the child who was her brother. Not that she blamed Jack or anything, but he surely was a four-foot-tall reminder of how far her father had slipped off his pedestal.

But then, she thought, Papa'd never asked to be up there where only the perfect could be comfortable. It was she and her sisters who'd taken care of that.

Then when he'd proven himself to be just a human being, Jo'd turned on him like a snake. Not a nice thing

to admit about yourself, but there it was. Papa's secret
came out and shattered them. If her own ever came out,
it would grind what was left of them into dust.

"You okay?" Jack asked, eyes narrowing as he
watched her.

"Yeah," she said, and reached out to push his hair
back from his brow. "I'm fine. But you won't be if
Nana sees you eating that before dinner."

"I'm almost done." To prove it, he grinned again and
plowed a heaping spoonful of ice cream and whipped
cream into his mouth.

"Right," she laughed and opened the truck door.
"Stay out here until you're finished, okay? I'll tell
Nana you're—" She came up blank. "I'll think of
something."

"'Kay."

Grabbing up her ever-present binder filled with job
files, she hopped down and started up the walk toward
the front door. The porch light shone in the twilight
like a modern-day candle in the window.

Shadows slipped from every corner of the house,
stretching out dark fingers to claim the night. The
flower beds needed weeding, the trim needed painting,
and the porch rail looked a little wobbly.

But to Jo, it was perfect. Home. The place where
she'd grown up. The place she'd run to ten years ago,
when her brand-new world had crashed and burned
around her.

The old Victorian meant safety.

Comfort.

She took the porch steps in two long strides, opened
the front door and stopped.

Sam was stretched out on the floor, hands over her

stomach, eyes closed, mouth grimly flattened into a tight, thin line.

From the kitchen came the nearly orgasmic scent of red-wine beef stew. Garlic flavored the air with enough strength to knock a less hardy soul to her knees, but she couldn't enjoy that just yet.

"Are you dead?" she asked, and kicked Sam's booted foot.

"If God is a good God, I will be soon," Sam muttered, without prying her lips apart.

Drama. One thing the Marconis all shined at. "What're you doing on the floor?"

Her sister pried one eye open and looked up at her. "Got dizzy. It was either lie down or fall down. This seemed easiest."

Jack clattered up the steps behind Jo and stuck his head around her. "What're you doing, Sam?"

"Resting."

"On the floor?" He sneaked past Jo into the hall.

"Seemed like a good idea at the time."

"Josefina, you are home," Nana called from the kitchen. "Step over your sister and comea taste the stew."

Sam's eyes opened.

Jo grinned.

Jack laughed and ran past his sisters to the kitchen. "I'll taste it, Nana!" Only a ten-year-old boy could polish off a double sundae and still be hungry.

"Is there no sympathy for the dying here?" Sam murmured pitifully.

"Fresh out," Jo said, and reached down to hold out a hand to Sam. Her sister grabbed it and held on when Jo pulled her to her feet.

"Okay?"

"Just a sec," she said, inhaling sharply, deeply as she swayed on her feet. "Okay, I may live."

"Good to know," Jo said, shutting the front door before facing her sister again. Sam's auburn hair only made her face look paler. Her blue eyes, Marconi eyes, looked wide and glassy. "What're you doing here, anyway? Don't you have a home? Husband? Daughter?"

"Yes, to all of it," Sam said, and headed into the living room to plop down onto an overstuffed sofa covered in faded tapestry cabbage roses. "I'm here, getting sick at the scent of wine and garlic"—she hissed in a breath and blew it out again—"because Nana spilled her guts."

"About?" Jo asked, and sat down next to Sam, waiting for the rest of it. She had a bad feeling about where this was going. Ever since the night Nana had spotted her and Cash out on the front lawn, Jo had felt the sword hanging over her head. Apparently, it was about to drop.

"You and Cash." Sam sent a horrified glare at the kitchen. "God, did she put like twenty cloves of garlic in that stew? It's like a toxic cloud. It's the garlic that ate Chandler."

Jo took a deep, appreciative breath. "Smells good."

Sam turned a cold stare on her. "I hate you."

"Love you back." Jo propped her feet on the coffee table, then crossed them at the ankle, hoping for a nonchalant pose that wouldn't give anything away. "And what about me and Cash?"

"Nana says he's your new honey."

Her feet uncrossed and her right boot clunked on the

tabletop. Damn it. She should have known that Nana would take the proverbial bit between her teeth and start off running. The old woman had probably already started a novena to Saint Jude—the patron saint of lost causes—for finally allowing Josefina to find a *man*. "Oh, for God's sake."

"Mike's going nuts." Sam dropped her head back on the sofa cushion and sighed. "She wants details and wants 'em now."

"Tough shit." Jo jumped up from the sofa and ignored Sam's moan of distress at the sharp movement. "There *are* no details. Never was, never will be, and if there were," she snapped, turning around to jab her index finger at Sam, "I sure as hell wouldn't talk about 'em to you two."

"Who else would you tell?" Offended, Sam sat up straighter.

"Nobody." She threw both hands high, let them drop, and shot a quick look at the empty doorway to the kitchen. Then she lowered her voice, because she so didn't need Nana throwing in her two cents' worth. But the conversation in the kitchen was still going strong between the boy and his grandmother, so she figured she was safe.

"I don't have the urge, like Mike, to tell every living soul whatever thought happens to drift through my mind," Jo said, stalking back to the couch. "And unlike *you*, I don't whine about my problems."

"*Whine?*" Sam stood up slowly, until she could glare at Jo, right in the eye. "I don't *whine*."

"Really? Then what's this?" She waved a hand at her. "All you could talk about was how much you wanted another baby. Then the minute you get pregnant, all you do is whine about how you're so sick, it must be a punishment for giving up your first baby."

"That wasn't whining," Sam said with a defensive sniff. "That was *talking* to my sisters who are *supposed* to listen to me."

"Oh, trust me," Jo said with a snort. "We listen."

Sam stood up too and momentarily thought she might have to make a break for the bathroom again, but she swallowed back the urge and glared at her sister. "Fine. Maybe I have been a little whiny—"

"A *little*?" Jo laughed shortly. "That's the biggest understatement since Custer said 'I think I see an Indian.'"

Sam sneered at her. "You try tossing your cookies every fifteen minutes and see how *you* feel."

"No, thanks."

"And since we're being so honest here," Sam continued, keeping her voice as low as Jo's as she leaned in to make her point. "I'd like to say that you deliberately switched this conversation around so that we're talking about *me* instead of *you*."

Jo jerked her head back and glared at her younger sister. Altogether, Sam was just too damn quick to miss much. Too bad.

Sam leaned in even further, until they were nearly nose to nose. "Something's definitely up with Cash or you wouldn't be so hyper."

"I'm not hyper. I'm annoyed."

"You're always annoyed, Jo. This is different." She stared hard into Jo's eyes, looking for something, and finally she smiled. "Hah!"

"What?" Jo backed up warily. Her sister looked too damn happy.

"You're *interested* in him."

She flinched inwardly but was pretty sure she covered it up on the outside. "Any woman would be. As a science experiment. The man is—"

"Yeah, yeah," Sam said, ending Jo's rant before it could get started. "Heard it all before. He should be castrated. A warning sign around his neck, blah, blah. But I don't hear you saying I'm wrong. Or that Nana's wrong."

She gritted her teeth, folded her arms over her chest, and lied. "You're wrong."

"Too late," Sam said, grinning now. "Wait'll I tell Mike. She's gonna love this."

Shit.

"But when you do have sex with him, no changing your life and running out of town."

"You think *Cash* could make me run when my own sisters haven't been able to manage it yet?" Jo murmured darkly.

"This is great," Sam continued, heading unsteadily toward the front door. "Plus, now Mike owes me five bucks."

It took a second, then it clicked in. "You *bet* on me?"

Sam looked over her shoulder at her. "Of course. Last summer."

"Last—"

"When you and Cash were at each other's throats all the time? I bet Mike five bucks that inside a year, you two would be doing the mattress bounce."

Jo's chin hit her chest. Nothing like family to take

your personal life and make it something worth betting on. "We haven't—"

"You will. And when *that* happens, Mike and I *both* want a report."

"Oh, for God's sake . . ."

"Samantha," Nana called out, "you take some stew home to Emma and your husband."

Sam hunched her shoulders and bolted for the front door. Frantic, she glanced at Jo. "Tell her I'm already gone. If I have to drive home with all that garlic in the car with me, I'll be pulling over to hurl every five minutes."

"What're you doing here?" Cash's grip on the edge of the door tightened reflexively. Everything inside him shuttered and closed as the dying sun sliced like a blade into his eyes.

His father smiled briefly, and stepped past him into the foyer. "Good to see you, too, son."

The cloying scent of Aramis announced his arrival, then stuck around to follow after him. Jared Hunter's black hair was dusted with gray at the temples and his features were blurred from too many years of too much booze. The body he'd once kept carefully maintained was starting to show some wear, but the smile was the same.

Empty charm and unfulfilled promises.

Once, Cash had hoped to be close with his father. Once, long ago, he'd thought that the two of them could build the family Cash had always wanted. But Jared hadn't been interested in knowing the son he'd made with a woman he barely remembered, let alone missed. And Cash had learned to stop wanting.

Closing the door, Cash leaned back against it, folded his arms over his chest and crossed his feet at the ankles. He wouldn't give the man the satisfaction of knowing that he could still get a rise out of him. "What do you want?"

Jared glanced around the impressive foyer, then shifted a look at his son. "Just happened to be in the neighborhood."

"Right." Cash pushed away from the door and stood on his own two feet. Didn't hurt that he was a good inch or two taller than the other man. "Since when is Chandler, California, in *your* neighborhood? Last I heard you were still living in Chicago."

Jared rocked on his heels, pushed his hands into the pockets of his well-tailored slacks, and took another appraising look around him. "Too cold. Thought it was time for a change."

A flicker of unease darted through him. "You're not moving here."

Jared smiled again. "That would be handy, wouldn't it? The Hunter men, together at last?"

Together.

Cash knew the only reason his father was here. The only reason he *ever* got in touch. And it didn't have a damn thing to do with family.

"Aren't you going to offer me a drink?"

Cash didn't really want to, but hell. He could use a beer himself. Without a word, he started down the hall and made a sharp left turn into the great room. The cathedral ceiling was high and wide. Four sofas were arranged in two different seating areas—one near the fireplace and the other staged to take advantage of the view.

A fire crackled in the river-rock hearth and the flames threw dancing shadows and the rich smell of burning wood into the room.

Beyond the wall of glass, the lake spread out, dazzled with the swirl of reflected color from the sunset. Trees dipped and swayed with the wind and a couple of ducks floated in mindless circles in the center of the water.

Cash didn't notice any of it. Instead, he headed for the wet bar in the far corner, stepped behind it and opened a minifridge. Grabbing up two beers, he set one on the bar and twisted the cap off the second one.

"You've done well for yourself," Jared said, snatching up the beer and wandering to the wide windows. "Too rural for me, of course, but very impressive nonetheless."

Cash had to force the swallow of beer past the tight knot in his throat. He hated that his father could still get to him. He hated having the man here, in the one place he'd been able to carve out for himself.

And at that thought, he told himself to relax. To remember that they were on *his* turf here. He had the advantage for a change. He inhaled sharply, tried to steady himself with the comfort of the familiar, and asked, "What do you want, Jared?"

The man smirked at him over his shoulder. "Is that any way for a man to talk to his father?"

He wouldn't be pulled down this road again. Wouldn't be manipulated the way he'd been as a child. Those days were long gone. "If I had a *father,* I'd be more careful."

Jared shrugged, tipped the beer up and took a long, healthy swallow. Then he studied the label on the bottle as if it were the Rosetta Stone. "Made yourself a home here, didn't you?" he murmured. "But I wonder if you'd have any of this if I hadn't paid for your education."

His guts felt cold and hollow. He didn't owe Jared Hunter anything. Didn't *want* to owe him. "I won that scholarship to college."

"Ah," Jared pointed out, before taking another sip of his beer, "you wouldn't have won it without the fancy prep school ties though, would you?"

Cash wouldn't be swayed. "Most people put their kids through high school."

"And most children appreciate it." He paced aimlessly around the room, lifting small vases, checking the bottoms, hefting a Remington sculpture as if he could judge the value of it by its weight.

Ancient aches reverberated through him, but Cash squashed them flat. He wasn't that kid anymore. The boy who'd hoped for family. A place to belong. He'd long since given up on that notion and accepted his "family" for what it really was.

His gaze locked on his father, Cash bit back the bitterness nearly choking him. The key to surviving his father's "visits" was to keep them as short as possible. Then all he'd have to do was bury himself in work to try to forget that the man was ever here.

"I was thinking maybe I'd just stick around for a while," Jared said as he set the sculpture down with a thunk, then shoved his hands into his slacks pockets and jingled the car keys within. "Spend a little 'quality' time with my son."

Quality time.

Jesus.

Rocking on his heels, Jared sent his son a smile.

"Think it'd be a good idea to settle in for a while. Meet the people here—introduce myself around."

"You wouldn't like it. Too rural, remember?"

Jared smiled again. "A man can get used to anything."

Cash's stomach fisted. Just having his father in his house made him want to get the place fumigated. The man really knew how to work a con. They both knew damn well that Jared didn't want to be in Chandler any more than Cash wanted him there. But just the threat of a long visit would be enough to pry Cash's wallet open that much quicker.

And that's what this visit was all about.

What they were *always* about.

Jared'd "dropped" in on him before. And the only way to make him leave was to give him the only thing Jared Hunter had ever appreciated.

Money.

And despite the fact that he wanted to throw his father out on his ass, he knew that he would pay. Because as much as Cash'd like to pretend that he'd come from a family, the truth of the matter was that he'd sprung from two selfish people who never should have met. He loved his mother, but in her own way, she was no better than Jared.

It was her way or no way.

Always had been.

But at least his mother had *tried*.

His father, though, had had no use for him until the money from Jimmy Holt's company had started pouring in. It was just as he'd told Jo earlier. People tended to treat you differently when they found out you had piles of money. Even his old man had managed to bury his disinterest in his only son for the sake of getting his "fair share" of his son's fortune.

It seemed, though, that Jared never really could get enough.

"How much this time?" Cash ground out, hating the taste of the words in his mouth. Hating knowing that he'd be willing to pay whatever it took to get this man out of his home. To have the invasion of his world reversed.

Jared stopped beside the hand-carved entertainment center and ran the tip of one finger along the detailed lines of the oak piece. Cash thought about disinfecting that piece as soon as he could get the man gone.

Taking another long drink of his beer, Jared mused aloud, "Well, if you'd rather I didn't stay here in Chandler . . ."

Cash stared at him.

Jared chuckled. "You should think about it, though, *son*. We could really make a hell of a team together."

"I don't think so." Jesus, the thought of becoming anything like his old man was enough to make Cash want to find the nearest cliff and jump off.

"All right then, if not here, I was thinking that it's time I moved to a warmer climate. A waterfront condo in West Palm Beach would be about right." He sighed, then smiled at his son. "I hear there are lots of lonely ladies there."

His insides clenched, then relaxed again. Fuck it. It was only money. What was a few million in the grand scheme of things? If it bought Cash solitude, it was well worth the price. Although, he thought, he should probably take out an ad in the local paper, warning women away from Jared.

Wouldn't matter, though. The older man still had the knack of turning women's brains to oatmeal.

Still.

Better Florida than California.

"Fine," he said, and stalked out of the room to get his checkbook.

Nine

The sun was hot, but the wind, sweeping in off the ocean, felt cold. Excitement jangled through Jack Marconi as he held on to his practically new baseball mitt with a grip tight enough to press his fingertips into the leather. His heart was beating really fast and his mouth was all dry and he felt like maybe he might be sick. Fear twisted with happiness and tangled up in his chest until breathing was really hard.

The grass needed mowing, the bleachers were only half full, and none of the kids had real uniforms, because Little League wouldn't start until June, but this was a really *real* baseball game anyway.

And he was on the team.

He smiled to himself as he sat on the bench in the dugout and listened to the other guys talking and laughing around him. He kicked his beat-up sneakers against the dirt, sending tiny brown clouds into the air. Pushing his hair out of his eyes, he pulled the brim of his hat down lower and looked over his shoulder at the bleachers behind him.

Moms and dads and brothers and sisters were laughing and talking and waiting for the start of the game.

He scanned the crowd until he spotted his sister Jo and Nana right in the middle of the crowd. Sam was there too and Emma, wearing bright red ribbons on her blond pigtails. Dumb name for a hairdo, he thought, but Emma said it was a girl thing and he wouldn't understand. Emma's dad, Jeff, was there too, and so was Lucas.

It gave him a nice feeling in his stomach to know all of them had come just to see him play.

Before he came to Chandler, it was always just him and his mom. His heart ached a little, remembering, but then he watched Jeff and Lucas laugh and something warm settled inside him again. It was better now, he told himself. Most of the time he wasn't worried so much about people leaving. Dying.

About being alone again.

Only sometimes.

Like late at night when the house was all quiet and he could remember a different room. A different life and how quickly it had all ended.

And alone in the dark, he worried.

He rubbed one hand under his nose, and blinked hard against the sunlight stabbing into his eyes, making them all blurry. Then he blinked and scanned the faces in the crowd one more time, searching, searching . . . until finally, *there* he was.

He *came*.

Just like he said he would.

Cash waved at him and Jack grinned and relaxed on the bench seat. Now he was ready. Now he wanted the game to start. So he could show everybody how much Cash had taught him.

· · ·

"I bring food, Josefina, now you eat," Nana said, reaching into the wicker picnic basket she'd insisted on bringing along to Jack's baseball game.

The field behind St. Joseph's elementary school hadn't changed much since the days Jo and her sisters had gone there. The grass was still more brown than green and the chain-link backstop had enough holes in it to be practically worthless. But it had never really mattered what it *looked* like. The important thing about a baseball field was how it *felt*.

Like summer.

"Josefina, you no eat, you no stay strong." Nana's lips thinned into a stubborn slash and her dark brown eyes narrowed. A cold wind rushed past them, but Nana's sausage curls were sprayed solid enough to withstand a hurricane. The hem of her black dress fluttered around her bony legs and the scent of White Shoulders took Jo right back to her childhood.

"Not really hungry, Nana," Jo answered, ignoring Nana's exasperated sigh as she shifted her gaze to the little boy in the dugout. If she wasn't still a little pissy at God, she might think of whispering a quick prayer that the kid did well.

Geez.

How did parents do this?

How did they let their kids go out and take the chance of failure? Of disappointment.

And when did she get so invested in a little boy she hadn't known existed a year ago?

Her own stomach was in knots.

A feeling apparently not shared by the rest of her family.

"I'll take a sandwich, Nana," Lucas said, leaning

over to stretch out a hand across Jo. "Gotta eat quick and get back to Mike. It's killing her that she can't be here, and when she's upset, she eats." He shrugged. "Kitchen's probably empty by now."

Happy, Nana reached into the basket for wax-paper-wrapped food. "You wanna sausage? Or maybe peppers and cheese? Or fresh salami and provolone?"

With the lid of the basket up, mouthwatering scents poured out into the fresh air and had everyone in the bleachers leaning in close.

Lucas inhaled deeply and sighed, "I'll take sausage, Nana, thanks."

"Make mine peppers," Jeff said, making the old woman smile like a kid at Christmas.

"And you, Samantha," Nana said, pulling another sandwich made on thick Italian bread out of the basket. "You no eat enough. Think of your *bambino*. *Mangia*."

"No, thanks, Nana," she said tightly. "I'll just sit here and groan quietly."

Nana muttered something in Italian, then turned around and invited the rest of the bleachers to dig into the bottomless basket of food. Eagerly, they leaped at her. Most people bought hot dogs at a ball game. Or at the most, they brought cookies and a thermos or something. Not Nana. She'd packed enough food for a week's stay. Plus she had jugs of Kool-Aid for the kids and iced tea for the adults.

Nana'd never met a crowd she didn't want to force-feed. As she dug into the bottomless basket again and again, Jo watched, amazed. Cannoli, lined up like sugar-dusted tin soldiers in a Tupperware container, were snatched up as fast as Nana unloaded them. There was cheese and bread, homemade chocolate chip cookies, and even a tray of cold veggies and spinach dip.

Baseball fans forgot about the game and got down to some serious scarfing.

"God," Sam whimpered, "did she have to use so much garlic in the spinach dip?"

"Whining?" Jo asked, pushing her knee gently into Sam's back.

"*Not* whining," she said, with a quick look over her shoulder. "Just saying."

"Right." It had been four days since their little chat, and to give her sister her due, Sam had really made an effort to cut back on all the complaining.

"Josefina," Nana said, huffing a little under her breath, "you no eat enough. You have some antipasto." She pulled out another Tupperware container the size of Delaware and snapped open the lid to release the mingled scent of garlic, basil, and just a touch of rosemary. Olive oil lay drizzled across broccoli tops, cauliflower, snap peas, and green and red bell peppers, cut into crunchy rounds.

Sam moaned and scooted down another row in the bleachers.

"Honey?" Jeff called. "You okay?"

Sam waved, Jo chuckled and dipped one hand into the tub for a piece of seasoned cauliflower. God knew if she didn't eat something, Nana would never give up.

"Is no enough." Nana clucked her tongue and passed the Tupperware down to Jeff and Lucas, who dug in like they were contestants on *Survivor*.

"I'm not hungry," Jo reminded her, dutifully chewing the vegetable.

"Is not good for you. This diet alla time. You are too skinny. One day," Nana foretold, wagging one finger at the sky as if calling down the heavens, "you will blow away, pfft!"

"I'm not skinny, and I'm not on a diet," Jo argued, but her heart wasn't in it. Instead, she had her gaze focused on the field where nine little boys were hustling out in their tattered jeans and worn sneakers to take their positions.

The sun glinted off a camera lens and she had to prop one hand over her eyes to see Jack, running out to right field. Her heart sputtered a little as she worried about him being able to play. This meant so much to him, and she knew if he screwed up, he'd be desolate. God, why was it easier to fail yourself than it was to watch someone you cared about do it?

"Josefina, your young man issa here."

"Huh?" She turned to look at Nana. *"What?"*

"There. Such a nicea boy."

Cash Hunter. Nicea boy? Not really. Nicea-*looking* boy, er, *man*? Oh yeah.

Lucas snorted and Jo stiffened, scowling at him ferociously. Instantly, he sobered up, and she had to admit that Mike was doing a hell of a job training him.

"New man, Jo?" Jeff asked, nudging her ribs with his elbow.

"Watch it, Weasel Dog," she muttered, gaze locked on Cash as he ambled toward the bleachers.

"Dog? Who issa dog?" Nana asked, her voice hitting a note designed to split eardrums.

"Ah crap," Jeff muttered.

"Nana, can I have a cookie?" Emma crawled across

her father, then Jo, to reach the promised land of Nana's lap.

"Pretty girls get *two*," Nana said, delving back into the basket that Jo was beginning to think of as just a little magical.

"Hi, Cash," Sam called out, and Jo thought about throwing a piece of cauliflower at the back of her sister's head. "Come on over."

Jo shifted her gaze to Tall, Dark, and Devastating. He strolled toward the bleachers like a man with all the time in the world. He was a walking testament to testosterone. Seriously. Black hair, ruffled by the wind. Black T-shirt, faded jeans, and those cowboy boots that looked as scuffed as if he'd been out on the range for decades.

Damned if Jo's heart didn't pound a little harder.

He stopped at the bottom of the bleachers and grinned up at her. Even from a distance, that smile was a hell of a weapon. And brother, he knew how to use it.

It had been four days since she'd seen him. And four even longer nights. God, it was a wonder she could maneuver at all during the day with the way dreams of Cash kept her waking up in a state of hunger so bad she shook with it.

"Come," Nana called, waving one hand while she kept the other arm wrapped firmly around Emma. "Come, eat."

"Nana," Jo said tightly, "maybe Cash doesn't want to—"

"Sure he does." Cash interrupted her and stepped up onto the bleachers, stalking up until he was seated right behind Jo.

Nana batted Jo's arm with her bony fingers and said, "Is good he wants to spend time with the *famiglia*. Josefina, get your young man something to eat."

Cash grinned at her again, clearly enjoying the whole show. But then, so were her brothers-in-law. And now that she felt the first flutters of irritation sputtering to life inside her, it was hard to remember waking up hungry for him in the middle of the night.

When the first pitch was thrown, the crowd concentrated on the game. Jo took the opportunity to half turn around and whisper, "What're you doing here?"

Cash shrugged and peeked inside the magic basket. At Nana's benevolent nod, he snatched up a wax-paper-wrapped sandwich and opened it. "Promised Jack I'd come."

"He didn't tell me he invited you."

"Any reason why he should have to?"

"No," she admitted, but she damn sure wished Jack had given her some warning. A hard smack of a bat on a ball had her head whipping around. She followed the hard-hit ball into left center field and let out a sigh of relief that Jack hadn't been responsible for fielding it.

Then turning back to Cash, she said, "Haven't seen you in a while."

His features tightened before he made a deliberate effort to relax them. "Been busy."

Why that should make her mad, she didn't know. But he'd been avoiding her and she didn't like it. Sure, she hadn't much liked it when every time she turned around, she'd practically tripped over him, either. But damn it, *she* was supposed to be the one doing the avoiding.

He was the one who was supposed to do the flirting,

play the little games he was so damn good at. The man was a maestro of seduction. Why the hell wasn't he trying to seduce *her*?

What? Was there something wrong with her? She wasn't good enough?

Frowning, she clapped hard as the second baseman fielded an easy base hit and threw the runner out at first.

She shifted uncomfortably on the bench seat and actually *felt* Cash sitting behind her. His knees brushed against her back and she fought the rush of something hot and steady pumping through her. She wouldn't look back. Wouldn't give him the satisfaction of speaking first. Not again, anyway. For God's sake, was she *hideous*? Had she all of a sudden become *grotesque*?

He wasn't interested, huh?

Well, fine.

Neither was she.

Her body tingled in direct contrast to her thoughts. Damn it. Of *course* she was interested. What? Was she *dead*? And now that she thought about it, she was pretty sure even a *dead* woman would sit up and take notice of Cash Hunter, the bastard.

Another batter stepped up to the plate, caught the first pitch and hit it high and right. Jo stood up slowly, her gaze locked on that ball as if, just by concentrating, she could guide the damn thing safely to Jack's mitt.

She sucked in a breath and held it.

Cash's hand came down on her shoulder.

Heat rushed through her.

Jack ran back, back.

Around her, she heard the collective intake of breath and knew her family was concentrating as hard as *she* was.

The ball fell from its sky-high arc and plummeted like a bullet toward earth. Jack ran, his usual clumsiness gone in the excitement of the moment. He held out both hands for the ball, still running, running, and then suddenly, *slam*.

The ball hit his glove, and his free hand trapped it within, just as she and Cash had shown him. He'd made the third out with no trouble at all. Jo hooted and shouted, jumping up and down on the narrow wood plank, high-fiving her brothers-in-law, and then planting a quick hard kiss on Nana's papery cheek. Adrenaline kicking, pulse pounding, she turned around to look at Cash and read the same rush she was feeling flashing in his eyes.

She wasn't sure how it happened.

Did she go up on her toes?

Did he bend down to her?

Did it *matter*?

One minute she was breathing, the next, his mouth was locked on hers and air was a secondary consideration. Her head spun, her blood raced, and as if from a distance, she heard the cheers from the rest of the crowd. In the celebration of the moment, he pulled her hard against him, and took her mouth like Grant took Richmond. Like Mike took a shoe sale. Like . . . hell, who cared?

Then he let her go abruptly, as if she were on fire or something and, hey, maybe she was. Her head was buzzing and she swayed unsteadily for a long second or two. Then she blinked hard, shook her head to clear her vision, and wobbly turned to watch her little brother.

Holding the ball high, Jack raced in from the field

triumphant, and Jo would have sworn she could read by the light shining in his eyes. Applause burst out around them like fireworks on the Fourth and Jack's grin was as wide as the sky as his team filed into the dugout to take their turn at bat.

Still revved, lips still humming, Jo turned around to look up at him, and his gaze locked with hers with a powerful slam of something hot and steamy and overpowering.

"He did it," she said, after swallowing a knot of something unexpected lodged in her throat.

"Never doubted it," Cash said tightly, jamming both hands into his jeans pockets as if to keep himself from touching her again.

That's fine. He didn't need to touch her again. She'd already gotten her bright idea. "I think we should talk."

His eyes narrowed and she felt him take an emotional step back. "After the game."

Jo inhaled sharply, deeply, then nodded. She'd waited this long. She could wait eight more innings. "After the game."

Cash tried to slip out after the game.

Get away clean before Josefina could arrange for the little *talk* she wanted. But there was no getting away. Not while Jack wanted to recount every play, every victory. Not while the rest of the Marconis closed around him, drawing him into the center of their lives, their world. Making him a part of the celebration as he'd never been before.

He glanced from one to the other of them and wondered if any of them had ever stopped to realize just what they had in each other. Probably not. People who grew up with love, with family, rarely appreciated it. It was just . . . *there*. Like air.

But for a man too much alone, it was impossible to turn away from it.

Even when he knew he *should*.

Since his father's unexpected visit, Cash had purposely kept his distance from Jo. He'd felt too . . . raw. Too close to the edge of a precipice he'd stepped away from years ago. He'd hidden out in the workshop. Buried himself in the work that had always been his salvation. Hell, he'd even avoided the kid. But he couldn't bring himself to break his promise to attend the boy's first game.

Now he'd kissed Josefina and the hole he'd been digging for himself had gotten a hell of a lot deeper. He couldn't afford to care. Couldn't indulge himself in affection that would only lead to disaster.

"Come, come," Nana announced, her high, thin voice cutting through the rush of conversation. "We go home now. Issa time for supper." She laid one gnarled hand on Jack's shoulder, then shot a look at Cash. Her wide brown eyes shone at him. "You come witha Josefina. We have gnocchi."

Tempting. "Thanks, but—"

Nana had already turned around, marching steadily toward the parking lot. "You havea supper with the *famiglia*. Issa good."

With shrugs and smiles, the rest of the Marconis fell into step behind the matriarch, leaving Jo and Cash alone on the empty field.

"Don't worry about it. You don't have to come," she said, before he could find an excuse to blow off the invitation. "Nana's just used to giving orders."

"You take after her, then?"

Jo's lips twitched. "Strong women run in my family."

"I've noticed."

"I've been noticing a couple things, too," she said, and glanced around as if to assure herself that they really were alone on the deserted playing field. When she looked back at him, she said, "For instance, I noticed that you're a pretty good kisser."

One eyebrow lifted and he knew he should head her off at the pass before she said any more. It'd be better for both of them if they just forgot all about that one little slip. Right. He still had the taste of her in his mouth and a sharp jab of hunger reminded him that they were all alone and one more kiss wouldn't be such a big deal.

"And?" he asked.

"And," she said, stuffing her hands into the back pockets of her neatly pressed jeans. "I don't actually *hate* you."

"I'm touched," he said wryly, and had the satisfaction of seeing her grimace.

"Anyway," she continued a heartbeat later, "like I said, that kiss was pretty good, so I was thinking that we should probably just have sex and get it over with."

He blinked at her. Damned if she didn't always find a way to surprise him. She stood there with that ponytail swinging, staring up at him through clear, sharp blue eyes, and invited him into her bed like another woman would say "Let's go shopping."

Everything in him yearned to grab her. Pull her close and devour her mouth again. To sink into the heat of her. Feel her legs wrap around him, drawing him deep.

And a second later, those images splintered and he snatched at reality.

"No."

"We could meet at your place and—*what*?"

"I said no, thanks," he repeated, though it cost him. Sleeping with her would be the easy thing to do. And maybe, in the long run, the safest. If they spent the night together, Jo would leave. He'd lose her. Lose the time they spent together. Lose hearing her laugh or snarl or bitch. Lose seeing her on job sites. Lose even the dream of her.

And he wasn't ready for that loss just yet.

"Why the hell not?" she demanded, jerking her hands from her pockets to slam them onto her hips. "You want me. I know you do. You *kissed* me."

From the parking lot came the muted roars of engines firing up, cars pulling away. In the distance, the ocean rushed to shore, sending a rhythmic heartbeat of sound reverberating through Chandler.

"Didn't say I didn't want you," he said tightly.

"Well, then, what's the big deal?" She threw her hands wide and let them slap to her sides again.

"If we have sex, you'll leave," he said flatly. Though it cost him some to admit the truth, he gave it to her. "I'm not ready for you to go."

Her eyes widened and her jaw dropped. Taking a half-step back, she stared at him in stupefied shock. "Are you *kidding* me?"

He shrugged off her anger. "You know what happens to the women I sleep with, Jo. Hell, you gave me enough shit about it last year."

"You're unbelievable."

"I'm right and you don't want to admit it."

Shaking her head briskly, she sent her ponytail into a wild fly-and-bounce. Then, as if she couldn't bear to stand still a minute longer, she paced around him in a tight circle, her steps quick, her boots pounding the sparse grass flat.

"I'm offering to go to bed with you and you say no because you don't want to 'lose' me."

"That's right." He turned in a circle, following her progress, mostly because he was getting the feeling it wouldn't pay to take his eyes off her.

"Well," she snapped, stopping suddenly to poke him in the chest with her index finger. "You can't *lose* what you never *had*."

A flash of heat shot through him and he welcomed it. Hell, even he couldn't believe he was turning her down. He should just sleep with her. Get her out of his system, reclaim his solitary life and be fucking grateful. But he couldn't do it. Couldn't make himself lose her before he absolutely had to.

It had been too long since he'd cared. Too long since a woman had *mattered* to him, on any level.

"You're just pissed because I turned you down."

"Damn skippy," she said, folding her arms across her chest, shooting one hip higher than the other, and tapping the toe of her work boot against the ground. "You've been flirting with me for a year. You wormed your way into my life. Buddied up with Jack. Charmed Nana. Hell, even *Mike* likes you and she doesn't like anybody!"

Cash gritted his teeth and fought down the snarl of anger nearly choking him. "You're saying I did all that to get to you? Hell, no ego problems with you, are there, Josefina?"

"Hah!" Her laugh was short, harsh, and sounded painful. "*You're* going to call *me* an egotist? The man who thinks that if I go to his bed, I'll then run away from my whole life because of the *glory* of his touch? Jesus, listen to yourself once in a while, will you?"

He was tempted. God, how he was tempted. But he bit back on his own hunger and dialed down the temper streaking through him. "It ain't gonna happen, Josefina," he said, with a slow shake of his head.

Jo felt every inch of her body humming with a fierce fury that had her trembling with the force of it. She'd expected him to say "sure" and take her off to his house. Hadn't they been building toward this for a damn year?

She had to have sex. It was time. Time to prove to herself one more time that she could do it.

And damn it, Cash was supposed to be ready and willing.

"Your problem is," she said, her voice just a low hum of fury, "you're afraid I'll shatter your damn Woman Whisperer reputation. When you sleep with me and I *don't* go, your rep is shot to hell."

"Whatever helps you sleep nights," he muttered, raking one hand through his hair.

"Oh," she said, snorting a laugh, "I'll sleep just *fine,* trust me."

She wouldn't, though. She'd been prepared to do the deed and prove to herself one more time that she was still whole. That her past hadn't really screwed up her present. That, damn it, she could be *normal.*

So now, she was more determined than ever to get him into the sack. On *her* terms. No Marconi ever turned away from a challenge. Whether Cash wanted her or not, she was going to have him naked and panting.

Soon.

She leaned into him, until her mouth was only a breath from his. Keeping her gaze locked on his, she watched flashes of heat he couldn't hide sparkle in his dark eyes and she knew she'd scored a point already. Foolish, foolish man. He'd already lost and he didn't even know it.

"You know what, Cash?" she asked, licking her lips and sighing just hard enough to brush her breath against him. "When I want you naked, I'll have you."

He forced a smile. "Is that a threat?"

She smiled, too, but there was no humor in it. "Baby, that's a *promise*."

Ten

"He said *no*."

"Wow," Mike said, staring up at Jo from her usual perch on the sofa she was slowly coming to loathe. "Can't imagine why."

Jo paced like a feral cat trapped in a hatbox. She snarled, she raged, she did everything but rip her own hair out with both hands. "Glad it's clear to you, because I'm clueless."

"Well, *duh*." Mike pushed herself up higher on the sofa and wished to hell she could stand on her own two feet. But the babies were taking up more and more of her body every damn day. Hell, she couldn't even remember standing up anymore. After an ineffective minute or two, she gave it up and flopped back against the pillows. "For God's sake, Jo," she complained, "you don't just walk up to somebody and say 'I think we should have sex.' "

"Why the hell not?" Jo demanded. "We're adults. What's the big deal?"

"Not exactly filled with charm and romance . . ."

"Who the hell said anything about *romance*?" Jo wanted to know. She wasn't talking about hearts and flowers. Or the magic and glory of *making love*. She didn't get that. Didn't understand why everyone had to make it all sound like some fairy-tale nonsense anyway. "I'm talking about *sex,* here."

"Are you *sure* we're related?"

"He kissed me," Jo shouted, stabbing her finger at Mike. "Yesterday. On the baseball field. In front of God and everybody."

"So naturally, you check your watch and say 'Time to have sex, big boy.'"

"Who the hell are you all of a sudden?" Jo said, coming to a dead stop to glare at her. "Until Lucas came along, I don't remember you wasting too much time worrying about the niceties. You used to be all about 'Get some and get gone.'"

"Well," Mike mused, "don't I feel special?"

"Sorry, sorry." Shaking her head, Jo started pacing again. "It's just . . . I finally decide, okay. Fine. I'll sleep with him. I mean," she continued, more to herself than to Mike, "he's been prodding me for like ever and it's *time*. I'm ready."

"What d'ya mean, it's time?"

"What?" She stopped again, then scowled. *Stupid.* She wasn't getting into this with Mike or anyone else. "Nothing. Didn't mean anything."

Mike watched her and saw more than frustration. She just wasn't sure *what.* "What're you not telling me?"

"What's who not telling you about what?" Sam came back into the room, looking pale, as usual.

Mike spoke up, never taking her gaze off her big sister. "Jo asked Cash to have sex with her—"

"You did?"

"—and he said no."

"He didn't."

"See?" Jo said, stabbing a finger at Sam, more grateful than she could say for the shift in the conversation. "*She* can't believe it, either."

Mike ignored her. When Jo was in a rant, it was pointless to try to get through. So instead, she turned to Sam, sinking into the sofa opposite her. "She says 'It's time' she had sex."

So much for the shift in conversation.

Sam frowned. "There's a specific time now?"

"That's what I'm wondering about," Mike said, narrowing her eyes on Jo, who was studiously avoiding looking at both of them. "So what is it we *don't* know?"

Jo stopped walking for a minute, but the toe of her work boot tapped against the cool blue floor tiles. "Could we stay on topic, here?"

"Which is?" Sam asked, lifting both feet to prop them up on the couch.

"How do I get the man naked?" Jo demanded. "Aren't you paying attention?"

"Thought I was," Sam said, but closed her eyes.

"That's simple enough," Mike put in thoughtfully, still curious about her older sister's evasion. Jo was usually about as subtle as a bulldozer. The fact that she was keeping something hidden worried Mike more than she wanted to admit.

"Tell me then, O great one," Jo said, sarcasm as thick as Nana's accent.

Mike shrugged. "Go over to his house naked."

"What?" Jo's eyes bugged out so far, it was a wonder they didn't just pop out and roll across the floor.

"Not naked-naked," Mike said with a pitiful shake of her head. "Wear a coat or something, but be naked under it. Then when you take it off, I'm guessing he'll be convinced."

Sam turned her head on the pillow to look at her. "You really used to lead an exciting life, didn't you?"

Mike shrugged and gave her a small smile. "We all have our strengths."

Wasn't as easy to get out of the house as she'd hoped it would be, Jo thought. Nana, of course, had to feed her first and then practically make her fill out a form detailing where she would be—which, naturally, Jo had lied about. But on the upside, Nana was *there*. Which meant there was someone at the house to look after Jack.

Standing in front of the mirror in her childhood bedroom, Jo belted her old gray raincoat and fanned the collar up around the back of her neck. Her fingertips ran along the lapels and she tried not to notice the trembling in her hands.

She kept her hair in a ponytail, since fluffing it up would only pique Nana's already rampant curiosity. Not much makeup, either, for the same reason. But because she was, despite Mike's doubts, a female, she brushed on some last-minute mascara and a quick coat of lip gloss.

Then she studied her reflection and saw not just herself, but the mirror image of the room that she'd grown up in. Dark green trim defined pale green walls dotted with posters of Paris, London, and Venice. No rock stars for Jo's walls. She'd wanted to travel. Tour the Louvre. Ride a gondola.

But that was *before*.

A soft wind slipped through the open window and fluttered the white eyelet curtains. Jo shivered, closed her eyes briefly, and instantly, Steve Smith's image rose up in her mind, haunting her as he had for ten long years.

Her eyes flew open again and her breath came fast, furious, as she fought to ground herself in the present. When she was back in control, she saw only her room. Like a museum, it held the memories of a younger Jo. A Jo who still had plans and dreams and still trusted that somehow, she would find all she wanted.

The girl who'd come home from college broken wasn't there. No memories of her time at UC San Diego infringed on this sanctuary. She'd erased every hint of those days as completely as she'd wiped them from her mind.

"Doesn't matter," she whispered, catching her own eye in the mirror. "He didn't win. It didn't affect me and I'm proving that *again,* tonight."

Grabbing up her purse, she started down the stairs, the heels of her black sandals clicking loudly on the wood. The phone rang and was snatched up before she hit the bottom of the stairs.

In seconds, Nana snarled, *"Bastardo,"* and slammed the receiver down with enough force to cause the holy cards tucked behind the wall phone to flutter to the floor.

"Was that Papa?" Jo didn't know why she bothered asking, since the answer was evident.

Nana stormed across the kitchen, snapped a dishtowel in the air, then flipped it over her shoulder. "I no talka to the *bastardo*."

The phone rang again almost instantly and the old woman whirled around and made a surprisingly nimble lunge for it. Jo was a step ahead of her, though, and grabbed the receiver first.

"Papa?" She walked into the living room, and ignored the stream of viciously shouted Italian rising in the kitchen like steam off a pasta pot.

"Josefina." Papa's voice carried through the phone, and just for a minute, Jo relaxed. God, she'd missed him. Even with things as unsettled between them as they were, she'd missed him.

Her hand fisted around the receiver and she used her free hand to block out Nana's raging from the other ear. "Papa. Why are you calling? You're coming home in another day or two."

"Ah . . ."

"What?"

"*Bastardos* no getta into heaven!" Nana shouted in English, just in case her Italian curses were being ignored.

"I thought," Papa said, and his voice seemed fainter now, farther away. "Well, Grace and me thought we might stay another week."

"Papa, no." Jo spoke up fast. "You've gotta come home."

"Something wrong? Is Jack okay?"

"Jack's fine," she said, and walked all the way across the living room to the front window, trying, and failing, to escape Nana's shouts. "But Papa, I can't do all this alone. It's too much. The business. Mike. Sam. Jack. Nana."

College, too, she added silently. *And memories, Papa. They're too thick. I can't think. I can't eat. And I can't do this all alone anymore.*

She stared out at the dark street and noticed that Mrs. Sanchez had a new porch light and someone had trimmed the hedges in front of her house. Money Fairy largesse.

And on the front lawn, Jack lay stretched out on the grass, his head pillowed on Bear's side.

"You're right, Josefina," Papa said, and even from a few thousand miles away, his tone was comforting, soothing. Like cool water on a fierce burn. "You're right. We'll come home. I'll see you soon. A few days. Maybe a little more."

"Good." She blew out a breath, amazed at the sense of relief pouring through her, and ignored Nana's shouts, despite the fact that they were getting louder, to say again, "Good. See you soon, Papa."

With a dial tone humming in her ear, she walked back to the kitchen, hung up the phone, then faced Nana, a tiny tyrant, both cheeks flushed with impotent rage. "I'm going out now, Nana. I'll see you later."

"The *bastardo*. He issa well?"

"Papa's fine."

She huffed out a breath, and nodded. "You go. You tell Jack to comea have his cookies."

"Okay." Moving on instinct now, she bent down and kissed Nana's cheek. "Don't wait up."

"I no wait up," Nana said, picking up a scrub brush to clean God knew what, since everything was blindingly clean already. "You go. Have a nicea time."

Nice? She wondered briefly what Nana would say if she knew her granddaughter was naked under her coat

and on her way to have hot sweaty sex? Then Jo's mind
boggled at the very idea of how many rosaries would
be said, so she shut that thought off.

Outside, she yelled good-bye to Jack, and headed
for her truck.

"Are you goin' to see Cash?" the boy asked.

"Yes."

"Can I come?"

"No."

"Aw man . . ." Jack stood up in disgust and kicked at
the grass.

"Nana says for you to go get some cookies."

"'Kay, c'mon, Bear."

The old dog stood up slowly, carefully, and if he'd
been an old man, Jo was sure she'd have heard him
grunting and groaning. Then boy and dog disappeared
into the house and she was alone with her plan.

She looked into the rearview mirror, yanked out her
ponytail, and fluffed her hair around her face. There
was no excitement in her eyes. Just determination.

And a determined Marconi couldn't be stopped.

Cash stalked through the house, temper flashing.

At the first sound of the doorbell, he'd gone into
fighting mode. All he could figure was that his father
had come back for more money. Wouldn't have been
the first time. And damn it, he was in no mood to deal
with Jared at the moment.

He wasn't in the mood to deal with *anyone*.

Since that kiss at the ball field the day before, he'd
been like a man on fire. Couldn't stop moving even
though he knew that running would only make the
flames that much hotter.

He hadn't been able to get his mind off Jo and he knew damn well that was a bad sign. Should have just done it, he thought. Do it and get her the hell out of his life.

He yanked the front door open and there she was. All the air left his body. Her hair was loose, long, and flowing over the shoulders of the ugly gray raincoat she wore. Her legs were bare and her feet were tucked into sandals with impossibly high heels.

She looked like temptation and smelled like heaven.

He slapped one hand on the doorjamb, just to steady himself. "What're you doing here, Josefina?"

"I'm here to have sex," she said, and shot one hip higher than the other. "With *you*."

Every cell in his body lit up, but he tamped 'em right back down again. "I told you—"

"I know what you told me," she said, and tugged at the belt of her coat. "Remember what I told *you* . . . ?" She opened the coat and gave him his first look at paradise.

Naked.

Gloriously naked.

His gaze locked on her and couldn't have been pried off by a nuclear blast. His hot gaze traced every curve. Every line. And then started over again at the top. Seconds ticked past. His mouth went dry. His groin went rock hard.

"Getting cold here," Jo said.

Gaze on her pebbled nipples, he said, "I noticed."

"So are we going to do this or do I tell everyone in town that *you're* the Money Fairy?"

He looked into her eyes and saw the challenge there. "Blackmail's an ugly word."

"I prefer 'extortion.' "

Nodding, he said tightly, "We shouldn't do this—"

"Why not?"

"—but we're gonna." He grabbed her, dragged her into the house, and lowered his mouth to hers. Hell, there was just so much a man could take. He had to have her. Had to feel her. Had to sink inside her before he exploded into a million jagged pieces.

Her mouth fed on his, giving as good as she got. His tongue tangled with hers in an erotic rush of need.

He slammed the door with a kick, then pulled her coat down and off her as he maneuvered her down the long hall toward the great room. A baseball game was playing on the TV, but the announcer's voice faded into a murmur under the heavy drumming of his own heart in his ears.

Stumbling down the two steps, he guided her, still kissing, still tasting, filling his hands with her curves, tweaking her nipples, feeling her jolt in his arms.

"Do it now," she said breathlessly as she tore her mouth from his. "Now, Cash."

"Oh yeah."

Screw reason. Screw logic. *Nothing* was going to get in the way of this now. He had to be in her. Had to feel her heat surround him and draw him deep. Had to look down into her eyes as she climaxed, as she rode the pleasure he would give her.

He tipped her back onto the closest sofa and while she lay there, naked, but for the high heels, watching him, he stripped out of his own clothes in record time. Then he was there with her again, sliding along her body, tasting every inch of her, swirling his tongue over her nipples, each in turn. She arched into him and moaned and Cash fed on the sound.

Eyes glazed with a passion that had been storming through him for more than a year, he dipped one hand to her center and found her damp. Not ready yet, but close.

She flinched at his gentle touch, then lifted her hips, looked him in the eye and said, "Now. I want you in me, *now.*"

A part of his brain clicked, but that little warning voice was too quiet, too distant, to really be heard. Instead, he listened only to her words—not whatever might be fueling them. His mouth claimed her nipples again, licking, nipping, teasing, as his fingers worked her center, dipping in and out of her heat, working her body until she rocked her hips in silent assent, invitation.

And when he couldn't stand it another minute, when her hands fisted on his back and pounded his flesh in insistence, he entered her with a quick push that jolted him to his bones and had her gasping and arching her neck.

He moved within her, diving in and out of her depths, and he watched her face, wanting to see the moment happen in her pale blue eyes. Wanted to see the flash of completion in her features, hear the satisfied whisper of sound that would slip from her mouth.

And he wanted to feel the quick contractions of her muscles pumping him dry. Wanted to know that even when she left him, he would have this one moment to remember.

"That's so good," she cried, her voice breaking. "So good. *Harder,* Cash, harder. *Faster.*"

His body a piston, he gave her what she wanted, moving on her, in her, with a fierce need and desire driving him. Release hurtled toward him. He felt the tension in her body as she tightened reflexively, legs locking around his hips.

And as his body erupted inside hers, she mirrored his own reaction.

Her hips lifted into him. She screamed his name and her body trembled from head to toe, just as it should.

She was all. She was amazing.

But most importantly, she was *faking it.*

His body still nicely buzzed, Cash drew away from her and helped her sit up on the couch. He watched her, trying to figure out just what had happened. For the first time in his life, he hadn't *touched* a woman. What the hell was going on?

The TV still blasted away in the background and puddles of lamplight gave the big room a golden glow. Jo sat in one of those puddles and the pale yellow light highlighted her unbelievably great body as she gave him an overbright smile.

"That was great," she said, and stood up. "Thanks."

"Oh, my pleasure, believe me." He watched her, stunned, as she moved across the room to scoop up her discarded coat and slip into it.

Feeling at a decided disadvantage, he grabbed his jeans and pulled them on before he stood up to face her. She was still smiling as she whipped her hair back from her face. "Don't look at me like that," she said on a laugh. "You didn't rock my world out of orbit or anything. I'm not running off to join the circus—or a convent—or Greenpeace."

"No?" he asked, voice tightly controlled—for which he gave himself silent applause. So, she wasn't affected by his "curse." Was it because that whole orgasm had been a fake? Was the secret to keeping a woman being a lousy lover?

"Nope. I'm going home and to work in the morning."

"Uh-huh."

"Where's my purse?"

"In the hallway."

"Oh." She stopped and looked at him. "What's with you?"

"Just curious," he said, walking closer to her as the baseball announcer in the background shouted in appreciation of some "miracle" play.

"About what?"

"About why the hell you're putting on such a great act."

Her eyes darkened and her mouth flattened into a grim slash. "I don't know what you're talking about."

"Sure you do," he said, reaching out to grab her upper arms and drag her close. "I know you faked that climax."

"I didn't."

"Bullshit," he ground out through gritted teeth. He was *good* at this, damn it. In her arms, he'd felt more than he ever had before and he had to figure out what had gone wrong for her. "And I want to know *why.*"

She squirmed in his grasp and her breathing quickened. Finally, she yanked free and he let her go.

"If you didn't want sex," he demanded, "why the hell did you come over here?"

She lifted her chin, looked down her nose at him and said, "I have sex every six months. It was time."

A harsh laugh shot from his throat as anger clawed at his insides. He'd just been used. Reaching up, he scraped both hands through his hair, dragging his nails across his scalp. Heart pounding, fury mounting, he looked into her eyes and saw walls coming up. There was some irony in here somewhere, he just couldn't put his finger on it at the moment.

"Now if you don't mind . . " She took a step and stopped, turning her head toward the television set.

Cash followed her gaze and saw the screen had shifted to a commercial. Steve Smith, candidate for state senate, filled the screen. An incredibly handsome man, he had one arm draped around the shoulders of his model-pretty wife. He smiled into the camera and promised that if people voted for him, it was a vote for integrity and a return to old-fashioned values.

Beside him, Jo coughed.

Choked.

Staggered.

Cash caught her, pulled her around to face him, and felt fear lap at his insides when he saw how pale she was. How wide and empty her beautiful eyes were. "Are you all right?" he demanded, and gave her a shake to snap her out of whatever it was that had such a grip on her. "Josefina!"

She sucked in air like a dying woman and, trembling, wrenched herself free of him. Eyes haunted, pain etched on her features, she stumbled back a step or two and, facing him, snarled, "You want to know why I didn't see the stars, Cash? Want to know why no blinding white flash erupted inside me when you touched me?"

"Josefina . . ." Instinctively, he took a step closer, but stopped when she lifted one hand to keep him at bay.

"Because," she said, breath hitching, voice breaking, eyes filling, "because *no* man has touched me—really *touched* me—" She slapped one hand against her chest. "Here. Inside. No one. Not since *him*."

She threw a glare at the television, and though the baseball game was back on again, she trembled anew as if she could still see the man and his wife.

"Smith?" he asked, though he knew. And a part of him knew what she was going to say next. Though it broke his heart to hear the words choke out of her strangled throat.

"The *honorable* Steve Smith," she said, lips twisting as a single tear spilled from the corner of her eye and snaked a silver trail along her cheek. "Ten years ago, that smiling son of a bitch *raped* me."

Eleven

Oh God.

Jo's eyes filled with tears, her throat snapped closed, and a ball of oily nausea rolled through her belly. She clapped one hand to her mouth and backed away from the horrified expression on Cash's face. He took a single step toward her and she stopped him fast with a shake of her head and one upraised hand.

"I've never said that out loud," she murmured thickly, still fighting the urge to run to a bathroom and be completely, thoroughly sick. "Can't believe I said that. Can't believe I—"

"Josefina . . ." His voice was a caress.

She groaned tightly and shook her head again. God, she couldn't let him touch her. Not now. Not when she might shatter like crystal. She glanced at him, then away again, but his image was burned into her brain. Broad, bare chest, tanned to the color of burnished copper. Muscles rippled as he helplessly fisted his hands over and over again.

"Josefina . . ." Her name again, said on a sigh of sound filled with anguish.

"No. Don't. No sympathy," she said, as a choked-off

laugh scraped her throat and brought fresh tears to her eyes. "Give me sympathy and I'll dissolve."

"You've got a right," he muttered, taking another half-step toward her.

"Don't—just—stay—" She scrubbed both hands across her face and felt the dampness of her own tears. Stubbornly, she rubbed them away, refusing to give Steve Smith one more ounce of moisture.

Over the years, she'd cried an ocean of tears and it hadn't changed a thing. Hadn't made her feel better. Hadn't faded the memories or eased the pain. And wasn't there a statute of limitations on tears? Shouldn't she be cried out?

"I still can't believe I said that out loud," she murmured, blowing out a heavy breath, looking everywhere but at Cash. For ten long years, the truth had been locked up inside her, chewing at her, gnawing on her, taking nips of her soul when she least expected it. And not once had she said the words aloud. Not even alone in her room. Not even in a whisper.

"I can't believe—he *raped* you?" Cash waved one hand at the TV where a baseball game was again playing out. "And he's running for office? How is that possible?"

It was possible because she'd never told a living soul—until tonight—what had happened on that long-ago night. Steve Smith had gone on with his life. Apparently he'd married, God help the poor woman, and he'd probably never once given a thought to the girl he'd left bruised and shattered on the floor of a frat house bedroom.

And just like that, it was all back. Here. Now. She

could smell the beer again. Hear the music. Feel bone-racking chills sweeping through her.

"God. I have to go. Have to—" She turned for the hall, anxious now to be . . . *away*. God, she didn't want to look into Cash's eyes again and know he knew. Know he could see what she'd been through. What that bastard had done to her. Turned her into.

"Josefina, wait."

"Why?" she snapped suddenly, riding a rush of bile that raced through her system like a toxic injection. "So I can tell you all the details? No, thanks. Don't want to think about 'em. Don't want to remember."

"You *do* remember already. Do you think I can't see it on your face?"

"You don't know anything about this, Cash. Don't pretend you do." Man, how had she let this happen? All she'd wanted to do was have her biannual roll in the hay.

She'd been in control. He'd touched her and she hadn't reacted. He'd kissed her and she hadn't let the fires combust. He'd pounded himself inside her and she'd refused to feel good. Refused to allow the tingling sensations coiled within to escape.

She hadn't had an orgasm—*ever*. She simply couldn't allow herself to lose control of the situation long enough to relax into one.

But tonight—it had been close.

For the first time, she'd *felt* something.

Almost.

Nearly.

There'd been a sensation of waiting, of expectation, and she'd thought—for a moment—about letting go.

Seeing if she was even capable of feeling what other women took for granted. But she hadn't been able to quite take that final step.

For years, she'd listened to her sisters rhapsodize about making love. About the fireworks they felt, the heat, the closeness, the tenderness. About doing what she should be able to do. And for years now, she'd played the game, made all the right noises, said all the right things. But it was all bullshit.

She'd never felt it.

Would never feel it.

All because ten years ago she'd loved the wrong man. *Trusted* the wrong man.

"You don't know," she said, tired now, the fury seeping out to be replaced by an exhaustion that went bone—no, *soul*—deep.

Cash's voice came again, soft, coaxing, as if he were trying to soothe a cornered wild animal. "I know you're in pain. I know you don't deserve it. I know I want to hunt down Steve Smith and bash his pretty face into the concrete for an hour or two."

Her gaze snapped up to his and she saw the truth of his words written in his eyes. She was unexpectedly touched and the tears sprang up again. Jo had to blink furiously just to see him, not two feet from her.

"Thanks," she said, and swallowed hard. "It's nice of you to offer. And a great visual, by the way."

He smiled sadly but kept his distance, as if afraid she'd bolt if he tried to touch her again.

And Jo was afraid of the same thing. But at the same time she was so tired. So tired of running, hiding, lying. She lifted one hand to her aching head and sighed. "Could I have a glass of water or something?"

"I think we can do better than that—" He half turned and then stopped. "Will you sit down or are you planning on making a break for the door the minute my back's turned?"

She gave him a wan smile, the best she could offer at the moment. "I'm not leaving. Yet."

She didn't trust herself to drive. Not with the way her hands were shaking—the way her vision was blurred by a sheen of tears.

"Good. Sit, then." He waved her toward the sofa they'd just made love on, but Jo wasn't quite ready to revisit the scene of the crime, so to speak. So she took a seat on the couch opposite. Oh, *good choice*. Now you get to *look* at the scene instead.

Nope.

Can't sit.

She jumped to her feet and shot a look at Cash, heading behind a wet bar in the corner of the huge room. Nerves danced inside her on football cleats. She felt the tiny spikes jabbing at her, poking at her, prodding her to move. To run. To hide.

But this time, she stood her ground.

Sort of.

Too much nervous, pent-up energy pumped through her to allow her to stand still, so she walked across the room, her heels tapping against the floor. Ordinarily, she might have taken the time to notice the beauty of the house. The glory of the wood and the building's simple clean lines. Tonight, though, she just couldn't manage it. She walked to the far wall and stared out the bank of windows at the black night beyond.

The moon reflected off the still surface of the lake's inky surface and shimmered slightly when a soft wind kicked up, rippling the water into echoes of each other that swam toward shore. Outside, night birds called, wind blew, the ocean roared.

Inside, there was only the still-muttering television, Cash, her, and *memories*.

God, they felt thick as summer gnats on the meadow, flying around her face, blinding her to all but the past. And as they raced through her mind, unfettered, Jo wanted to curl up and groan until they passed. But this time, she wasn't at home. She couldn't turn out the lights and burrow under her covers. She stiffened her spine and lifted her chin, to fight that inclination.

Cash walked toward her, carrying two chilled glasses of white wine. He handed her one and she instantly took a sip, letting the cold, tart liquid slide down her dry throat. After a moment, she said, "Thanks. And um, sorry about the meltdown, but seeing him like that really hit me hard and—"

"Don't," Cash said, and was forced to make a conscious effort to dial down the fury churning inside him. "Don't apologize to me."

She turned her back on the view and leaned one shoulder against the glass as she looked at him. "I don't respond much better to anger than I do to sympathy."

"Tough shit. You get 'em both." He looked down into his own glass and studied the wine as if trying to read a crystal ball. The truth of the thing was, he'd lowered his gaze to keep Jo from seeing just how much her admission had affected him. "I can't help feeling sorry for what happened to you so long ago—or for wanting to beat the shit out of that guy, *now*."

She inhaled sharply, deeply, and blew it out again in a rush. "You don't need to feel bad for me. I'm fine. I survived."

"This is surviving?" he demanded, as the anger crashed and rolled inside him like storm surf. "Faking your way through sex you obviously didn't want or enjoy?"

She stiffened. "Didn't mean to take a punch at your ego."

That little dart hit home with an almost surprisingly sharp sting. "You think *that's* what this is about?"

"No." She said it quickly, without hesitation, and Cash knew she meant it. He could see it in her eyes, those pale blue depths that shone with more emotion than he'd ever seen there before.

She took another sip of wine, and used her free hand to idly pull at the belt of her raincoat. "I know that's not what you meant, so now I guess *I'm* sorry."

He hated knowing she was in pain. Hated seeing her emotionally beaten. He'd much prefer her spitting and snarling, arguing, threatening to hit him with a hammer.

This Josefina broke his heart.

"Don't be sorry," he said softly, and took a chance, reaching out to lay one hand on her arm. When she didn't shake him off, he didn't know if he was pleased or sorry. He wanted to comfort, but more than that, he wanted her to not *need* comforting.

Jack lay on his bed, staring up at the ceiling. Moonlight speared through the open curtains and lay in silver strokes across the whitewashed beams. Bear's big head

on his leg felt like a comforting blanket, and he stroked
the dog while his mind wandered.

It wasn't too bad here, he thought. Nana liked him
and Jo was turning out to be pretty nice. Cash was great
and now Jack was on the baseball team. So that was
good and stuff, but there was still something that tick-
led his stomach and sort of made him nervous.

Papa was coming home.

He loved his father, but right now everything was
good, and once Papa got back, things would be different. He wouldn't see Cash so much and Jo would go
away, back to her own house. And, he realized, he
would miss her. She didn't talk to him like he was just
a little kid. And she was fun, too, and knew lots of
stuff.

"But maybe," he said softly, and the big retriever
lifted his head and perked his ears as if he were listening to the boy. Jack grinned. "Maybe tonight they're
gonna *kiss* and get all mushy together and then I can
show Jo and Cash that it'd be good to have me around
and then maybe they could get married or something
and then I could live with them. What d'ya think,
Bear?"

The big dog snorted, laid his head back down, and
closed his eyes. Jack ran his head over the dog's
smooth head and smiled. Didn't really matter what
Bear thought, he told himself.

It was a good plan.

"What happened?" Cash kept his voice quiet, careful.

Her mouth twitched, then flattened out again just before she took another sip of wine. When she'd swallowed, Jo cupped the glass between her hands and

Cash saw the straw-colored liquid slosh against the sides of the glass as her hands trembled.

"It was a long time ago," she said softly.

"It was yesterday," Cash argued.

A moment ticked past and then another. Finally, she sighed. "You're right. Ten years ago and it's as fresh to me as if it had happened last night."

"Tell me, Josefina," he urged, keeping his voice low, hardly more than a whisper. Tentatively, he cupped her cheek in the palm of his hand, and stared into her eyes. "Talk to me, Josefina. Trust me."

She sucked in a breath and slowly released it again as she shook her head gently. "Trust isn't something I'm long on, Cash. Not anymore."

"Can't say as I blame you—but I'm not *him*."

"No," she said, stepping away from him and taking another long drink of her wine. "You're really not. You irritate me sometimes, Cash," she said, forcing a smile that didn't reach her eyes. "But you don't scare me."

He hated knowing that she'd been scared before. That she'd had to fear anyone. But he felt only relief to know that she didn't fear *him*. "Glad to hear it."

"He didn't, either," she said. "Scare me—at first." She walked, taking slow steps, around the edge of the sofa closest to the window, to the far wall where she stared up at an abstract painting—vivid splotches of red and blue paint bisected with swirls of green. "We'd been dating for three weeks. Spent almost every day together. He couldn't seem to see enough of me. He was gorgeous—tall, funny, charming. He said all the right things," she admitted, and turned around to look at him.

Moonlight washed over her, making her face look

paler, her soft blue eyes nearly silver. Even from a distance, Cash felt the pain rippling off her in thick waves. It took everything he had to keep from going to her. But he knew it was more important to give her the room she needed to keep talking.

"He took me to a party at his frat house." Jo shuddered, took a long sip of her wine, and wrapped both hands around the glass, her fingers smoothing up and down the heavy crystal. "Every kid in school was there, I swear. Could hardly move for all the people. Music blaring, guys shouting, girls laughing. I can still smell it. Beer, perfume, cigarettes, and sweat."

She shook her head, blew out a breath. "He said he wanted to show me something up in his room. A surprise, he said." She lifted one hand and rubbed her right temple gently. "I was excited. Happy. God. His room was a wreck," she remembered. "I actually thought it was cute. Guy, pigsty. Didn't realize it was the personification of his soul."

She shook her head and got back on track. "He closed the door and grabbed me. At first, I thought, Ooh, manly. So strong, so sexy. God, how pathetic. I kissed him back—I kissed him back and then he tore my shirt and told me that it was time. He'd waited long enough." She frowned. "I remember being confused." She choked a laugh. "Jesus. *Confused.* And asking him what he was talking about. What he was doing. I'd already told him that I was saving myself. Stupid, I guess, but I was like the last living virgin in California. Too much Catholic school probably, but—"

Ah God. Empathy washed over Cash and did battle with the fury crouched inside him. He wanted that bastard's face beneath his fists. Wanted to hurt him as he'd hurt Jo. Wanted to make it all go away and erase the shattered glint in her eyes.

And he couldn't.

"Josefina—"

Her head snapped up, she took the last swallow of wine and met his gaze. "No. I started this. I'll finish it. *He laughed at me.* I still hear him in my dreams sometimes. That laugh, as he pushed me onto the narrow bed." Her eyes glazed over and there was a faraway tone to her voice, as if she'd slipped into the past and was trapped there. "The sheets were dirty and bunched up under me. The room smelled like stale sweat and rotten food. The music pounded up from downstairs, shaking the windows. I heard them rattle behind my head and I remember thinking that whoever'd built the place had done a crappy job. Stupid thing to be thinking while being raped, but—" She shrugged halfheartedly. "He unzipped his jeans, tossed my skirt up, and tore my panties off. I screamed then, but he hit me and told me to keep quiet."

"Damn it, Jo—"

She shivered, a bone-racking chill that sent a matching cold to the pit of Cash's stomach.

"No one had ever hit me before—" she said. "The pain . . . blossomed, kept getting bigger, but I was too shocked to really feel it. But I kept quiet. Really quiet. I was screaming inside, but stayed quiet so he wouldn't hit me again. I remember I kept thinking, This isn't happening. Not really. It's just a nightmare. Wake up, Jo. Wake up! But it wasn't a nightmare and I couldn't wake up. Couldn't get away."

"I'm so sorry . . ."

"He used a condom." She spoke up quickly, avoiding his sympathy as if she were dodging a bullet. Then she coughed. "At least he was a careful rapist. He was on me in a second and while he—he grunted in my ear. His breath felt hot and smelled like beer."

She wrinkled her nose in memory and Cash knew she was back there. In that tiny room. Reliving every moment of it all.

Cash felt his chest tighten until breathing was nearly impossible. His heartbeat thudded heavily and the roaring in his ears almost drowned out her voice. God, he wished he didn't have to hear this. Wished she didn't have it to tell.

"It seemed to last for *years*," she said, her voice hardly more than a sigh. "And when he was finished, he stood up and looked down at me. I was crying. Still quiet, though, because he still seemed so mad. I was sure he was going to hit me some more. But he didn't. He zipped his jeans and he told me to get over it. It was just sex. Everybody did it and God knew I was nothing special. Then he left me there and went back to the party."

She cupped one hand across her mouth and looked at him through eyes brimming with tears that tore at him.

"I don't even remember how I got back to my dorm room across campus," she said. "But I did."

"You didn't report him?"

"No."

"Why?"

"I—couldn't," she murmured, and set her empty wine glass down onto a nearby table. "I showered for a few hours, and then the next morning Papa called to tell me Mama was sick."

"Jesus." He couldn't even imagine. He hadn't had a

close family, but he'd seen Jo's in action and there was none closer than the Marconis. They had a bond that could withstand anything. That would have encircled Jo with the kind of love and support she so desperately needed. Yet she hadn't told them.

"I couldn't tell them then," she said, walking again, back to the windows overlooking the lake. She stared past her own reflection at the night beyond. "When Papa called, the whole world shifted. But—"

"But what?" He took a chance and walked over to her. Every step measured, Pounding loudly against the hardwood floor. She didn't back away, didn't turn from him or raise her defenses. And a part of him was sorry. If she'd taken a battle stance, she would have been the Josefina he knew. This woman was fragile, ready to splinter into a thousand pieces, and Cash didn't have a clue what to do or say.

She glanced at him, then turned her gaze back to the moon-washed lake outside. Bending her head forward, she rested her forehead on the cool glass and closed her eyes. "The rape—that's not the worst part."

"Jo—"

"When Papa called," she whispered brokenly, "and he told me that Mama was so sick, all I could think was, Thank God."

Surprise flickered through him. "Why?"

"Because it gave me the reason I needed to leave college. To run away. To run home." When he didn't speak, she turned her face to him and, with tears swimming in her eyes, she said, "Don't you get it? I was *grateful* that my own mother was sick. How twisted is that? How *hideous* is that? I used my mother's pain as an excuse to run from my own problems. I've always felt guilty about that. It's like her dying was partly my fault."

"That's nuts." He grabbed her, but she yanked free of his grasp instantly.

"No it's not," she said firmly, "it's *karma*."

"You can't seriously believe *you're* responsible for your mother's death."

Jo's brain snapped back into focus at the incredulous tone in his voice and for one brief moment, she wanted to kick her own ass for opening this little can of ugly worms. But too late now, she told herself. She'd opened her big mouth and told him things she'd never said aloud before. Had barely admitted to *herself* before.

Maybe he really *was* some kind of hypnotist.

"Not logically," she said, feeling an inward twist of fury at the situation, herself, *him*. "I'm not an idiot. I know I didn't cause my mother to die just by being a coward. But there's that little voice inside me, the one that keeps me from walking under ladders, that has me knocking wood for luck. The same voice that halfway believes Nana really can cut a storm in half by clacking two sticks together. *That* part of me believes."

He cut through everything she'd said and homed in on one thing—one word—that had been buried in the avalanche of words. "How are *you* a coward?"

Jo wanted more wine. Actually, she wanted a vodka tonic with extra lime. But as shaky as she was at the moment, she so didn't need liquor on top of it all. Instead, she'd face Cash down and finish this. She'd say it all. Everything she'd felt, everything she'd lived with for ten long years. And when she was finished, she'd lock it away again.

Flipping her hair back behind her shoulder, Jo lifted

her chin and met his gaze. "I'm a *Marconi*," she said, her voice flat, quiet, despite the decade-old fury clawing at her insides. "I should have fought him."

"You did what you could."

"No I didn't. I just *lay* there and cried." Bitterness filled her mouth and she swallowed it down like a vile medicine she was too accustomed to taking. "But he didn't win," she murmured now, feeling fire erupt in her belly, snaking out tentacles of heat to chase back the bone-deep cold. "I didn't let him win. He didn't turn me away from men completely. He didn't take my *life*. Just my virginity. I didn't hide away," she said, her voice firming, her breath quickening. "I have sex every few months. Whether I'm interested or not. Just to prove to myself that I beat him. That *I* won, in the long run. He was nothing more than a bad blip on my radar screen."

"You're wrong."

"What?"

"I said you're wrong," Cash repeated, reaching out to stroke her hair back from her face. "He's still winning."

"He's won *nothing*. Weren't you *listening*?" Her features twisted and her eyes flashed.

"I was," he said, "but I don't think you were."

"What the hell are you talking about, and by the way, what the *hell* do you know about it?"

"I know you have sex and don't want it," he said, capturing her gaze with his, staring at her until she felt as though she were tumbling forward into the rich, dark depths of his eyes. "You don't—*won't*—enjoy it."

"Who says I don't?" she whispered, and heard the strain in her own voice.

"*I* say it." Cash cupped her face between his palms.

"I felt it. Your body was here, Josefina, but *you* weren't."

And he was the first man who'd ever noticed. What did that say about her?

About *him*?

She reached up and plucked his hands from her face, while at the same time stepping back and away from him. It was the only safe thing to do. The only *smart* thing to do. She couldn't allow herself to have strong feelings for him. Couldn't let herself wonder what her life might have been if she'd never dated Steve Smith.

Shaking her head, she kept backing up, until she was nearly at the door of the great room. She needed to go. Needed to get home. And if that was running away, then she'd just have to live with it.

But as a Marconi, she had to take the last shot.

"Did you ever stop to think that maybe *you're* the reason I didn't see the 'stars' during our little encounter?" She watched his eyes narrow, then delivered the last barb. "Maybe the great Woman Whisperer finally found a woman he couldn't reach."

Twelve

The worn-out shingles on the Meyerses' roof bit into the seat of Jo's jeans and made her shift uncomfortably in the hot sun. She glanced skyward and winced at the brassy beauty of the cloudless expanse of blue.

Spring was already shaping up to be a warm one, which could only mean that summer was going to be hot. She scowled a little at the thought, since usually summer in Chandler was just about perfect. This year, naturally, would be different.

Just as too many other damn things in her life were different these days.

She drew her knees up and dangled her hands between them, idly swinging her favorite hammer in a metronome fashion. She dropped her gaze to the scarred, metal head of the hammer and blindly watched as the sun glinted off the metal like stray sparks from a downed electrical wire. Her eyes felt gritty and she was bone-tired.

But then, that's what happened when you lanced open a puddle of poison in your insides, then stayed awake all night reliving it.

Sex with Cash was supposed to have been recuperative, for chrissake. The man was an artist, according to all reports.

A Mozart in the bedroom.

The modern-day Don Juan.

A freaking walking *orgasm.*

She'd expected . . . Hell, she wasn't sure what she'd expected. Maybe just to get through another sexual encounter with her pride intact. But no, not Josefina Marconi. Why settle for something subtle when you could go all out, make a complete ass of yourself, and *then* leave? Never let it be said that a Marconi did anything in a small way.

"Oh God, I can't believe I told him," she muttered, and realized that she was beginning to sound like a tape recorder stuck on repeat. She'd been saying the same thing over and over again all night long and through most of the morning. And every time the words left her mouth, she saw Cash's face again. The shock in his eyes. The fury—and then the *pity.*

She'd given a hard blow to an ego that had to be the size of Mount Everest by now. Every other woman who'd spent time in his bed had not only seen the stars, they'd run off to save the world. Not Jo, though. Her, he hadn't even been able to reach.

And wouldn't you know he'd notice?

"Hey, need some help?"

Jo's gaze snapped up and she watched her sister Sam's head pop up over the edge of the roof. She grinned at Jo from between the rungs of the aluminum ladder. Sunlight caught the red streaks in her sister's hair and for a brief moment made it look as if her head were on fire.

"What're you doing here?" Jo asked, fighting down

the spurt of worry that jolted up inside her. "And why the hell are you on a ladder, for God's sake?" She scooted toward the edge of the roof, sliding the soles of her boots along the raggedy shingles.

Sam only grinned and slowly handed over a tray bearing two coffee cups and a paper sack with the Leaf and Bean logo on it. "Are you gonna help with this or what?"

Jo took the tray then watched as Sam sprinted up the last few rungs of the ladder and stepped out onto the roof with an ease that spoke of years of practice. Glancing at the two-story drop-off, Jo then shifted her gaze back to her younger sister. "You sure you should be up here? This is no place to get dizzy."

Sam waved a hand at her, then walked up the slope of the roof to its crest. There she plopped down and drew her knees up, as at home as she would have been on the sofa in her living room. "I feel *great*," she said, flinging her arms wide and grinning up at the hot sun. "Woke up this morning and it was like the baby just decided, Hey, let's cut Mom a break."

She did look better, Jo thought. For the first time in months, Sam didn't have a green tinge to her face. And her eyes were a clear, pale blue, unlike her own that were as red streaked as a closeup shot of a city map.

Walking back up the roof to take a seat beside her sister, Jo made herself comfortable and pulled one of the cups out of the cardboard tray before handing the other one to Sam. "Latte?"

"God, yes," her sister said on a heartfelt sigh. "The doctor said I could have one a day. And this is the first day I've felt good enough to enjoy one." She took her first sip, sighed dramatically, then reached into the paper bag for a cinnamon roll. Only after she'd taken her first bite did she really look at Jo. "So what's with you?"

"What?"

"Nice try, but you heard me," Sam said, and frowned as she chewed and swallowed. "You look like shit."

"Gee, thanks for stopping by." Jo took a long gulp of her latte and felt the hot milk sear her throat.

"Spit it out."

"The latte?" Jo asked, deliberately misunderstanding. "You must be nuts."

"Back atcha if you think that little stalling tactic is going to throw me off. Now tell me what's wrong."

"Would it do any good to tell you to mind your own business?"

"What do you think?" she asked with a snort of laughter.

"I think life would have been much simpler as an only child."

"Nah. You would have found a way to complicate things anyway," Sam said, still smiling. "It's your nature, Jo. Go with your strengths."

Jo looked at her and laughed shortly. Damn if she hadn't missed her smart-ass sisters the last few months. Even when they were driving her nuts, they were at least a distraction.

Taking another sip, she glanced at the pile of paper-wrapped shingles stacked at one side of the roof beside a roll of tarpaper. "With you here, we should be able to get most of the roof done today. Finish it off tomorrow or the next day," she said quickly. "And we've got to get out to Mrs. Phillips's house to give her an estimate on expanding her back porch and screening it in."

"Uh-huh," Sam said, taking a small sip of her latte. "I heard the Money Fairy had been by over there. Loretta Phillips has been wanting to enclose that porch for years."

The Money Fairy.

Cash.

Damn it, even when she wasn't actively thinking about him, he found a way back into her brain. Was that fair? And thinking about Cash naturally brought up memories of the night before and something cold and ugly gnawed at the pit of her stomach as she recalled the rest of it.

Telling him about Steve.

Reliving that long-ago night until it was all as fresh and clear in her mind as her last trip to the dentist.

"Okay, talk."

"About what?"

"About whatever's putting that look on your face."

Jo frowned, deliberately made the attempt to smooth out her features, and looked at Sam through wide, innocent eyes. "Finish your latte and let's get to work."

"Josefina Angela Christina Marconi," Sam said softly, "I never thought you'd be too scared to tell me what you're thinking."

She flinched at the use of both her middle and confirmation names. That was pulling out the big guns. "Nobody said anything about being scared."

"So?"

"Fine." She blew out a breath, looked dead into Sam's eyes and said, "I had sex with Cash last night."

Sam's eyes popped open wide enough that Jo was pretty sure she could see right through them to the back of her sister's skull. "Well, that's disappointing."

Not the reaction she'd been expecting. "Why?"

"Because I've never seen you look more miserable. He's either not very good at it, which his reputation clearly indicates is not true—" She tilted her head to one side to stare at her. "Or there's something else you're not telling me."

And for the first time in . . . *ever*, she thought about it. Oh God, she seriously thought about telling Sam the truth. For about five whole seconds, before she dismissed the idea completely. And how sad was that? she asked herself silently. That she could tell *Cash Hunter* the whole truth, but couldn't face her *family* with it?

Her throat tightened as she fought to breathe, to drag air into lungs that felt sealed shut. Stupid. Opening up that wound last night had left it raw and bleeding and too easily noticed. She hadn't been able to hide her misery from Sam today—and she'd been pulling it off successfully for ten years. So how was she going to manage to hide it all again? To push it back into the cold black pit of her heart where it had festered so long in silence?

Panic reared up inside her. She couldn't. Couldn't tell them. Couldn't see their faces fill with pity or, worse . . . *shame*.

She'd simply have to find a way to face her past and let it go.

Sure. No problem.

"Nothing satisfies you, does it?" Jo snapped, taking another long gulp of her coffee in a vain attempt to ease the chill beginning to crawl through her. "I finally tell you what you want to know and you think there's got to be more."

"Isn't there?"

Jo pushed to her feet and automatically shifted into the cautious position she used when walking around a roof. She might be on edge, but she had no intention of going over that edge and hitting the ground like an overripe watermelon. "No, there isn't. I'm fine. Cash is fine. Sex is fine. Now can we work?"

"Jeez," Sam muttered as Jo stomped off across the roof, sending loose shingles falling like black rain to the ground. "Who knew *having* sex could make you crabbier than *not* having it?"

Cash felt as if his guts were on fire. On fire and being twisted. By a giant, cold hand.

Yeah. That about covered it.

Opening the door to the guest cottage, Cash stepped inside and paused to take a quick look around. He smiled, despite the rampaging thoughts thundering through his brain. No matter how messed up the rest of his life might look at the moment, at least *this* was coming together.

It was finished.

Or should be.

Technically, the place had been completed six months ago. But he'd kept finding new things to add. New things to tempt his mother with. He wasn't such an idiot that he didn't know what he was doing.

He wanted to make Kate Hunter a place so nice that she'd finally want to stick around. To put down roots. To be more than a kind stranger in her own son's life.

The windows were covered by lacy swatches of fabric that swung low across the glass and then were gathered back by more lace, tied into bows. Sunlight splintered through the leaded windows and lay in diamond-shaped patterns on the gleaming wood floor. The walls were a pale golden oak, much like the main house, but here, there was something more feminine about it.

He'd hung pictures on the walls, spread area rugs on the floor, and furnished the place with feather-soft chairs and lamps that looked as if Tiffany himself had designed them. There was a tiny kitchen filled with every convenience he could think of. The small bedroom had a mural of a cloud-filled summer sky on the ceiling, courtesy of Sam Marconi. And the luxurious bathroom boasted a spa tub that Mike Marconi had wired complete with stereo speakers fitted into the garden window. The Murphy bed Jo had built for the living room would do for any of Kate's friends who might like to stay over, and the deck spearing off the back of the house held a brick fire pit and built-in padded benches.

"This time she'll stay," he murmured, and ran one hand across the smooth edge of a built-in bookcase as he walked through the cottage to the back door and the deck beyond.

There were just a few more things to finish back here, then it would be ready. He stepped outside into the cool shadows of the pines surrounding the house and took a deep, satisfying breath, grateful to have thoughts of Jo gone—and just like that, she was back.

Front and center in his mind.

And the twisting fury that clamped at his guts returned in full force. He wanted to go into the city, find Steve Smith and beat the living shit out of the man. But it wouldn't change anything. Wouldn't help Jo. Wouldn't change what had happened—or *hadn't* happened—between them.

Absently, he picked up the propane torch, turned it on, then snapped the sparker in front of the escaping gas. A blue-white flame shot from the end of the torch and Cash reached for the goggles he'd left on one of the benches.

He bent then to focus the heat on the planks of the picnic table, running it carefully back and forth against the grain, giving the table the look of aged wood.

Ordinarily, work helped. Distracted him. Forced him to concentrate. But Jo was too deeply entrenched in his mind to be ousted that easily.

"Damn it," he said aloud, since no one was there to hear him anyway. "She thinks she's dealt with it. Thinks she's moved on." But she was still too trapped in the past to see the present, let alone the future.

It had stung more than a little, knowing that she'd held back from him the night before. Even with her in his arms, he'd sensed her distance. Known that she wasn't participating. Heard every false cry and rehearsed moan and felt it slap at him.

Always before, he'd found a way to touch a woman without being touched himself. He'd protected his own heart, safeguarded it by taking more pleasure in *giving* pleasure than in receiving. Not that he was a saint or anything. He enjoyed sex. He just didn't want to get involved.

So why the hell was he involving himself *now*?

Because Jo *hadn't* enjoyed herself? Was being a lousy lover the secret to making a woman stay?

Scowling, he left the torch flame in one spot too long and saw the wood blacken and begin to curl. Irritated as hell, he shut it off and set it down before he set fire to the whole damn place.

No.

This wasn't about getting a woman to stay.

Jo wouldn't be staying with him.

Neither of them wanted that, anyway.

And yet . . .

Knowing that he had touched her flesh, yet had never come close to touching her soul, tore at him.

And just for a minute, he wondered if any of the women he'd been with over the years had felt the same way about *him*.

Jack led the way.

He'd been to Cash's house so many times, he figured he could ride his bike there in the dark. But he was just as glad it wasn't dark. He had the feeling the woods were probably pretty spooky at night time. But right now, with sunlight coming through the trees, it was kind of pretty.

Not that he'd say that out loud or anything.

"How far away is it?" Justin demanded from behind him.

"Really close," Jack shouted back, amazed again that Justin was like his best friend now. Once Cash had taught him how to throw and he'd made the baseball team, Justin had stopped teasing him and now they were friends.

Maybe living in Chandler wouldn't be too bad after all.

Especially if he could make Jo and Cash like each other enough to get married. And then he could live out here in the house by the lake and he and Cash could go fishing like Cash said they were gonna do sometime. Cash was really great. He never got mad and he knew lots of cool stuff and he didn't mind showing Jack how to do it, too. Like working with his tools and stuff.

"You gotta see it," Jack said, still really excited because Cash had let him help finish the deck on the cottage.

"You got to use the tools?" Justin didn't believe him, not really, but that was okay. Sometimes even friends needed proof.

"Yeah, even the torch, and that was really cool 'cause you have to use goggles for safety and everything—"

"Wow." Justin kicked it up a little until his bike rolled right alongside Jack's. The heavy rubber tires jolted over the rocks in the road but neither boy seemed to mind. "My dad never lets me help him do stuff. I think it's 'cause he cusses so much when he works on stuff in the garage."

"Cash doesn't cuss," Jack said, and enjoyed having a guy to talk about. His papa was really nice, but he wasn't like the other fathers. He was kind of old and didn't really have a lot of time to do fun stuff or anything.

When the boys rounded the bend in the road, the guest cottage was there, sitting in a splash of tree-dappled sunshine and looking like something out of a fairy tale. They dropped their bikes on the front yard and raced each other around the side of the house to the back deck.

"That's really awesome," Justin whispered, and took the steps in a couple of quick jumps. His sneakers hit the wood deck with a thump and he walked around in a slow circle looking at everything.

Jack was right behind him and he shoved his hands into his jeans pockets and rocked on his heels a little, like Cash did sometimes. "I helped him make that fireplace, too, and mixed cement and everything."

"Cool. So what'd you use the torch on?"

"The table," Jack said, and pointed to where the propane torch and starter were still lying in the sun. "You use the flame to make the wood look really old."

Justin frowned. "But it's new."

"Yeah," Jack shrugged. "But people don't want it to look like it is."

"That's dumb."

Jack thought so, too, but he wasn't about to say so. "Cash says it's called 'distressing.' "

"Show me how you do it."

A ping of caution erupted in Jack's chest. He looked around, half expecting to see Cash come walking out of the woods to ask what they were doing. But he didn't. He must be at the workshop up by the big house. But then why'd he leave the torch? Maybe he was coming right back.

"Come on, show me," Justin was saying as he picked up the torch and shook it.

"Don't do that," Jack said, and moved to grab it from his friend.

Justin swept his blond hair back from his head and

frowned. "Then show me. What's the big deal? You said Cash lets you do it."

"Yeah . . ." But Jack'd never done it by himself before.

"So?"

"Okay," he said, figuring he could turn on the torch and show Justin and then have it all off and put away before Cash came back. Nobody would have to know.

Carefully, he put on the goggles, and when Justin laughed, he did, too, forgetting about the nervousness sliding through the pit of his stomach like black oil. Then he turned on the propane tank and heard the hiss as the colorless gas escaped.

"Sounds like snakes."

"Yeah," Justin said, and picked up the spark maker. He liked this part best, because it was sort of like magic. Just press the sparker thing together in front of the gas and the little spark set off the propane and made fire.

The whoosh of flame smothered the hissing sound, and Justin said, "Cool."

Jack grinned to himself as he aimed the stream of flame at the tabletop. The wood blackened and smoked as he moved it carefully, just like Cash had shown him how to do.

"Lemme try it," Justin demanded.

"Just a minute," Jack argued.

"C'mon!" Justin gave him a shove and Jack shoved him back.

"Wait your turn," he warned.

"You had your turn, now it's mine," Justin said, and grabbed for the propane torch.

Jack laughed and yanked it out of his reach, but

when Justin grabbed again, Jack stumbled and his grip on the torch dissolved.

It clattered onto the deck, rolled a few feet, and still spitting flame, landed up against the wall of the cottage.

"Uh-oh!" Justin's eyes bugged out and he took off, running for the front yard and his bike.

But Jack couldn't go.

Flames were licking at the bottom of the wall. "Oh no . . ."

Fear licked at his insides as quickly as the flames were beginning to chew at the wall. He ran to the torch, but when he tried to pick it up, he burned his hand and dropped it again. Tears blurred Jack's vision, but he saw the torch roll away from him until it landed near a pile of old paint rags.

Terrified, jack felt the blistering heat reach out and punch at him as, in the next second—*whoomph!*—the torch and rags created a giant fireball.

Thirteen

Cash smelled the fire before he saw it.

For a second or two, he stood stunned outside the workshop, trying to figure out what the hell was burning. Then he saw the smoke twisting up from the treetops in sinuous swirls of gray and black and knew it was the cottage.

He broke into a run, his long legs eating up the distance in seconds, and as he ran, he pulled his cell phone from his jeans pocket.

The thick stench of acrid smoke reached for him and stung his eyes and throat. He heard the snap and crackle of flames devouring wood and punched in 911 on his cell.

"Fire!" he shouted when the operator answered. "On the lake road, behind the Van Horn house."

He was already snapping the phone closed when he heard the high-pitched scream.

Heart in his throat, he left the road and took a short-cut, pushing through the trees and bushes separating him from the guest cottage. The wind kicked up, sending the smoke at him in thick waves driven by heat. Long branches tore at him, swiping at his face and arms.

"Cash!"

Jack's voice lifted again, higher this time, colored by panic and pain.

Blood hammering through his veins, heartbeat crashing in his chest, Cash fought the mind-numbing fear threatening to choke him. Plunging through the last of the overgrowth surrounding the tiny house, he stepped into a clearing filled with the bright, wavering light of flames.

Incredible heat washed over him and he felt the sharp sting of it searing his skin. His eyes watered, his breath strangled. He coughed, and held his forearm up to his face. The fire roared at him with a kind of savage hunger as if daring Cash to come closer.

But Jack was there, huddled on the deck, trying to inch away from the inferno gathering strength with every second.

Forgetting everything but reaching the boy, Cash jumped onto the deck and raced to Jack's side. Kneeling beside the boy, he felt the incredible heat of the fire singeing his back and a part of him wondered if his black T-shirt was on fire. Didn't matter if it was. He had to move Jack. Get him to safety. Couldn't wait for help. "Are you hurt?"

"My arm and my hand," the boy said, tears making clean streaks in the soot smeared across his face.

The kid's left arm looked . . . *wrong*, and there were blisters forming on his right palm. Tiny cuts up and down his arms bled tiny streams of red and there was a knot on his forehead the size of Cash's fist.

"I didn't mean to—"

"It's okay," Cash said quickly, scraping his hands up

and down the kid's body checking for further injuries with a brusque thoroughness that belied the trembling inside him. "Don't worry about it. Everything's okay. Fire department's coming. And I'm getting you out of here."

He scooped the kid up carefully, cradling him against his chest, and when he stood up, he winced at Jack's soft moan of protest. Everything in him tightened like piano wire pulled to the point of snapping. He felt the boy's pain and fear as if it were his own and the tremors within kept right on coming.

Glancing over his shoulder then, Cash watched as the flames lifted, reaching for the overhang of roof and the new shingles. Fresh paint on the walls buckled and peeled away from the wood, dropping into the hungry flames like snowflakes into hell.

The hiss and crackle of the flames sounded like demonic laughter and as he watched a section of the roof collapse he knew the joke was on him. All the time and effort he'd put into this place and now it was going to be nothing more than a pile of embers in the woods.

Even as he heard the sirens approaching, though, Cash turned his back on the burning cottage. Holding the boy close, he stalked off to get help.

Jo raced into the hospital lobby with Sam just a step or two behind her. Their boots sounded overly loud in such a quiet place. They made a sharp right turn into the narrow waiting room that smelled of antiseptic and fear, the two of them slid to a stop, and the silence was suddenly deafening.

The TV, mounted high in the corner, flashed with

some soap opera, peopled by fabulously dressed and impossibly pretty actors, but the sound was muted. Two rows of scoop-shaped green plastic chairs dotted the green-flecked linoleum and the mint-green walls finished off the slightly nauseating color scheme.

Jo hardly noticed.

The Marconis were gathered.

Sam's husband, Jeff, and her daughter, Emma, were already rushing toward her, Nana paced slowly in her black orthopedic grandma shoes, and Lucas Gallagher was standing beside the ugly chair where a *very* pregnant Mike was perched uncomfortably.

"Mike?" Jo crossed to her youngest sister. "What're you doing here? You shouldn't be up."

She frowned. "Like I could just sit at home?"

True. No Marconi would be able to stay away when one of them was threatened.

"Have we heard anything?" Sam asked, sweeping Emma up close for a quick, tight hug, as if reassuring herself of at least *one* child's safety.

"Nothing yet," Lucas said, dropping one hand onto his wife's shoulder. "The doctor's still with him."

Mike reached up and covered his hand with hers, their fingers interlocking. "Nobody's talking to us." She waved a hand at the receptionist in the far corner. "She won't even look at me anymore."

"Maybe you shouldn't have threatened to kick her ass," Jeff said quietly.

Mike jutted her chin at Sam's husband. "Don't start with me, Weasel Dog," she warned. "I'm *way* too pregnant to put up with much more."

"Down, tiger," Lucas murmured, tightening his grip on his wife.

"For God's sake, Mike—" Exasperated, Sam blew out a breath.

"Is Jack gonna be okay?" Emma asked no one in particular.

"Sure he is," her dad reassured her.

"Is there *anybody* we can talk to?" Jo demanded, looking from one face to another.

"The doctor will come," Nana said, holding up one hand like a traffic cop.

"While we're *young*?" Jo demanded.

"Dial it down," Sam told her, wincing as Jo's voice hit a pitch that was better suited for a football game.

"We pray now," Nana said softly, and fingered the shining, blue crystal beads of the rosary dangling from between her gnarled fingers. A stray beam of sunlight shot through the window, hit the rosary just right, and briefly lit up Nana's black dress in a rainbow of color before just as quickly winking out again.

Pray.

Yeah. That'll help.

Jo hadn't done a lot of praying lately. Well, not since last year, when she'd stopped by St. Joseph's church just long enough to tell God to kiss off. Nice move, she told herself now, as she rubbed at her forehead, trying to ease the headache crashing against the inside of her skull. Piss off the Big Man and see how screwed things get.

"You might as well sit down, Jo," Sam's husband Jeff said as he stroked his wife's shoulder in a slow, gentle caress. "We can't do anything until somebody comes out to tell us what's going on."

She nodded, but knew she wouldn't sit. How could she sit when she didn't know? Didn't— "What was he doing at Cash's house anyway?" she asked, not really expecting an answer.

"Is that really important right now?" Mike snapped, then eased back as Lucas stroked his fingers through her long blond hair.

Jo noticed the gestures passing between her sisters and their husbands. Maybe they were all so used to those tiny signs of affection that they didn't pay attention anymore, but suddenly *she* was. Idle touches, gentle pats, a look, a smile, a whispered word. All tiny signs of the connection they shared.

And for the first time, Jo was envious of it.

Not just the affection part, but the *bond*. The thread that tied them so closely together that one of them wasn't complete without the other. For so long, she'd told herself that she didn't need a man in her life. That she was fine on her own. And she'd believed it—or at least she'd convinced herself she believed it, which was pretty much the same thing.

Yet now . . .

Now she was thinking about Cash. About the night before. About how she'd almost . . . *God*.

So not the time.

"Is Jack gonna die?" Emma's voice came thin, worried.

"No." Jo said it before Sam could answer her daughter. Dropping to one knee, she looked into Emma's tear-streaked face and reached out to swipe those tears away with careful fingers. "Jack's not going to die." She said it firmly, as if by being confident, she could make it so. "He's going to be fine. You'll see."

Sam stroked one hand over her daughter's pigtails and chewed at her bottom lip.

"Rocket Man," Mike said into the following silence, "why don't you go find us all some coffee?"

Lucas nodded, then looked sternly at the woman he adored. "You're not getting out of that chair, right?"

She swept her fingers across her heart, then lifted them into a perfect imitation of a Girl Scout salute. "Swear to God. I'll be right here when you get back."

"All right." He bent down and kissed her forehead, then turned to Jeff. "Give me a hand?" Not waiting for an answer, he hurried out of the waiting room.

Jeff gave Sam a quick pat on the rear, then followed Lucas out.

Alone but for Emma and Nana, the sisters huddled together. Sam took a seat beside Mike and pulled her daughter up onto her lap. "What'd the hospital say when they called?" she asked.

Mike shrugged and looked at her grandmother. "The hospital called the house, Nana called me. All I know is, Cash brought Jack in."

Nana nodded. "The hospital say Jack issa hurt. I call Michaela."

"And I called you guys," Mike said.

"Where the hell'd Cash go?" Jo wanted to know, looking around the room as if half expecting him to morph right out of the wall or something. "Why isn't he still here? What? Did he just dump the kid and keep on going? What's that about?"

"Issa no importante where is Cash," Nana said softly, sneaking up on Jo from behind like some tiny, Italian ghost. "Now issa time for worry about Jack. We pray."

"You go ahead, Nana," Jo said, and took a step back, shaking her head. She wouldn't go running to God in time of crisis when she hadn't bothered talking to Him in months. She would at *least* not be a hypocrite.

Mike eased back in her chair, winced and rubbed both hands over her truly impressive belly.

"You okay?" Sam asked, drawing Emma closer as she slumped tiredly in the chair.

"Are the babies okay?" Emma wanted to know.

"We're all fine," Mike answered, and found a smile for her niece. "We're just a little crowded."

"Josefina," Nana said, poking at her arm, apparently unwilling to let this whole praying thing go. "Why you no want to pray with me?"

Jo gritted her teeth and took a deep breath. "I'm too worried to pray," she said, hoping her grandmother would leave it alone.

A foolish hope at best.

"When you are worried, issa best time to pray. God knows." She lifted her hand and pointed her index finger skyward. "He listens."

"If He already knows, then I don't have to pray," Jo said, wondering how in the hell she'd been sucked into this conversation while her little brother was back in the bowels of this damn hospital going through God knew what.

She scrubbed her hands over her face, then stuffed both hands into her jeans pockets. Nerves jumped inside her and her mouth was dry as dust. She needed to *do* something, damn it.

"Nana," Sam was saying quietly, "maybe now's not a good time to—"

The middle child. Always looking to make peace. Even though she was rarely thanked for it.

"Say a rosary for me, too, Nana," Mike threw in, hoping to take the heat off Jo.

"I say a rosary for *all* my grandchildren," Nana muttered, shooting a meaningful glance at Jo. "And especially for Josefina, I think."

Guilt pooled in the pit of her stomach, but she was used to that. You couldn't grow up Italian *and* Catholic without learning how to live with guilt. "Thanks, but I'm fine, Nana. Jack's the one in trouble."

"I'm not so sure," the old woman whispered.

Jo checked her watch, threw a quick glance at the reception desk where a bored blonde sat filing her nails, then looked back at her sisters. "I gotta get out of here for a while. Need some air. I'll be back."

She turned and crossed the green-flecked lobby tile in a few long strides and heard Mike explain to Nana, "It's okay. Jo just needs to go kick something. She'll be back."

Kick something.

Sounded good, but it wouldn't help, she knew. Reaching up, she grabbed the bill of her baseball cap and pulled it down snug on her forehead. She hit the glass doors with both hands and gratefully left the scent and silence of the hospital behind.

Sunlight hit her tired, gritty eyes like a sledgehammer and she winced and sucked in a breath. Didn't help. She still felt as if she'd been run over and kicked to the curb. Stomping to the side of the hospital, she stepped into the shade of the building and leaned back against the cold stucco. The rough texture poked at her through the fabric of her Marconi Construction T-shirt and she welcomed the distraction. Propping one foot behind her on the wall, she stared down the slope of the hill toward the meadow that stretched along the outskirts of town.

In that meadow, the local growers were setting up their stalls and lining up the flowers they'd be selling beginning this weekend. The Flower Fantasy was about to kick off, and soon busloads of tourists would be flooding Chandler. The whole town would be filled with the commingled scents of hundreds of different blooms, and growers from all over central California would be happily counting up profits.

In other words, the world marched on while she stood here wondering what the hell was going on with her little brother.

"He'll be all right."

She jerked away from the wall and spun around when Cash walked up. His black shirt was torn and filthy. Soot streaked his forehead and his black hair looked a little singed around the edges.

In short, he looked great.

Damn it.

"What happened?" Her voice sounded choked, strained.

"There was a fire. At the guest cottage."

"How'd it start?"

"I'm not sure." Cash pushed one hand through his hair, shifted his gaze from hers, then let his hand drop listlessly to his side. He'd been sitting in his truck for the last half hour. Waiting. He couldn't leave the hospital without finding out about Jack, but he hadn't wanted to wait inside with the Marconis, either. When he saw Jo stomp outside alone, though, he'd had to follow her.

"I was at the workshop. Smelled smoke." He shook his head and squinted into the distance, staring down the hill at the workers setting up booths. He wasn't really seeing them, though. Instead, he was watching the flames, feeling that rush of gut-wrenching fear again.

"Heard Jack scream," he said tightly. "Found him on the deck, trying to get away from the fire."

"Jack started the fire?"

"I don't know." He shrugged and blew out a breath. "Whatever happened, it was an accident. And my fault."

"You weren't even there," she pointed out.

"My place. My fault." His chest hurt and he slapped one hand against it, rubbing absently. "Think he tried to use the propane torch like I showed him last week."

Last week. Felt longer ago than that. He remembered the flash of excitement on the boy's face, and in his mind, that expression faded now into the pain he'd seen only an hour ago. Shaking his head as if to wipe away the unwanted images, he said, "I saw the torch. In the fire—casing exploded."

"Oh God."

"He could've been killed." Each word was squeezed out of his throat, as painful as if they'd been jagged shards of glass.

"He wasn't."

Cash looked at her, saw the fear shining in her pale blue eyes, and fought down his urge to comfort her. He couldn't take that step. Not now. He was way too close to the edge.

"Why the hell aren't you pissed off?"

"At you?"

"*Yes*." He scraped one hand over his jaw, then across the back of his neck. "He was hurt at *my* place. It was my fault."

"Jesus, Cash," Jo said, "how is it your fault that my brother went to your place and burned down a building?"

"I shouldn't have left the torch there."

"And he shouldn't have touched it."

"He's a kid."

"Exactly."

"Don't you get it?" he snapped, grabbing her shoulders and yanking her close enough that she had to tip her head back to meet his gaze. "He could have *died* in that fire."

" 'Could have' doesn't mean a damn thing. Jack's alive. You found him. *You* saved him."

He let her go and swallowed hard past the knot of tension lodged in his throat. "You still don't get it."

Before she could speak, the door behind her flew open and Sam stuck her head out. "Jo— Hey, Cash." She grinned at him. "The doc was just in. Said we can see him. Jack's okay."

Relief washed through him and left him nearly as weak-kneed as the fear had an hour ago. When Sam ducked back inside, Jo turned her gaze on him. "You want to come in?"

God, yes.

And no.

He backed up, instinctively pulling back from any kind of emotional attachment. He was connected here, but it wasn't too late to sever that link.

"It's not your fault," Jo said.

Cash laughed shortly. "When it comes right down to it, Josefina, *all* of this is my fault."

Then he turned and left her watching after him as he walked across the parking lot, alone.

"Am I in trouble?"

Jack looked pitiful. A small boy with a still-dirty face, his left arm was in a cast and Band-Aids dotted his face and right arm. He moved his feet under the sheet, as if trying to find a way to make a run for it.

For the moment, Emma, Lucas, Jeff, and Nana remained in the waiting room, giving the sisters time with their brother. But who knew how long that would last?

"What do you think?" Sam asked, reaching down to stroke his hair back from his face. Glancing at the grime clinging to her palm, she wiped her hand on her jeans and shrugged.

"I didn't mean to do it," he said, then looked past them at the empty doorway. "Where's Cash?"

"Good question," Sam muttered, shooting Jo a quizzical look.

Jo ignored her and focused on their brother. "What happened?" she asked, gripping the metal rail at the edge of his bed. Around them, people in the emergency room came and went, machines hummed and clicked, and somewhere down the hall a baby wailed.

Jack started talking, pulling at the sheet with his fingertips and shooting uncertain glances around the room. The Marconi sisters gathered around their little brother as he told them all about the fire, how it had happened and how Cash had jumped practically into the flames to carry him out.

"And then he brought me here in his truck, and he

drove really fast and said that he'd call you guys and I told him I didn't want you to know, but he said you had to know and I told him I'm sorry and stuff, and he said it was okay, so—" Jack took a deep breath and blew it out again. "Is it okay?"

"It will be," Sam said, and held out one hand. "You'll have to talk to Cash about this. And we'll have to find a way to pay for the damage . . ."

"Hey," Mike told him, as she laid her hand on top of Sam's, "we'll work it out. Besides, you're not a true Marconi until you do something *really* stupid."

"Trust Mike on that," Jo told the little boy staring up at them with a tremulous smile on his face. "She knows all about *stupid*."

"Funny," Mike whispered.

Jo laid her hand atop her sisters'.

"So," Sam asked with a wink. "You gonna join in on the Marconi shake?"

"Really?" Jack looked from one to the other of his sisters in disbelief. For nearly a year, he'd watched them link hands like this and he knew just how special it was to them. And now, for the first time, he was being included.

"You're a Marconi, aren't you?" Jo asked, smiling at him as if she weren't really mad at all.

"Yeah," Jack said, and winced as he reached out to lay his small right hand on top of his sisters'. "I guess I am."

"Jack he will be fine, the doctor tells me," Nana said as Jo pulled into the driveway.

"Yeah, I know. I just felt bad leaving him at the hospital overnight."

"Is better he issa there, with the bump onna head."

True. The doctors just wanted to be sure he wasn't concussed or something, and hey, Jo was all for being careful. But leaving a little boy all alone in a hospital just didn't feel right. Still, she couldn't leave Nana alone, either, could she?

Man.

She bent over and rested her forehead on the steering wheel. Every inch of her body ached and pounded. Her brain kept racing with "what might have beens," and to top the whole mess off, she couldn't stop thinking about *Cash.*

Hell, he wasn't even *Italian* and he'd picked up the guilt banner and was running with it. Key word there being "running." He hadn't been able to get away from her fast enough. So much for their little "moment" the night before. So much for her thinking that all of his flirting over the last year had meant diddly.

"Josefina." Nana's voice came as soft as the hand she laid on Jo's back. "You are *praying.*"

She stiffened and turned her head to look at her grandmother. In the late afternoon shadows, every line and crease on the old woman's face stood out in sharp relief. But her eyes were sharp and clearly pleased.

"Nana, would you just let it go?"

"What issa 'let go'?"

She sighed. "Never mind." Opening the driver's-side door, she hopped down, slammed the door shut hard enough to rattle the window glass, then stomped around to the passenger side. She opened the door, looked in, and said, "Come on, Nana. I'll make you some tea."

"You're a gooda girl, Josefina," Nana said, gingerly

climbing down out of the truck as if trying to balance on raw eggs. "This I *always* say."

"Thanks," Jo said, steering her grandmother up the narrow walkway to the front porch. With one hand on the elderly woman's elbow, Jo guided her up the steps, then opened the screen door and turned the worn, brass knob.

"I think we both have some tea, eh?" Nana asked, a dry chuckle grating from her throat. "Issa busy day for all."

"I'll say," Jo muttered, following her grandmother into the living room. "And I could really do with just a little bit less drama for a while."

"Josefina!" Hank Marconi's booming voice preceded him into the room and he strode toward her, arms extended, inviting a bear hug, his wide, bearded face beaming with benevolence.

"Papa?" She took a step forward—but before she could get that hug, Nana Coletti struck like a snake.

Jumping in front of her son-in-law, the old woman reared back and slapped him full across the face. *"Bastardo!"* she shouted, lifting both hands to heaven and shaking them as if she were calling down thunder and lightning. "You no here when *la famiglia* need you! *Bastardo!* Living inna sin! God issa *watching!*"

Had she really wished for *less* drama?

Hank winced, reached up and rubbed his cheek. "Hello, Maria," he said. "Good to see you, too."

He turned to watch the old woman stomp past him into the kitchen, still muttering in what sounded like vicious Italian.

Fourteen

"I called the hospital," Papa said as he stepped onto the front porch with his morning cup of coffee. "They say Jack is okay and I can come and get him."

"Good. I'm glad." Jo took a sip of her own coffee. "Maybe Nana will ease up once he's home again."

"Maria has issues."

"Issues?" Jo laughed out loud as her father took a seat beside her on the top step. "Since when do you talk like Oprah?"

He shrugged, a little embarrassed. "Grace says everybody has issues. Maria more than most," he added quietly.

Though things were still a little iffy between her and her father, Jo was glad to have him home. And grateful as hell he and Grace had caught an earlier flight. Even if it had meant listening to Nana rant and rave for hours the night before.

To give Papa his due, though, he hadn't argued with his mother-in-law. He'd simply sat still and taken the abuse Maria Coletti seemed determined to heap on his head. She'd continued her one-woman assault this morning, too, standing outside Papa's bedroom and clanging two saucepans together as a hideous, home-made alarm clock.

The fact that it had also jolted Jo out of bed didn't seem to matter. The point was, at least in Nana's esti-mation, that she was making Papa suffer.

Jo'd originally planned to move back to her condo as soon as Grace and Papa came home. But after hav-ing a ringside seat for the Nana-versus-Papa battle of the Titans, she'd decided to stay a while longer—as sort of a buffer. And though that argument sounded extremely logical, even Jo knew there was more to it than that. When it came right down to it, she really didn't want to be alone at the moment. Even putting up with Nana's rants was better than being wrapped up in silence so thick that the only thing to do was *think*.

"Papa," she said, before she could change her mind, "if you want me to, I'll just stay on here with you and Jack until Nana goes home."

His whole face lit up. If she'd needed reassurance that her decision was the right one, she'd just found it.

"Thank you," he said, and took another hesitant sip of his murderous coffee. He shuddered visibly, then added, "I know you'd rather be at your own house—"

"It's okay, Papa."

From inside the house, a pan clanged hard against the stove and Nana shouted something unintelligible.

Papa winced. "She's very angry."

"Yeah." And maybe *because* the older woman was so determined to inflict punishment, Jo felt more in-clined to be understanding than she had been before. "Nana shouldn't keep on you like this."

Sighing, he took a sip of coffee, and scowled as he chewed.

Jo hid her smile. Nana had made *two* pots of coffee. An excellent one for Jo and another, complete with coffee grounds, for Papa.

He stared out at the raggedy-looking front yard, the street beyond, and over to Mrs. Sanchez's house, where Precious was outside, walking the perimeter. The little dog looked hungry.

"She has a right to hate me. Sylvia was her daughter."

"And my mother."

He nodded and stroked one hand across his almost snow-white beard. "And you, Josefina? Can you say that you forgive me?"

When she didn't answer, he patted her knee and sighed again. "It's okay. I know you are ashamed of your papa, and I understand."

"How can you?" she whispered, wanting the ache inside her to dissipate. "When I'm not sure even *I* understand me anymore?"

Henry studied his oldest daughter and wished that he could hold her. That she would welcome his embrace. That she could tell him what caused the pain he saw in her eyes. Because he knew it wasn't just his own disgrace that had caused it. He'd known for years that his oldest girl had troubles that she wouldn't share.

And if he hadn't known before, he would have now. Between trying to break his eardrums and burning his morning coffee, Maria had taken him to task on his parenting skills just a few minutes ago.

"Josefina is no happy. Is something wrong. Her heart is hurt and you must fix this. You are a *bastardo* still, but you are her father. Josefina, she needs you now. Go. Be a papa."

The trouble was, he didn't know how to reach her. Josefina had always been the strongest of his girls. The most self-contained. She was always ready to listen to someone else's troubles, but her own she kept locked away, so no one would see. And now . . . she'd somehow slipped so far from him that the road back to where they'd once been looked impassable. Still, he had to try.

"Josefina," he said, his voice caressing her name as his hand itched to stroke her cheek. "When your mama was sick—"

Instantly, a shutter dropped over her eyes and her back went as stiff as a two-by-four. "No, Papa . . ."

She tried to get up, but he laid one hand on her knee to keep her in place. Facing her, he waited for her to look at him. Then he tried again to find his way back into his daughter's heart.

"When your mama was sick, I was scared. More scared than I've ever been before in my life." He closed his eyes briefly and remembered the bone-wracking terror that had crouched inside him during those lonely days. He'd had no one to tell his fears to. He couldn't burden his children. His wife was already suffering. A priest? What did a man of God know about losing the woman who meant more to you than your own soul?

He shook his head, opened his eyes again, swallowed the bitter taste of his own shame, and looked deeply into Jo's wary eyes.

"My Sylvia was in such pain. And every day, she became less. Less herself. Less of this earth. It was . . ." He paused and searched for the words, even knowing there were none sufficient to explain. "Like watching her die with every breath. I worried. For her. For you girls. For me. And alone at night, I cried. There was nothing for me. No comfort. No way to ease the emptiness coming for me."

"Papa . . ."

He'd been understanding. He'd given her nearly a year to come to grips with his slip from grace. He hadn't wanted to push—to risk shoving her even further away from him. But the time had come at last. There'd been enough hiding.

"No. It's time, Jo." He tightened his grip on her knee and let the tears flow unchecked down his face. He wasn't ashamed of them. When a man loves with his whole heart, what are a few tears? "When I met Jack's mother, Carol—"

"I know the story," she interrupted, holding up one hand, trying to make him stop.

"Fine. You know. Then you know how I met her. She was kind and alone and I was more alone than I'd ever been."

"You had *us,* Papa."

"I know that," he said, and wondered how to make her understand what it had been like for him to face losing her mother. "But you were children. How could I worry you more than you already were?" He shook his head again. "You were still in school then. Sam had just come home and Michaela was running away every time I turned around. Your mama was leaving us and my family was crumbling around her."

Jo scowled and her dark eyebrows drew together as

they always did when she was thinking hard about something. It gave him hope.

"It was wrong, Jo. I know that. I knew that *then*. But I—*needed* to feel alive. To be reminded that life would keep going on. That the whole world wasn't dying along with my Sylvia."

Taking a chance, he reached out, cupped her chin and turned her face to his. "And as much as I'm ashamed and sorry that I hurt you and your sisters, I can't regret Jack. I can't wish him out of existence to change things between us."

"I know that," she whispered, and carefully covered his hand with hers. "Neither can I."

A fragile bubble of hope expanded within him and Henry clung to it desperately. He needed to be right with his daughters. He needed to reach Jo to be able to help her with whatever it was that was tearing at her so.

"Losing your mama like that made me crazy. I couldn't run away like Michaela. So I ran away the only way I could. Can you try to understand, Jo? Try to forgive me for failing you? For letting you down?"

Jo swallowed hard and a single tear streaked down her cheek, but she quickly wiped it away with the back of her hand. She *did* understand. Finally and completely.

Sylvia Marconi's illness and death had shattered them all in different ways. Mike had run away almost weekly until the night she hitched a ride with the wrong guy and ended up in a hospital bed. Sam had given away her own child in an effort to not burden their already broken family.

And Jo had run from the man who'd destroyed her trust. She'd taken her mother's illness and used it for her own purposes. She'd buried her heart and her shame and her fears in the care of her mother. How could she possibly blame Papa for running in the only way he could?

"I do understand, Papa," she whispered as tears choked her, tightening her throat until oxygen became a serious issue. "Better than you know."

"Ah, Josefina," he soothed, "can't you tell me what's hurting you? Can't you take me back into your heart?"

"Oh Papa, you never left my heart," she said through her tears. "Not really."

"Then tell me, Josefina. Talk to your papa."

She smiled to herself as she heard the slight flavor of Italy in his voice. Only when he was most moved, most overcome with emotion, did the accent he usually buried arise to color his words. And somehow, that was enough to splinter the rest of the ice around her heart.

She set her coffee down and leaned into her father. His beefy arms came around her instantly and his big hands stroked up and down her back while she talked, while she spilled her heart and emptied her soul of the blackness she'd hidden for too many years.

She felt him stiffen, felt the outrage bubbling within him, and then sensed when the anger gave way to sorrow as he held her tighter, closer. And she wondered how she'd managed to live nearly a year without losing herself in one of Papa's hugs.

"If I could," he murmured, kissing the top of her head, "I would go back in time to tear this man apart with my bare hands."

"I know, Papa," she said, smiling into his shoulder. Papa and Cash both had wanted to beat her attacker into the ground. She only wished that she'd had the courage to handle it herself ten years ago. Maybe if she'd faced him down then, she wouldn't have had to wait so long to feel . . . *free.* "And I love you for it. But it's over now."

"Is it?" Her father eased back, his gaze sweeping over her face, checking her eyes, studying her features carefully. "Is it? Or is he still deciding how you should feel?"

"*What?*" All those nice warm fuzzy feelings evaporated instantly. Hurt, she tried to pull away, but her strength was no match for her father's.

"Jo," he said softly. "You've been ashamed for years, when the shame was always *his.* You've done nothing wrong and yet you hide while he goes on about his life."

"But—"

"You left school because of him. Gave up on your dreams—"

"Yes," she argued hotly in her own defense, "but I went back! The last year and a half, I've been going to night school. I picked up my credits. I'm going to graduate, Papa. In three weeks."

"This is *good* and I am so proud of you." His eyes sparkled madly and Jo understood completely why the kids of Chandler were so convinced her father was really Santa Claus.

Then the twinkle in those pale blue eyes faded. "Graduating is wonderful. But you have a *full* life to live. You cannot allow one evil man to color how you look at your whole world, Josefina." He stared directly into her eyes and the kindness she saw there softened his next words. "There is only *shame* if you continue to hide the truth."

• • •

Mike sneaked through the living room and into the kitchen—feeling pretty much like a hippo trying to tip-toe through a river. But now that she'd been up on her feet, she so didn't want to go back to lying on her ass.

The cool blue tiles felt cold against the bottoms of her feet and the morning sunlight glanced off the surface of the lake and sliced into the kitchen like a spot-light sent directly from God. Gorgeous. She only wished she could be outside to enjoy the day. Maybe ripping out someone's sink.

"No offense, guys," she whispered, stroking her hand across her belly, "but if you don't get out of there soon, mommy's gonna go to a nuthouse and then where will you be?"

"Will you at least lie down in the nuthouse?"

A deep voice, right behind her.

Mike shrieked and turned around. "You know, if you're trying to *scare* me into labor, you're doing a great job of it."

Lucas shook his head. "You're pitiful, you know it?"

Guilt rose up and took a nip at her, but she gamely bit back. "Geez, Lucas, give me a break." She lifted her left hand and ticked off her fingers, one by one. "Jack's in the hospital, Nana's making everybody nuts, something's bugging Jo—she hasn't growled at any-body in at least a week, Sam's back to work without me, and I've been pregnant for freaking *ever*." She leaned in at him. "I'm a woman on the edge, Rocket Man."

He tipped her chin up with his fingertips. "Jack's going home today, Nana's been bugging you for years, Jo will growl again as soon as she has the time, you'll be back at work making some poor homeowner crazy in no time, and you're *supposed* to be lying down."

Here came the guilt again. Mike wondered idly if she'd have the same capacity for guilt if she'd been raised Protestant. Then she figured that being Italian would have been enough.

"Ah, come on, remember that edge I was telling you about? I just wanted to sit up to eat some ice cream." She blinked her eyelashes furiously and tried a smile.

"Is that supposed to convince me?"

Mike blew out a breath and gave it up. "Fine. Sexy I'm not." Then she perked up. "Can you be bribed?"

"Depends on the bribe."

"Ah," she said, getting into the spirit of the thing now, since at least he hadn't pushed her into a chair yet. "So you *can* be had, you're just not *cheap*."

"Exactly."

"I can respect that."

"Glad to hear it," he said, moving past her to the freezer. "Chocolate chip?"

Victory! "Is there any other kind?"

"Not according to my lovely wife," he said and grabbed the carton. Then tugging on a brass parrot pull, he opened a nearby cupboard, took down two bowls, and carried them to the kitchen table. "Sit."

"You joining me?"

He went back for spoons. "Somebody has to keep an eye on you."

"Great," she said, enjoying the sensation of warm sunlight spraying across her back. "Don't forget the whipped cream."

He nodded, opened the fridge, grabbed a red and white can, and said, "Just got an e-mail from Bree."

Mike took the spoon and bowl he handed her. Bree Gallagher, Lucas's late brother's widow, was back in Ireland, living with her family and raising her son. Good thing Mike liked her or she'd be pretty pissy about Bree's already having gone through the whole birth thing.

"How's she doing?"

Lucas scooped ice cream into her bowl and grinned. "She says little Justin is smiling and rolling over now. Wants us to visit after the babies come."

Mike frowned at the ice cream that had seemed so important a minute or two ago. "The babies are *never* coming, Rocket Man. They're gonna be in there forever. Bree's already skinny again, I bet, and here I sit looking like the Plumber Who Ate California."

"Just southern California."

"Gee, that makes me feel better."

Lucas dropped to one knee in front of her. Lifting the hem of her shirt, he bent his head and kissed her belly, sending a shiver of something warm and delicious moving through her.

Then he looked up at her and smiled. "You are the most beautiful woman I've ever known. And you humble me every day."

Tears blurred her vision and love filled her heart. Sighing, Mike reached for him and cupped his face between her palms. "You are the best thing that ever happened to me, Rocket Man."

"I know," he said, grinning now.

"But I still want my ice cream."

"I know that, too."

• • •

Cash walked through the pile of rubble that had once been a perfect little guest cottage.

He spotted the lacy white curtains, now soggy wet and filthy, draped over a charred timber. Most of the fireplace and chimney were still standing, spearing up from the destruction like a monument to better days. His boots crunched and squished as he kicked crap out of his way and looked for something—*anything*—that could be salvaged.

But the sad truth was, there just wasn't a damn thing that had come through that fire. And despite it all, he'd been lucky. The fire department had managed to contain the blaze, so that the woods were pretty much unaffected and neither his house nor Grace's had been in danger. Strange how bad "lucky" felt.

He lifted his head and squinted into the late afternoon sunlight spearing through the copse of trees in golden shafts. A soft wind kicked up and rustled the leaves as it carried off the stench of charred wood and soggy fabric.

"Well," a quiet voice said from inside the tree line, "this *is* a mess, isn't it?"

Grace Van Horn, Cash's aunt, stepped out of the shadows and gingerly picked her way through the ruin.

He forced a smile that didn't quite reach his eyes. "Heard you were home. Good trip?"

"Oh," Grace said, skimming the tips of her fingers through her impeccably styled snow-white hair. "It was wonderful. Henry and I had a lovely time." She frowned as she came up beside him. "In fact, he just left. Told me he'd been to see you."

"Yeah." Cash shook his head and kept his gaze focused on the glistening, blackened heap in front of him. "He wanted to pay me for the damage."

Cash still couldn't believe it. He'd expected that Jack's father would have wanted to wring his neck for endangering his son. Instead, he'd been the one apologizing and trying to make good on what Jack had done. None of the Marconis blamed him—but they didn't have to. Cash knew damn well why this had happened. Because he'd allowed Jack into his life. Because he'd gotten sloppy. Careless.

He'd forgotten that the most important rule was to *not care.* That the only way to keep yourself safe was to let no one in.

"That's very like him," Grace said, nodding in silent approval. "But I'm guessing that you didn't allow that?"

"Of course not," Cash said, "I've got insurance. I don't need him to pay for something that almost got his son killed."

"Most people in your position would be angry at Jack. Thinking about suing his parents."

"Yeah, well I'm not most people, am I?" he asked, swinging his gaze to the aunt he'd loved since his childhood. It was only through Grace Van Horn that Cash had *ever* known anything about a normal life. Had experienced even slightly the kind of family ties he'd always hungered for. "It was *my* fault, Grace," he muttered thickly, wondering why nobody understood that but *him*.

"I'm sure you see it that way, but—"

He cut her off. "It's the truth. I left that propane torch out. *I* taught Jack how to use it. *I* let him come over here all the damn time. I spent time with him. Got too close to him. Never should have," he muttered, his

voice dropping as his mind once again painted pictures
of what might have been.

"Cash . . ."

"No." One word. Harsh. Painful. "The kid could
have been killed."

"He wasn't." Her voice came soft, patient.

"Just lucky," he said, and winced when somewhere
beneath the rubble something broke with a groan.

"Accidents happen, Cash." She laid one hand gently
on his forearm.

That touch calmed him, but did nothing to change
the resolution pounding through his head. All night, all
day, he'd been seeing Jack lying on the deck, bleeding,
burned, in pain. He saw again the fire sweeping closer
to him, inch by hungry inch.

The sting of dozens of tiny burns on his own back
reminded him just how close to disaster they'd all
come. And he wouldn't let it happen again.

"Cash," Grace said, her voice firming, as she willed
him to look at her. "I know you feel bad about Jack, but
when you care about someone, you take the risk of
pain."

"Funny you should say that," he said through gritted
teeth. "I've just been telling myself the same damn
thing."

"Take a hike, Lucas," Jo said as she marched into
Mike's house.

"Excuse me?" Her brother-in-law was wearing a
T-shirt and a pair of flannel pajama bottoms. He looked
completely comfortable and completely baffled at the
sudden invasion of Marconis.

"Forgive her," Sam said from right behind Jo. "She's got a bug up her butt about something and won't even tell me why she dragged me out of the house and brought me over here."

"I'm *going* to tell you," Jo snapped, shooting a glance into the empty living room. "As soon as we're alone, the three of us." She gave Lucas another long, meaningful look. "Where's Mike?"

"In the kitchen," he said. "More ice cream."

"Perfect," Jo declared, and stomped across the entryway to the closet. Yanking it open, she reached inside for Lucas's jacket. Then scooping his car keys off the hall table, she tossed them at him.

This could have waited until the morning, but Jo didn't want to wait another damn minute. She'd told Papa the truth and that had been the hardest part. Now, she needed to tell her sisters. She needed to finally, and at last, stop hiding.

But she wasn't about to do it in front of Lucas.

"Can't I just go upstairs?" he asked, a little wistfully.

"No, you can't. Go away," Jo insisted, shoving his jacket into his hands.

Sam patted him absently. "Go to my house. Jeff's watching *The Terminator*."

"The first one?"

"Does it matter?" Jo asked.

"Yes, the first one," Sam answered, ignoring her and focusing on Lucas. "Jeff says the third one doesn't count, and in the second one, Linda Hamilton is just way too intimidating."

"Yeah," Jo snapped, "and I just hate the way she did her hair in that one. Can he go now?"

"Good God, Jo, can you *please* take a pill of some kind?"

"I want *five* minutes of my sisters' time," Jo argued, throwing both hands high. "Is that *really* so much to ask?"

"You don't ask. You demand," Sam pointed out.

"If you guys are gonna argue," Mike shouted from a distance, "at least do it back here where I can join in!"

"Okay, ladies," Lucas said, juggling his keys as he put on his jacket. "I'm gone." Then he shot a look over his shoulder. "You two promise to keep Mike off her feet?"

"Hell, I'll tie her to a chair if you'll just go away!"

Lucas laughed at her and Jo had a minute to realize the man was getting way too used to the Marconi way of life. They didn't scare him at all anymore.

Once the door closed behind him, Jo took Sam's arm and half dragged her to the kitchen. Mike was seated at the table, a half-eaten carton of ice cream open and waiting and a bowl of whipped cream right in front of her.

"What's going on?" she asked, licking her spoon before dipping it back for more.

"That's what I want to know," Sam said, grabbing a spoon out of a drawer before sitting down beside Mike. She dipped into the ice cream, pulled out a tablespoonful and stared at Jo. "So. You gonna talk, or what?"

"Yeah," she said, lifting her chin and swallowing, despite the suddenly dust-dry condition of her throat. "I am."

"You wanna sit down?" Mike asked.

"No."

"You want some ice cream?" Sam offered.

"No."

"Must be serious," Mike muttered.

"God, will you two shut up and let me *talk*?"

Now that the moment was here, Jo's tongue felt thick and her mouth was dry. But she'd done enough hiding. Enough lying. She grabbed another spoon and went to join her sisters. After a big bite of chocolate chip ice cream, she blew out a breath and hit the highlights.

"Two things. First, I went back to school to get my degree. I've been going nights for almost two years. I graduate in two weeks and I want you guys there."

Both of her sisters erupted into applause and Jo felt a swell of pride and pleasure that almost helped her say the rest of what she'd come here to say.

"And the reason I *left* school ten years ago, is . . ." *God. Why am I still so damn ashamed?* Papa was right. Cash was right. She'd done *nothing* wrong. It was all on him. All of it. And she'd let him get away with it for too damn long. "Because Steve Smith raped me."

Stunned silence.

The kitchen clock, a parrot, naturally, swung its long tail feathers, making a tick, tick, tick sound that felt as though it were reverberating up through the floor.

Jo pulled in another shaky breath and waited. She didn't have to wait long.

"The no-good, scum-sucking, lying, miserable son of a bitch bastard," Sam said finally.

"Where is he now and how much can we kill him?" Mike wanted to know.

Releasing her breath on a sigh, Jo looked from one of her sisters to the other and knew that she was finally on the road to getting her life back.

Fifteen

"Next stop on the road to freedom."

Jo said the words out loud just to remind herself why she was sitting in her truck, parked in Cash's driveway. Since talking to her sisters the night before, she'd done a lot of thinking. True, they'd said almost the same thing her father and even Cash had said.

That as long as she hid away from life, Steve Smith was still winning.

So it was past time for her to take charge. To admit that she'd been wrong ten years ago and every day since. To acknowledge that on that long-ago night, Steve had stolen something precious from her.

Her ability to have a normal life.

Which was why she was here.

"So why aren't you getting out of the truck?"

Fine. She could do this. Not saying it would be easy, but she could do it. She opened the door, stepped down carefully, and when her left foot slipped on some loose gravel, she cursed herself for going all out with high heels. But damn it, the man had never even *seen* her in a dress.

Smoothing her hands down the hips of her short,

black dress, she felt the wind's icy fingers dip down the low-cut back before slipping under her hem to tease her bare thighs. Jo blew out a breath and glanced down at her less than impressive cleavage. The low-cut scooped neckline displayed her charms as best it could, but just for a minute, she wished she'd gotten some of the boobs in the family.

Mike, selfish bitch, had pretty much claimed them all.

"What's going on?"

Her head whipped up as Cash stepped out of his workshop, dusting his palms together. In his worn jeans, battered cowboy boots, and dark blue T-shirt, the man looked almost *too* good. Almost.

"I need to talk to you," Jo said, then cleared her throat, since she sounded as nervous as she felt. Which was just stupid since she'd already slept with him, for God's sake.

He shook his head. "If this is another Marconi attempt to pay for the damn cottage, forget it. I already told your father I wasn't interested."

"No, I—"

"And if you're here to tell me to stay the hell away from Jack, don't bother," he added, half turning to go back to the workshop. "I already figured that out for myself."

"I didn't say—" For Pete's sake, would the man not shut up long enough for her to proposition him?

"And," he said, cutting her off again and making her grit her teeth, "don't worry, I'll be at the Phillipses' house tomorrow to help you with the roof."

"Do I *look* like I'm here to talk about work?" she shouted, suddenly and completely out of patience. "Or

Jack? Or the cottage? Or any of the other damn things you're going to say next?"

His gaze swept her up and down and she watched something flash in his eyes. Something hot enough to singe her even from ten feet away. "Then why are you here, Josefina?"

Here it is, she thought. The big moment. Make it count. "I'm here to go to bed with you again."

"Who asked you?"

Another woman might have been insulted. But Jo was a Marconi, born and bred, and they fought fire with fire. Insult to insult. Eye for an eye.

"You want me bad and you know it," she said, feeling a hell of a lot more at ease, now that she was headed into battle.

His mouth quirked. "I've had you bad, remember?"

"Okay, yeah. I do." She took another step toward him and cursed her heels again when she wobbled. "The thing is, I want to have you 'good.'" She frowned. "That's not grammatically correct, but you know what I mean."

He folded his arms over his chest and watched her, giving nothing away with his closed expression. "I don't think I do. Why don't you explain it to me?"

"I told my family," she said, lifting her chin, just in case another salvo had to be fired. "About Steve. About what happened."

"Good." His features softened. "I'm glad."

She shifted uncomfortably. "Yeah. And the thing is, you were right about something."

One corner of his mouth tipped up. "Oh, this I've got to hear. Josefina Marconi admitting *Cash Hunter* is right about something."

"Don't get used to it."

"I'm waiting."

"You were right when you said that I was cheating myself. That as long as I didn't enjoy sex, then I was letting him win."

He straightened up and watched her through dark eyes that were suddenly unreadable.

So she kept talking. "The thing is, Cash . . . I *want* to know what it feels like. I don't want to be cheated anymore."

"Josefina . . ."

"And I—trust you."

He blew out a breath, reached up and shoved both hands through his too long hair before letting his arms fall back to his sides. "I don't know if that's a good idea."

"Cash, I'm not asking you to marry me," she sputtered. "It's one night, for God's sake."

He thought about it. "Are you sure about this?"

"I'm sure," she said, then added her last bit of temptation. "I brought you a pan of Nana's lasagna. I thought we could have dinner together—*after*."

He gave her a slow smile. "What if you're too exhausted to chew?"

She swallowed hard. "Maybe we should eat first."

Cash looked her up and down, letting himself feast on her. Josefina in her ironed jeans and freshly pressed T-shirts drove him to distraction. In that little black dress, she damn near killed him. One look at her, and all he'd wanted to do was grab her and pull her close.

But he'd made his decision after the fire, after Jack was injured—nearly died: no more getting involved. No more idle fantasies about Josefina, because somehow or other she'd become too important to him already.

Now, he realized that whether she knew it or not, she'd given him exactly what he needed. If he could heal her, help her to actually *enjoy* sex, to have the orgasm she'd avoided for years—then she'd leave.

Like everyone else had.

And his problems would be over. Not that he *wanted* her gone. But he knew she'd leave eventually and better that *he* decide exactly *when*.

"Are you gonna say something or what?" she demanded.

Cash smiled. The woman had a temper like a cornered rattler and the patience of a three-year-old. Damned if he didn't like her.

"No more talking, Josefina," he said, and reached out for her. Cupping his hand around the back of her neck, he pulled her to him and took her mouth in a slow, deep kiss that promised a glimpse of heaven.

"You okay now?" Papa asked, tucking the blanket and sheet around Jack until he was outlined on the bed like a perfect little mummy. "You need anything?"

Jack shook his head and looked up at his father. It was good to be back at home. And even better that nobody was mad at him or anything, because they felt sorry for him because of his broken arm, which was totally cool even though it hurt a little. Nana had even made him chocolate milk and lasagna and it was really good, except Papa's lasagna got burned by accident or something. She'd promised Jack some cake, too.

But he was still worried about something. "Is Cash mad, Papa?"

"No," his father said, easing down onto the side of the bed. "He's happy you're all right. Like all of us are."

"Good," Jack said, and pulled at the edge of the sheet. He didn't want Cash to be mad 'cause he had a plan and he didn't want to get it all screwed up before it could come true. "Papa?"

"Yes?"

"If Jo and Cash get married, can I go and live with them?"

"What?"

"Don't be mad," Jack said hurriedly, when he saw the shock on his father's face. "It's just that Cash knows how to play baseball and you're all busy and stuff and I think it would be good if I lived with them because Jo might get lonely without me now." He didn't want to hurt his father's feelings, but he really liked being around Cash. "You'd still be my papa and everything," he told him, reaching out to pat the man's hand reassuringly.

Papa shook his head, opened his mouth, closed it again and then opened it to ask, "Jo and Cash are getting *married*?"

"Maybe." He hoped.

"And you want to live with them."

"Uh-huh."

"I was only gone *three weeks*," he muttered.

The lasagna was in the kitchen, there was an open bottle of wine on the bedside table, and Jo was thinking about getting naked.

Stupid. Stupid to be scared. She'd had sex *lots* of times. Hell, she'd had sex with *Cash* already. What's the big deal? But even she wasn't buying that.

Outside, clouds had rolled in off the ocean and even now the first drops of rain were beginning to pelt the wall of windows that overlooked the lake. The trees bent in the wind, the reeds at the water's edge dipped and swayed as if they were dancing, and a swell of music rose up from the stereo downstairs.

Something soft, haunting. Violins and harps, bleeding together into a symphony of sound that sounded both joyful and desolate.

"Boy, he takes his work serious," Jo muttered, and sat down on the edge of the bed, before hopping right back up again as if she'd been scalded. To calm herself, she looked around the room.

The huge master suite was completely male and yet warm and welcoming. The bed was one of Cash's own creations—the headboard was carved with intricate vines of ivy that entwined and curled around each of the four bedposts and down to the footboard. Two tall dressers stood on either side of a flat-screen plasma TV hanging on the wall opposite the bed, and bookcases crowded with paperbacks ringed another wall.

"Dance with me."

She started, then spun around to look at Cash, standing in the open doorway.

"Dance?" she repeated. "You want to dance?"

"For starters."

"Ah. Like an appetizer." Great. Talk about food. But that's Italians for you—when things get tough, open a fridge.

"Dance with me, Josefina." He crossed the room, took her hand and swept her into a slow, sensuous sway that both calmed and excited her. If she felt foolish dancing in the late afternoon wash of rain and watery light, that feeling faded as soon as his arms came around her.

They swayed to the music, perfectly in synch. He held her close, one hand running up and down her spine in long slow strokes that kindled a fire deep within. A fire she'd always kept carefully banked. Until tonight.

Jo took a deep breath and told herself to relax. To concentrate on the feel of his hands on her, on the warmth skittering through her, on the soft sigh of the music surrounding them.

"You're thinking," Cash whispered, dipping his head to nibble on her shoulder. "No thinking allowed, Josefina."

"Right." She nodded and bit down on her bottom lip as his mouth trailed damp kisses along her throat and up to the curve of her jaw. "No thinking. Only . . ."

He lifted his head and looked down at her. Shadows crossed his face, flickering with the wavery light from outside. "Only what?"

"Only, I'm a little nervous."

"Yeah? Me, too."

Jo laughed and immediately felt better. "Sure. You. Nervous."

His hands lifted to cup her face. His thumbs stroked her cheekbones, his fingers speared into the silky strands of her hair. "I've never made love to a virgin before."

She stiffened instantly. "I'm not a virgin."

He kissed her. Once. Twice. "In every way that really matters," he said gently, "you *are*."

Then he scooped her up into his arms and carried her to the bed. His practiced fingers moved quickly, and before she knew it was happening, Jo was naked and lying back on cool, white sheets. She watched as he stood up, stripped out of his own clothes, and then stretched out alongside her, running the palm of his hand up and down the length of her body.

Jo shivered and fought for air when his fingers caressed her nipples, tweaking, tugging, creating a sensation that she'd never allowed herself to feel before. And now, now she couldn't have stopped if she'd wanted to.

He dipped his head and his mouth took over what his fingers had begun. And as he suckled her, drawing deep on her hard, sensitive nipples, each in turn, his left hand swept down her body to the center of her.

Jo pressed her head back into the pillow and stared unseeing at the ceiling. Her vision blurred, clouded and cleared again, as if her brain were shutting down. And hey, who needed a brain, anyway?

She lifted one hand to his head, boldly holding him in place. Her fingers scraped through his thick, soft hair and she sighed as her touch seemed to inflame him. His hand dipped low, sliding between the thighs she'd managed to keep locked together.

Now, for his touch, she parted them slowly, carefully. And he slipped into her warmth. One finger, then two, he dipped into her damp heat, stroking, caressing, fanning the flames he'd created until she felt as though she were burning alive from the inside out.

"Something's happening," she croaked, surprised her voice could work at all. "Cash . . . something . . ."

"Don't think," he whispered, lifting his head to stare down at her. "Just feel, Josefina. Let yourself feel. Let go and let it happen."

"I can't— Oh God . . ." Her hips rocked as he touched her, as his fingers slicked across one small, sensitive piece of flesh at the core of her. Electric jolts shot through her and she wouldn't have been surprised to see smoke lifting off her body.

She couldn't do this. Couldn't lose control. Couldn't . . . *stop*.

"Don'tstopdon'tstopdon'tstop . . ."

Her hands clutched at him, fingers digging into his shoulders, holding on to him as the world around her rocked unsteadily. She lifted her hips into his hand and he gave her more. "Cash—" She fought for air. "Cash—"

"Come, Josefina," he said, his voice a hush of sound nearly drowned out by the harps and violins that continued to ache in the air around them. "Look into my eyes and come for me."

She shook her head, licked her lips, and ground out, "No. Not until you're inside me. Be there. Be with me when it happens. When it *finally* happens."

"Stubborn, hardheaded woman," he said on a groan. But he moved quickly, tearing his hand free of her body, then shifting to cover her. He entered her in one, smooth stroke that locked them together in ways neither of them had imagined.

"Look at me," he ordered, his voice tight with need. A need that she shared. That she finally and completely *shared*. "I'm with you, Josefina," he said, and rocked his hips against hers, pushing higher, deeper inside. "Be with *me*."

"I'm with you, Cash," she managed to say even as she moved with him, into him, against him. More, she wanted more. Wanted to feel it all. As if a dam had burst inside her, she was drowning in sensation and hoped she'd never surface.

Her gaze locked with his, she whispered, "Show me *everything.*"

She was still staring up into his dark, fathomless eyes when the first explosion shattered her body. She cried out his name, but didn't close her eyes. She couldn't look away and so she saw herself reflected in Cash's eyes. Saw the woman she had been dissolve— and watched as she became the woman she was always meant to be.

While her body celebrated and her heart began to heal, she felt Cash's surrender and she cradled him to her as he fell.

Three hours later, most of the lasagna was gone, the wine bottle was empty, and the two of them were sprawled across Cash's mattress like survivors of a shipwreck.

He turned his head to look at the woman lying beside him, but instead, came eyeball to eyeball with her pink polished toes. One eyebrow lifted as he raised his head and looked down the bed at her. They'd been eating, sitting opposite each other, when they'd each collapsed, stretching out where they were.

"I feel you moving," Jo said without lifting her head. "And whatever you've got in mind—" She paused, then smiled. "Give me five more minutes to recuperate and then you're on."

Grinning, he reached out one hand and skimmed it along her muscled calf and up the inside of her thigh.

"It just occurred to me that since we're in this position anyway . . ."

Now she *did* lift her head. *"Really?"*

Cash laughed out loud, surprising himself. He couldn't remember the last time he'd had such a damn good time. "I've got to hand it to you, Josefina," he said, winking at her. "You're a slow starter, but you catch up quick."

His fingertips brushed the joining of her thighs and she sucked in a fast breath before she sat up, stark naked and completely comfortable. "I've got a lot of time to make up for," she said and caught his hand in hers.

"Yeah," he said, his gaze moving from her tousled brown hair to her kiss-bruised lips and then up to her eyes. The woman awakened something in him that hadn't been touched in years. And though a part of him enjoyed the sensation, the more logical side of his brain was already trying to warn him to get out. Get out now. "I guess you do."

"And I've made a decision," she continued, pushing her hair back from her eyes as she leaned over him, dusting her rigid nipples across his chest with the touch of a butterfly.

"Well," he managed to say even though his body was suddenly hard and raring to go again. "I liked the last decision you made. So what's the next one?"

She dropped a kiss onto his mouth and he waited, braced for what was coming. She'd had an orgasm. *Plenty* of 'em. Now, he was pretty sure she was going to announce that she was leaving. *Thanks very much for the good time, I'm off to Africa to save the spotted elephant*, or some damn thing.

His stomach fisted, but he told himself this was how he'd wanted it. She was healed and now she'd be gone. And he could get back to doing what he did best. *Alone.* No ties, no connections. No caring.

But damned if Josefina Marconi didn't surprise him again.

"I'm going into the city. I'm going to see Steve Smith and tell him just what I think of him."

"What?"

She grinned. "What's the matter? Did you really think that I'd be rushing off to save the world or something?"

"Well . . ." *Yeah.*

"Nope. I've got a life," she said. "And it's right here. But I will say that this afternoon has given me the strength to do what I should have done ten years ago."

"Which is . . . ?"

Her pale blue eyes narrowed and her full lips went as thin and sharp as a razor blade. "Kick that son of a bitch's ass."

Two days later, Jo walked into the tall steel-and-glass building and gave her reflection in the elevator doors the once-over. Her long brown hair was held back from her face with a thick, gold-toned barrette. Her makeup was perfect, thanks to Mike, and she was carrying Sam's good black purse for luck. Black slacks, green long-sleeved blouse, and her square-toed, thick-heeled boots—good for either kicking or stomping, whichever was required—completed her look.

Then her gaze shifted to the man coming up behind her. He wore a black jacket over a white shirt, but he hadn't turned in his jeans or his boots. She still wasn't sure if she was glad Cash had invited himself along or not. But the fact was, he was here now and she just had to deal with it.

He'd been treating her . . . *differently* since their long, luscious afternoon together. It was as if the closer she felt to him, the more he set himself back from her. He was running while standing still. A clever, if annoying, trick.

"You sure you're ready for this?" he asked quietly.

She shifted her gaze to the list of names on the building's directory. She stabbed "Steve Smith, Attorney at Law" with her index finger. Glancing at Cash, she said only, "Suite 305."

"Right." He hit the button for the elevator and they didn't speak again until they were inside and headed up. "You don't have to do this alone, you know."

She looked up at him. "Yeah, I *do*."

He nodded, but said, "Fine. But I'll be right there in case you need backup."

The elevator hummed, the engine, a slow one, lifted them past the second floor. "Why are you really here, Cash?"

He pushed back the edges of his jacket and stuffed his hands into his pockets. "I didn't want you to be alone."

"You've been leaving me alone for two days."

"What're you talking about?" he asked irritably. "We've been working together, haven't we?"

"Working, yes, talking, *no*."

"What's there to say?"

Annoyed, Jo tapped the toe of her boot against the plain gray carpet. "You know, you're the one who started all this between us—"

"Meaning?"

"*Meaning,* you idiot," she snarled at him, "that for a year, you've been flirting and teasing and trying to get me into the sack. Now that you've had me, it's *over*?"

The third-floor button lit up, the elevator dinged, and the doors opened with a groan.

"Is now really the time to talk about this?" he asked.

Annoyance flickered into anger and from there it was just a short hop to downright fury. "You know, maybe it was the right time. Because trying to talk to you put me in exactly the right frame of mind to face that bastard now, let me tell you."

She stomped past him, out the elevator, across yet another gray rug to the receptionist's desk. There, a dark-haired woman in her fifties lifted her cautious gaze and asked, "May I help you?"

"Yes," Jo said, straightening up and lifting her chin until it was perched at a completely defiant angle. "I'm here to see Steve Smith."

"Your name?"

"Josefina Marconi," she ground out. "He'll remember me."

"Do you have an appointment?" the woman asked, already flipping through her daybook.

"Yep," Jo said, out of patience and sailing past the clearly stunned woman as she leaped out of her chair to stop her. "Made it myself, ten years ago."

Jo threw open the cherrywood double doors and entered the bastard's lair.

"What's this about?"

He hadn't changed much, Jo thought absently. His blond hair was a little thinner, his face a little thicker, and his eyes a bit shiftier. But all in all, he was still the

pretty boy with the black heart. It was a wonder there
wasn't an oil spill oozing down the sleeves of his impeccably cut suit jacket to pool on the top of his desk.
He stood up and the city of San Francisco was spread
out behind him in a glorious vista that he probably
never noticed.

"I'm sorry, Mr. Smith," his assistant was saying
from directly behind Jo. "I couldn't stop her."

"Fine, Linda," the great man himself said, waving
one hand at her in dismissal. "I'll take it from here."

The woman left, but Jo didn't hear the door close.
And even without turning around, Jo knew she and
Steve weren't alone in the room. She could *feel* Cash
standing right behind her. And though she'd told him
she could handle this herself, she could acknowledge,
at least silently, that she was grateful for his presence.

"Jo Marconi," Steve said as he came around his
desk, a small, private smile on his face. "Isn't it? Long
time."

"Not nearly long enough," Jo said, but added, "It's
taken me a while, but I've got a few things to say to
you."

"Who's he?" The man's blue gaze shifted briefly to
Cash and back again.

"A . . . *friend*," Jo said, without turning around. She
didn't take her gaze off the man standing opposite her.
Hard to believe, but during the last ten years, her memories had become so overpowering that she'd somehow
convinced herself that he was bigger, stronger. When
in reality, he was a little shorter than Cash and *much*
smaller.

He looked at her, his cool gaze as deceptive as the

smooth surface of a toxic lake. "Why not lose your 'friend' and we'll talk about old times?"

"We don't have any 'old times' I want to remember, let alone talk to you about."

"Fine." Steve dismissed Cash, leaned one hip on the corner of his desk, crossed his arms over his chest and shook his head. "What could you possibly have to say that I would want to hear?"

"You *raped* me, you rat bastard."

He didn't even blink. Instead, he flicked at a piece of imaginary lint on his lapel, then lifted cold eyes to hers. "Not how I remember it. But it's quite an accusation."

"It's the truth and you know it."

"What I know," he said, straightening, "is that you're looking at a slander suit if you say that to anyone else."

"Slander?"

He took one step toward her, then stopped, flicking a wary glance at Cash. "Please. We were kids. Grow up and get over it already."

Get over it?

"You left me battered and bruised on the *floor.*"

His lips quirked. "You had a good time."

Fury quickly devoured whatever nerves had been left, swimming in the pit of her stomach. She looked at him and couldn't believe that she'd let thoughts of him, memories of him, rule her life for the last ten years. She should have fought him then.

But she'd make up for that, *now.*

"I want you to drop out of the race for the senate," Jo said, her voice quiet, every word a stone.

He laughed at her. "You've got to be kidding."

"If you don't," she promised, "I'll go to the media. Tell them everything."

In the outer office, Linda Sandoval listened intently, heart racing, stomach spinning. Excitement coursed through her and she wanted to cheer. But there was something more important to do, she reminded herself as she kept listening, making mental notes. Something she'd wanted to do for years.

Now, it was finally time.

Steve Smith's practiced smile slipped from his face and the *real* man became evident for the first time. He stepped toward her, leaning in close enough that Jo could have counted the pores on his leanly sculpted nose. "One word out of you and I'll sue you for everything you've got. I'll make it my business to make your life hell."

"Josefina?" Cash's voice came soft, steady. "Need some help?"

"What're you gonna do?" Steve sneered at her. "Have your 'friend' *hit* me?"

She inhaled slowly, deeply, letting the air slide through her body like a balm. Then she half turned to smile at the man who'd helped her come this far. "No, but thanks. I can handle him."

"Is that right?" Steve laughed.

Jo drew her right arm back, gave it everything she had—and decked him.

Sixteen

"Damn it, Maria," Hank yelled as he stomped down the stairs from his bedroom to beard the lioness in her den-kitchen. His best dress shirt gripped in one tight fist, he waved it like a flag at a bull.

The old woman stood at the kitchen table, forming dough into tiny, crescent-shaped gnocchi. She lifted her head and when her gaze locked with his, Hank wanted to cross himself.

If ever he'd seen an "evil eye," this was it. Not that he didn't deserve his mother-in-law's contempt—but a man could only take so much.

He looked away from her hot, dark gaze and noticed a separate pile of pieces of gnocchi dough—flattened, misshapen, poisonous little bites—and he knew instantly which pile she intended for *his* dinner.

Gritting his teeth, he hissed in a breath and faced her again. "Enough, Maria," he snapped, tossing his good shirt across a chair. The scorched imprint of an iron decorated the back of the pale blue fabric and just seeing it set his teeth on edge again. "Say what you have to say and get it over with."

She drew herself up to her less than impressive

height, narrowed her eyes on him and looked about to
spit fire. "You *bastardo*," she accused, wagging one
gnarled finger in his face. "*Diavolo!* You cheat on my
Sylvia while she issa dying. *Abbindolatore!* Cheater!
You have no heart. No soul. You are worse than a dog."

Bear, sleeping under the table, reacted by lifting his
head and thumping his tail against the floor, before settling back down again.

Hank tried to remember that this was his mother-in-
law. That she had a right to her anger. To her pain. But
damn it, he had a right to decent coffee he didn't have to
slice with a knife. To clothes that weren't either burned
by irons or mysteriously shredded in the washing machine. He wanted to eat food that wasn't burned and
stop looking over his shoulder for a cleaver-wielding
Italian maniac to attack him when he least expected it.

He took another breath, held it for as long as he
could, then released it while he counted to ten. Then
twenty.

Then he gave it up.

Throwing his hands wide, he said, "I know what I
did was wrong. I can't feel any worse about it. But I
can't change it, either. What would you have me do?"

"*Penance!*" she shouted right back at him.

"I do, Maria. Every day I pray that Sylvia will forgive me."

"She no forgive." She lifted one hand and slammed
it onto the table. "*I* no forgive."

All the air left him and Hank's shoulders sagged. No
matter what he said or did, nothing would ease Maria's
pain. Nothing would wipe away his sin. And in his
heart, Hank knew that she was right. There was no for-
giveness for him. Sometimes mistakes lived forever.

"Fine. You no forgive. Torture me forever if it gives you peace." He leaned down until they were eye to eye. "But what happened that summer—what I did—is between me and Sylvia. Not you. If she spits in my face when I see her again . . ." The thought of that broke his heart, but it was something he would just have to face when the time came. "If she can't forgive me, then I'll go to hell. I'll pay there."

"She no forgive." Maria's deeply lined, aged face was set in stone but for her darkly burning eyes—a perfect sculpture of an avenging mother. And he couldn't even blame her. Damn it.

"Maybe not." He picked up his former best shirt and crossed the room to toss it into the trash. Glancing at her again, he said, "If it makes you feel better to torture me, I understand."

Seconds ticked past and the only sound was Bear, snoring his morning away.

Finally, though, Maria looked at him again. "It no bother you for me to make you pay?"

"No," he said, surrendering to the inevitable. "I deserve it. And more."

A stream of viciously muttered Italian left her as she gathered up the misshapen gnocchi and set about redoing them. "Iffa you no mind, it'sa no fun anymore. *Bastardo*."

Stunned, Hank took what he could get and left the kitchen quick—before Maria could change her mind.

"How's your hand?"

Jo flexed her fingers, winced, then sighed with satisfaction. "Hurts like hell," she admitted, then slanted him a glance. "But I'm betting Steve's jaw hurts a lot more."

"You should've let me hit him for you."

"Not a chance," Jo said, smiling at the scrapes on her knuckles as if they were medals won in glorious battle. "I had to do it myself. Though I wouldn't put it past him to have me arrested for assault or something."

Cash laughed and took the freeway exit for Chandler. "Are you kidding? He'd be too embarrassed to admit a woman clocked him. Besides, he can't take the chance of your explaining to a cop *why* you hit him."

"There is that." It was too late now to report him for the rapist he had been ten years ago. She had no proof. Only the memory of innocence lost. And it would be her word against Steve's. Still . . . he wouldn't risk her talking to the police.

"I'm proud of you," Cash was saying. "It took guts to face him down, but you did it."

"Thanks," Jo said, smiling. "Took me ten years, but I'm pretty proud of me, too."

He drove slowly along the coast road, and on his left, Flower Fantasy spread across the meadow. Thousands of blooms, in every color imaginable, crowded the open field and filled the air with the heady scent of spring. Tourists flocked up and down the rows of booths and a carnival atmosphere clogged the main road into town. Cash slammed on the brake to avoid a Volkswagen that cut in front of him, and Jo rested her head against the seat back.

"What're you gonna do now?" he asked.

"Go to Disneyland?" she quipped.

"Funny."

"I don't know," she admitted. "But I feel really . . . *good*. You want to help me celebrate?"

"What've you got in mind?" He stepped on the gas again, cutting around a carload of gawkers that weren't even pretending to be moving.

"I was thinking we could go back to your place and—"

Just like that, Cash's features shut down. She watched him fist his hands on the steering wheel and the cab of the truck suddenly felt like a refrigerator.

"Well, guess that answers my question."

"I just don't want you getting the wrong idea, Josefina."

"Really? And just what idea is that?" Oh, she wished her hand didn't hurt so bad, because she had the almost overpowering urge to use it again. On an even *harder* head.

He didn't answer for a long minute. Instead, he pulled the truck off the highway, into a scenic turnoff designed to give tourists a perfect Kodak Moment shot of the shoreline. He parked between two other cars, threw the truck into gear, cut the engine, and swiveled his head to glare at her.

"You're supposed to be gone."

"Excuse me?"

"We had sex," he reminded her. "You had an orgasm . . ."

"Several . . ."

"Exactly!" His shout startled a kid skateboarding along the sea wall, but Cash didn't notice. He slammed both hands against the wheel. "So why the hell are you sticking around? That's not how this works. We sleep together, you leave. That's the deal."

Jo finally understood that old saying about "seeing red." The edges of her vision went cloudy, grainy, and there was a decidedly red tinge to the whole thing. In fact, there was a *ring* of red around Cash's face.

Not unlike a target.

"You're serious." Amazing. "You actually expected me to run off and join the circus? Or a convent or something? One night with you and I see the stars?" Of course, she *had* seen the stars, but that was beside the point.

"Well," he said, nodding. *"Yeah."*

Outside the truck, the ocean roared, seals barked at the tourists, demanding handouts, car horns blared and traffic staggered along the road. *Inside* the truck, Jo was looking directly into the eyes of an idiot.

"You self-satisfied, egotistical—" Words failed her and she sputtered to a stop. The one time she most wanted to call down curses on a man's head and she couldn't think of anything low enough. Wouldn't you know it?

She unbuckled her seat belt and reached for the door handle. He stretched out and grabbed her hand first.

"Move that hand or lose it, Cash."

"Damn it, Josefina—"

She snapped him a look. "Don't call me that. Never call me that again."

He let her go and eased back into his seat. "Why the hell are you so pissed off? You've been keeping me at arm's length for a year. You never wanted this to be anything. God knows you told me that often enough."

True, all true. And when had that changed? When

had she stopped looking at him as an annoyance? When had she started thinking of him as someone she could trust? Someone she could count on? God, he wasn't the only idiot in the truck. "I changed my mind."

"I didn't."

"Why?"

"Because I'm not doing this again, that's why."

"Excuse me?" She pinned him with a look that should have fried him to the black leather seat. *"When* have we done this before?"

"Not *you* and me," he said, *"me. I'm* not doing this again."

"Fine. You know what? I don't even care what that means. I don't want to know. You're right," she said, opening the truck door and climbing down. She swung her bag up over her shoulder and glared in at him. "This could never be anything. I spent the last ten years running scared, Cash. Now I'm finished. You're *still* running."

He shifted his gaze out to the wide sweep of ocean in front of them before looking back at her. "You don't know what you're talking about."

"Oh, I think we both know I'm right about this." She slammed the truck door hard enough to make him wince.

"Jo—get in the damn car, let me take you home."

"You can't take me anywhere I need to go, Cash," she said, glaring in the window at him. "So why don't you do us both a favor and just . . . go away?"

She walked away from him and never looked back.

Cash knew that for a fact, because he watched her until she disappeared into a crowd of tourists.

• • •

Three days later, Cash still felt like shit. He worked
with Jo, but she wouldn't talk to him. Hell, she
wouldn't even look at him. And he missed her. Missed
arguing with her, missed laughing with her. Missed
having the right to touch her.

His guts twisted, his heart ached, but he figured that
was just the price he had to pay to protect himself from
devastation later.

What the hell did she want from him, anyway? She
should be grateful, not pissed. He'd helped *heal* her,
for God's sake. He'd done her a damn favor and now
he was letting her go. Couldn't she see how goddamn
noble he was being? Damn the woman!

Grumbling, he ran his thumb over the smooth edge
of the rocker he'd designed and built. Made of rich,
dark walnut, the elegant yet comfortable rocker
swayed under his touch and made a welcome sound in
the stifling stillness.

"That's neat. Did'ya just finish it?"

Cash turned around as Jack Marconi raced into the
workshop. He hadn't seen the boy since right after the
fire. He'd made it a point not to.

Running scared? Jo's accusation rose up in his
mind, but he shut it down fast.

"What're you doing here, Jack?"

"I rode my bike over. Papa said I could if I was
careful."

"Well, I've got work to do and—"

Jack wasn't listening. He swung his hair back out of
his eyes. " 'Cause this lady's coming to the house and
Papa said she wouldn't want lots of people there and
stuff, so he said I could come see you."

"What lady?" Curiosity. Meant nothing.

Jack sat down in the rocker and gave it a push with both sneakered feet. He set his cast down on the left arm of the thing and looked up at him. "I don't know her name or anything, but she's been on TV and everything. Papa says her husband's a senate or something."

"Senator?" Jack asked.

"Yeah, that's it." He gave the rocker another push. "This is great. It's like so big and everything. Can you show me how to make one?"

"Why's she coming?"

"Who?" Jack blinked at him.

"The senator's wife?"

"I dunno. She wants to see Jo, I guess." Jack sprang up from the rocker and grinned up at him. "You wanna sign my cast?"

Steve Smith's wife coming to see Jo? What for? What was the bastard up to? And why hadn't Jo told him about this? Even if she was pissed, wasn't he a part of this? Did she think she could shut him out? Damn hardheaded woman.

He didn't trust Steve Smith as far as Jo could throw him, and any woman stupid enough to marry the prick couldn't be much better.

"Your sister," he murmured, "is a—"

"What?"

"Pain in the ass," he wanted to say, but he couldn't really say it to a ten-year-old. Damn it, if Jo thought he was going to stay away when she was still dealing with this shit, then she was headed for real disappointment. He was in this and he was *staying* in this, until Smith was a distant memory.

Once Cash was sure she was safe—when he knew she'd be all right . . . *then* he'd let Jo go.

"I'll sign it later," Cash said, steering the boy out of the workshop. He picked up the bicycle from where Jack had dropped it in the driveway, and then set it in the truck bed.

"Where we goin'?" Jack asked.

"Your house," Cash answered.

"Bastardo," *Nana muttered. "You are inna my way. Move over."*

"Maria," Hank whispered, "if you don't be quiet, we won't hear anything."

"I *hear* everything," *she warned, a steely look in her eye.*

"Great. Super-Nana." Hank forgot about his mother-in-law and focused his attention on the scene playing out in the backyard.

"I had to see you."

Jo sat in one of four lawn chairs pulled up beneath the shade of an oak that had been standing in the Marconi yard since long before there was a house there. She leaned back into the green plastic chair with the wobbly front leg and studied the woman opposite her.

Steve Smith's wife, Melanie, was as pretty and soft as her name sounded. Her blond hair was cut into a feathery-looking do that left little wisps framing her pale face. Her green eyes looked huge under perfectly arched brows, and rose-colored lipstick gave her milky-white skin some color. She wore a cream-colored suit with beige heels and a beige bag.

It was as if she were deliberately trying to be invisible.

"How'd you find me?" Jo asked after a long minute.

Melanie smiled uneasily from her perch on the edge of a matching lawn chair. "It wasn't difficult. Linda—Steve's assistant? She knew your name. Looked you up on the Internet."

Great. Thank you, Google.

Across the yard, from inside the house, she knew her father and grandmother were posted at the windows, watching. She shouldn't be glad they were such devoted snoops, but at least someone was going to be a witness to this.

"Did Steve send you out here to—" She stopped, unsure just what his motive could possibly have been to send his wife out to see his rape victim.

"No." One word. Fast. Melanie jumped to her feet and clenched her hands together at her waist. "He doesn't know I'm here. He *can't* know I'm here."

"Okaaaayyy . . ."

The agitated woman took a few short steps, her beige heels sinking into the Marconi lawn, before she turned around and came back again. "He hurt you, didn't he?"

"He raped me." No easier to remember, but it was getting easier to say. What did that mean?

"Oh God." Melanie lifted her left hand to rub her forehead and her wide gold wedding band glinted dully in the sunlight. "I thought so. Linda said you . . . hit him and I—"

It dawned on Jo finally that this visit wasn't about *her*. It was about Melanie. Fear rippled off the woman in little sonic waves and Jo's instinct to protect kicked in. "Are you all right?"

She laughed. "No. No, I'm really not."

"What's he done to you?"

Melanie's gaze shot to hers. "I didn't say he—"

"Relax," Jo said, her voice low, soothing, as she stood up carefully, making no fast moves. She had the feeling that Melanie was already regretting her visit and was, in fact, on the verge of bolting. "You're safe here."

"Jo?"

"Damn it." She saw Melanie flinch and tried a smile. It wasn't easy.

Cash Hunter came around the edge of the house from the driveway and his long legs were making short work of the distance separating them.

"Who is that?" Melanie demanded.

"A . . ." Good question. Just who the hell *was* Cash, anyway? Friend? Lover? Annoyance? "Long story," she said finally, then added, "He's okay. A pain in the ass, but okay. Trust me."

"Issa Cash."

"I can see that, Maria," Hank snarled. "What's he doing here?" He was still dealing with the fact that his daughter had taken Cash with her, instead of her papa, to face down the son of a bitch who'd raped her.

"He's a good boy," Nana whispered in that throaty half-shout of hers. "Not cattolico, but good boy just the same."

Hank gritted his back teeth and squinted into the sun, trying to see past the light to the patch of shadows under the oak. "I don't care if he's Catholic, for God's sake. And him being a 'gooda' boy doesn't tell me why he's here."

"He inna love with Josefina."

"What?"

"Basta! He no know it yet."

Hank spared a glance for the old woman beside him. Crazy? Undoubtedly. Right? Who the hell knew?

"What's this about?" Cash asked as he stepped up to align himself with Jo. "Is everything okay?"

"I'm fine, go away."

He snorted. "Not likely, I'm in this. Right here with you."

Now Jo snorted, almost forgetting about the other woman as she sneered at Cash. "Sure you are."

"What's that supposed to mean?" he demanded.

"You know just what it means," Jo snapped.

"I have to go." Melanie grabbed her bag and turned to leave.

"Damn it!" Jo reacted in a heartbeat. Shooting Cash a furious glare, she stepped around him to grab the other woman's arm and draw her to a stop. "Don't leave. You came here for a reason, didn't you?"

Green eyes flashed quickly toward Cash and away again. "Yes."

"Then ignore him and tell me."

"So what is it, Melanie?" Jo asked, fixing her gaze on the other woman. "What brought you all the way out here to see me?"

Several long seconds ticked past and the only sound was the sigh of the wind through the trees and the rumble of Nana's whispers from the kitchen.

Finally, though, Jo's valiantly maintained patience was rewarded.

Melanie took a deep breath to steel herself, then blurted out, "I have to leave him before he kills my baby. And I need *you* to help me."

Seventeen

"The last time I was pregnant," Melanie said, pacing nervously, digging her heels out of the grass over and over again, "Steve—*hit* me." She stopped, looked over at Jo and corrected herself. "No, that's not true. He'd hit me before, but that night was different. He beat me until I was on the floor, begging him to stop. He didn't want children, he said. Had no intention of having an anchor around his neck. Then he kicked me in the stomach."

She shuddered and reached for the back of the lawn chair. She curled her fingers around the top rung and held on until her knuckles went white. "I lost the baby."

"Oh God."

"After that, I was careful," Melanie said, not reacting to Jo's sympathy, not allowing herself to be silent—as if she'd been quiet for too long already. "I wanted children, but after that, I was careful. Until now." She shook her head. "This pregnancy was an accident. Steve doesn't know about it yet and it terrifies me to think of what he'll do when he does find out."

"And you *want* his baby?"

"I want *my* baby."

"Then why don't you leave?" Jo felt bad for asking it, but dear God, to stay with a guy who used you for a punching bag?

"Because he wouldn't allow it." Melanie huffed a breath and almost laughed. "He said he needed me to get elected. I look good in pictures. Know all the right people—my father sat on the State Supreme Court until he died two years ago."

"What about your mom? Does she know what's going on?" Cash asked.

"My mother died five years ago. And *no* one else knew about the abuse until today." She looked at him. "Who'd believe me? He's rich, handsome, charming. People don't expect snakes to come in such a nice package."

"What're you going to do?" Jo asked. "And why did you come here? To me?"

Melanie's gaze shifted to hers. "You stood up to him. You *hit* him. When Steve came home that night, he was furious. I thought sure he'd turn on me, he usually does. But he didn't. He was so angry he couldn't speak, but he just locked himself away in his study."

Good, Jo thought, relieved she hadn't been responsible in some way for Melanie taking another beating.

"Linda, his assistant, told me that *you* had hit him, and I knew that's why he was so furious. Because a *woman* had stood up to him. And who knows, maybe that's why he steered clear of me that night." Her gaze locked with Jo's. "All I know for sure is that when I found out about you, I thought—maybe there's a way. Maybe I could get out. Take my baby and get out."

"You should go," Jo said, then worried. "Is there anyone you could go to? Somewhere you'd be safe?"

"My sister lives in Michigan. I could probably go to her. Yes," she said, and nerves tugged at her lower lip. "Probably. Most likely. But the more I think about this, the more I think that coming here was a mistake."

"No. No it wasn't," Jo said quickly, moving to lay one hand on the other woman's arm. "It was brave of you to come."

"Brave." Tears welled up in soft green eyes and Melanie sighed. "If I were really brave, I'd have left him before he killed my baby." Her hand moved to cup her still-flat abdomen, as if she were already trying to protect *this* child. "But I was just too scared. Too tired. Too hurt to think of trying to cross him. And he won't let me go. Won't let himself look bad to the constituents."

"But if you stay now, you'll lose this child, too."

She covered her face with her hands. "God, I can't—I'm just not as strong as you. I thought I could be, but—"

Jo understood. God, she understood that mind-numbing fear and the sense of humiliation that somehow, without even noticing how, you'd lost control of your life. Her heart twisted as she looked at the broken woman in front of her. Steve had done this, too. But he hadn't completely succeeded yet. Melanie was broken, but she wasn't shattered.

Reaching out, Jo took Melanie's hands in hers and pulled them away, so that she could meet the woman's eyes. "I *do* understand what you're feeling. Because he put me through the same thing. The terror. The shame—"

Melanie gripped Jo's hands hard, as if clinging to a lifeline—and maybe she was.

Taking a deep breath, Jo continued, "It's not easy for me to admit this, but it took me *ten years* to find the guts to look Steve in the eye and tell him what I think of him. Courage isn't always that easy to find."

"I don't know if I can do this," Melanie said softly. "I know what I *want* to do. I just don't know *what* to do."

"It's a big step," Jo agreed. "But it's a step worth taking and you already know that, because you're *here*."

"Talking about it's one thing. Actually *doing* it is something else."

"Believe me," Jo said, "I *know* that."

Melanie gave her a brief, wistful smile. "I'm glad I came here," she said, "talked to you. Whatever happens, I feel better for it."

"I'm glad." Releasing the other woman's hands after a hard squeeze, she urged her to "Just think about it. You don't have to make up your mind this minute."

She wished she could do more to help. Old feelings of guilt resurfaced and simmered on the oil slick floating in the pit of her stomach. No matter how much she wanted to jump in with both feet and fight Melanie's battles, she knew that sometimes, you had to find the will all on your own. No one else could decide for you.

To fight your demons, you had to do it standing on your own two feet.

"It won't be easy," she said, meeting Melanie's eyes and trying to will strength into her. "But if I *can* help," she promised, "I *will*."

Jo waved until the dust cloud behind Melanie's BMW had settled back onto the driveway. Only when she was sure the other woman couldn't see her, did she spin around and screech, "That son of a bitch!"

"I wish to God you'd have let *me* hit him." Cash's growl came, filled with heat and ice.

But Jo hardly heard him. Her insides jittered, her stomach quivered, and her blood was pounding in her head. Fury, raw and unshakable, held her fast. "This is all my fault."

He grabbed her upper arm and turned her around to face him. "How the hell do you come to *that* conclusion?"

She yanked free of his grasp and squinted up into the late afternoon sun to look at him. "If I'd stayed at college, pressed charges, Jesus, even *told* people about that bastard ten years ago—Melanie would never have been in this position."

"I don't believe this," he ground out. "You're going to take the blame for what's happening to Melanie?"

"It's not just her." Jo kept going, riding a swell of incensed rage that had her eyes glazed over and her breath hitching. "Who the hell *knows* how many women he's brutalized over the years?"

"You can't take the blame for this."

"If I'd had the guts to take him on ten years ago, he might have gone to jail," she shouted, waving her arms as if looking for something to hit. "And he sure as hell wouldn't be running for state senate now."

Cash grabbed her shoulders and pulled her close. Anger churned in her eyes, but sorrow and misery were there, too, and they tore at him, damn it. "This is that smooth-talking, rat-faced bastard's fault, and nobody else's."

She got that stubborn look on her face, so he kept
talking.

"You were a victim, too, Josefina." God, it cost him
to say that. To remember that she'd once been young
and vulnerable and alone. "He hurt you as much as
he's hurt Melanie. Don't you dare take the rap for
him."

Her mouth worked, but some of the misery faded
from her eyes, disappearing behind a flash of temper
he was glad to see.

Pulling free of him again, she took a step back and
said, "Fine. Okay, even I know I can't take the blame
for all of this. But don't you get it?" She slapped her
chest. "I understand her. I know just where she is, because Melanie's right where I was ten years ago. She's
scared. Ashamed. Alone."

"You're not that girl anymore."

"No, I'm not. And I'm not afraid to take him on."

Pride filled him as he watched her find her balance
again. Find her strength. The woman had more spine
than anyone he'd ever known.

"I want to help you in this."

She almost smiled, a soft tug at the corner of her
mouth. "Thanks, but this is something I have to finish
alone."

He felt a door slam in his face and realized that he
was being shut out. And what's more, he didn't much
like it. Made no sense, of course, because hadn't he
been trying to shut *her* out lately? Hadn't he convinced
himself to let her go so that when she left it would be
on *his* terms?

But this was different.

"You don't have to do every damn thing on your

own, Jo," he said, with more control than he was feeling. "Alone's not always everything it's cracked up to be."

"Is that right?" She looked him up and down, then frowned at him. "Well, if you think alone sucks so much—why are you so determined to stay that way?"

He didn't have an answer for that one. Not that she'd have heard him if he had. While he stood there like a statue carved out of stupid, she turned on her heel and marched off to the house.

Leaving him more alone than he'd ever been.

"So what're we gonna do about this?" Mike demanded from her spot on the couch.

"Yeah, assemble the warriors," Sam cried, lifting one fist in a power salute. "Let's go to the city and take this creep out."

"Good plan," Jo said, nodding. "Get the bazooka."

Sunlight washed through the wide front windows of Mike's house and lay in a thick slice of gold across the matching green sofas that sat facing each other. The area rug beneath the couches looked like a life raft on the imaginary sea created by the cool blue tiles on the floor.

Jo paced a wide circle around that area rug, shooting her sisters occasional eye rolls as the two women shouted out ideas on how to kill Steve Smith and get away with it. Tempting. Too damn tempting. The heels of her polished work boots rang on the cool blue tiles as her mind raced along, looking for ideas. Hell, *any* idea would do. Okay, an idea that wouldn't put them all in jail for the rest of their young lives.

It had been three days since Melanie's visit and Jo

had hardly slept. She kept worrying about the other woman. Was she safe? Had her bastard of a husband beat the shit out of her again? And what could Jo do about it?

"Come on, we should be able to do *something* about this guy," Mike complained.

"Don't see what," Jo said, stopping suddenly to drop onto the end of the couch. Lifting both feet, she rested them on the coffee table and crossed them at the ankles. "If we go busting in, then Rat Boy's going to know that Melanie's been talking. Which won't make life any easier on her."

"True, but—"

"No buts. We can't do this *for* her." Jo studied the shine on her boots and faced the one truth she hadn't been able to shake. "If Melanie's not ready to leave, there's no way we can do anything about it."

"Fine, if you're going to use logic," Mike sniffed. "Hand me that cookie, will you?"

"Aren't you afraid you're gonna pop?" Jo asked, reaching for the snickerdoodle and tossing it to her sister.

"Actually, I'm sort of hoping I *do,*" Mike whined around a bite of cookie. "Shelley says I could go any day, but the babies are *so* not cooperating."

"Apparently they didn't get their patience from *you.* Just don't give birth at my graduation, okay?"

"Oh please." Mike snorted, licked one finger and used it to snag the crumbs off her bodice. "I want a hospital and *lots* of drugs."

"All right, you two, back on track," Sam said, reaching for Jo's thick work binder. "If we can't save the world, or kick a deserving ass, we should at least figure out the jobs for this week."

Jo's eyes bugged out and she made a panicked lunge for the binder. "Give me that."

Sam pulled it away and out of reach. "God, you are so freaking territorial. Take it easy, will you, I just—" Her voice faded away as she pulled a loose sheet of paper from the binder. "Hmm. Someone seems to have written the word 'Cash' a few hundred times. Now what do you suppose that's about?"

Jo snatched the paper, crumpled it into a tight ball in her right fist, and felt her cheeks flush as both sisters stared at her. "I was worried about cash flow. I was *working*. Doing the spreadsheet. Figuring out the bills . . ."

They were nodding, smiling—okay, *smirking*.

"Fine," Jo muttered, stuffing that wad of paper in her jeans pocket. "I wrote his name. *Shoot me.*"

"Ah," Mike said on a dreamy sigh, "pit bulls in love."

"Pregnant or not, you watch it, twit."

"And is Cash writing *your* name on *his* homework, too?"

"You know," Jo said, glaring at Sam, "*you* were the sister I actually liked."

"Uh-huh," Sam said, clearly unconcerned with the sarcasm—and why wouldn't she be? The Marconi girls had gotten their sarcasm inoculation as children. "You're avoiding the question. Does Cash Hunter feel the same about you?"

"You know," Jo said, slumping farther into the feather-soft couch, until it looked as though she were being swallowed by the cushions. "Sometimes there's a *reason* for avoiding questions."

"So he doesn't love you?"

Jo glared at Mike. "Who said anything about *love*?"

"I think you did," Sam pointed out.

"God, why was I cursed with know-it-all sisters?"

"Just lucky?" Mike ventured.

"That can't be it," Jo said. "Trust me."

"Well," Sam snapped, "he's clearly not good enough for you."

"Thanks for that anyway."

"What the hell's wrong with him?" Mike wanted to know.

"How much time have you got?" Jo snarled, crossing her arms over her chest in self-defense, though she knew it was a useless gesture against her sisters.

"How much time do you need?" Sam asked.

The small, hard ball of hurt and misery inside her slowly deflated into a puddle of goo. They were willing to sit and moan with her. Willing to listen to her talk even if it took *days*. Damn it. Just when she thought Mike and Sam were about the most annoying human beings on the face of the earth, they went and did something nice. Something touching. Something . . .

"I'm in *love*." Jo reached up and yanked at her hair in frustration over her own stupidity. "In love with *Cash Hunter*."

"Yeah," Mike said. "We got that much."

"The question," Sam asked, "is what're you gonna do about it?"

"What the hell am I supposed to do about it?" Since she couldn't sink any farther into the couch, she gave up on it altogether and leaped to her feet instead. Immediately, she felt better. She was through hiding away from what she was feeling. Never again was she going to bury herself under a blanket of lies and secrets. "Why do *I* have to do *anything* about it?"

"Atta girl. Don't go after what you want. Stand here and complain." Mike choked out a laugh and stretched her hand toward the last couple of cookies.

"Who's complaining?" Jo asked, shoving the plate of cookies closer to Mike.

Her youngest sister blinked, shook her head, then thumped the heel of her hand over her ear. "Geez . . . sounded like you."

"Funny."

"Did you tell Cash?" Sam asked.

"Why the *hell* would I do that?"

"Uh, so he'd *know*?"

"Like I want him knowing. For God's sake, he's made it perfectly clear he didn't want a 'relationship,' and Lord, I hate that word." Jo bent down, grabbed up one of the cookies and took a bite.

"Hey!" Mike shouted.

Jo ignored her. "He says he 'healed' me and now I should go away."

"He *what*?"

"Thank you," Jo said to Sam. "Exactly how *I* felt."

"Just how did this mystical healing take place?" Mike wondered.

Scowling, Jo took another bite of cookie. "I went back to his place. Forced him to have sex with me again—"

"Forced him?" Mike interrupted. "Did he cry?"

"You really do love the sound of your own voice, don't you?" Jo finished off the cookie and reached for another, but Mike was too quick for her and grabbed up the last three, as if she were a survivalist planning on not getting another meal anytime soon. "The point," Jo said, "is that this time, I, uh, you know, I . . ."

"Saw fireworks?"

"Exactly." Jo pointed a finger at Sam, as if she'd just won the grand prize on *Jeopardy*. "So anyway, I'm all, This is great, and Hey, fabulous, and really trying to not say anything stupid like 'I love you, you big moron,' when he pulls out the 'We've had sex and now you'll leave to join the Peace Corps' thing."

"To give him his due," Sam said, "that *is* what most women who've been with him have done."

"Yeah, but *I'm* not most women, am I? I'm not going anywhere. And I told him so."

"No doubt in quiet, genteel tones," Mike guessed.

"Cute."

"And he said . . . ?" Sam asked.

"He said I should go now, because I'd be going eventually anyway, so basically, Here's your hat, what's your hurry?"

"Bastard." Sam scowled in disgust.

"Totally," Mike agreed.

"Moron," Jo said, feeling that wadded-up paper with her squiggled words of affection burning a hole in her jeans pocket.

"So," Sam said, "do you still want him?"

"I'm just stupid enough to, yes," Jo admitted, though the truth was so galling she wanted to spit.

"Then you're going to have to take the risk and tell him how you feel."

Humiliation rose up inside her and Jo could feel her

stomach twist into tight little knots of *defiance*. There had to be an easier way.

"He's not interested," she said.

"You don't know that," Sam said.

"He told me so himself."

"He didn't know you love him."

"It won't make a difference," she said stubbornly. "If anything, it'll just make him push me away even faster."

"His loss then." Sam held one hand out in front of her. "But you'll never know for sure if you don't try."

"Amen," Mike said, laying her hand on top of Sam's. "And if he's really too dumb to see how great you are and how good you'd be together, then he's *so* not good enough for you."

Jo looked at the two women in the world who meant everything to her. Unfailing loyalty. Unquestioning love. This was family. This was what Cash couldn't seem to get. And maybe she could understand why.

But that didn't mean she was willing to let him blow off a future because he didn't like his past.

Laying her hand on top of her sisters', she said, "Okay. I'll tell him. I'll make him listen to me if I have to hit him in the head with a hammer."

"Atta girl," Mike snorted. "Use your charm."

Jo ignored her. "Then when I've had my say, if he still won't wake up and see what we could have together . . . I'll be the one to let *him* go."

Eighteen

Waiting to hear from Melanie Smith was making Jo nuts.

She felt as if she were stuck in neutral, her engine revving, but there was nowhere to go. She couldn't face down Steve Smith and she couldn't have it out with Cash, either. Well, she could, but she wasn't going to. Not until she had her life in order. She wanted her past cleaned up and disposed of before facing down the man who could be her future.

Lying out in the cool grass of the Marconi family backyard, she stared up at a wide, starlit sky. Behind her, she could hear the homey sounds of Nana fussing around in the kitchen and the low-pitched hum of the television as her father no doubt fell asleep in his recliner. Jack was probably upstairs doing his homework and she should be inside writing up the bid on the Stevenson job.

And yet . . .

She couldn't help worrying about Melanie, and besides, from a completely selfish point of view, she wanted this finished. So she could go deal with Cash.

Maybe he would still tell her to go. Maybe he wouldn't be interested in knowing she loved him. But by God, he was going to have to listen to her. The man couldn't become a part of her life and then walk away without at least letting her say her piece.

"Who're you mad at?"

Jo tipped her head back on the grass and got an upside-down view of her little brother strolling across the yard toward her. His jeans were too baggy, his hair too long, and his sneakers looked as though Bear had been chewing on them again.

"Who says I'm mad?"

"Your foot's tapping hard on the ground. Usually you only do that when you're mad."

"Hmm." Geez, Cash didn't even have to be in the vicinity to affect her temper. She deliberately stilled her right foot, stared up at the sky again and said, "You're way too smart."

"Yeah, I know. My teacher says I'm gifted."

She laughed as he stretched out in the grass beside her. "Is that right? Well hey, I think that's a first for the Marconis."

"What'cha lookin' at?"

"Just the stars," she said, lifting one hand to point. "There's Mars."

"Yeah? How do you know?"

"Because Mars is called 'the Red Planet.' But from here, it only looks a little yellow-orangish, see?"

"Yeah." He leaned his head against her shoulder and kept looking. "Know any other ones?"

Thoughts of Cash and Melanie drifted away. "Um, that's Jupiter there and way over there? That's Saturn."

"The one with the rings."

"Hey," she said, giving him a nudge in the ribs, "you *are* gifted."

He laughed and Jo smiled into the darkness. "I've

got a telescope back at my house. This summer we'll pull it out and look at all of 'em a little close up."

"Cool. How do you know this stuff?"

"I took an astronomy course in college last year." And almost flunked it. But Cash had ridden to the rescue with his *Astronomy for Dummies* book. Blast the man, there he was again. Up front and center in her mind.

"Jo?"

"Hmm?"

"How come Cash hasn't been around much?" He tapped his fingertips on his cast. "Is it 'cause of me? You know, the fire and everything?"

"No." She patted his good arm and turned her head to give him a smile. Learning fast on the guilt meter, wasn't he? "It's not you, kiddo."

"Then why?"

"I don't know," she said at last, because it was the only thing she could say. "Guess you'd have to ask him."

No way was she going to try to explain to a ten-year-old that the closer she felt to Cash, the further away he pulled. Nope. Let the great man himself take on that little task.

When her cell phone rang, Jo was grateful for the interruption. Digging it out of her jeans pocket, she checked the caller ID, then sat up straight and whipped it open.

"Melanie?"

The next morning, while Jo was on her way to San Francisco, Grace Van Horn walked down the Lake Road to her nephew's house.

The morning was cool and the wind that sighed through the trees sounded like whispers from an interested crowd. She tugged her black cardigan a bit tighter around her and stepped carefully in her black mules. Sunlight dappled the dirt road and she took her time, walking slowly. Not so much to enjoy the morning, as to put off the chat she'd have to have with Cash.

He was the son she'd never had and she loved him more than she could say. But a more hardheaded individual she'd never met. Still, she wasn't looking forward to giving him news she knew would cause him pain.

When she rounded the bend, she saw that he was already in his workshop. The pounding beat of classic Rolling Stones rushed through the open double doors to greet her as she approached.

He hadn't heard her come up, so just for a minute or two, she studied him unaware. He'd always been a loner and for that she blamed her younger sister Kate, Cash's mother. Kate loved her only son, but she loved herself more, and Cash had never really accepted that. He pretended differently of course, but Grace knew that a part of him was still waiting for Kate to be the mother she should have been.

And now, Grace was going to have to give that lingering hope another kick.

"Morning, handsome," she called, forcing cheer into her voice.

He looked up from the table leg he was carving and gave her a smile that could light up a small city. "A little early for you to be out, isn't it, Grace?" he asked, turning back to his task.

He scraped the razor-sharp edge of a carving tool

along the table leg and pushed out a thin curl of wood that dropped to the floor to join hundreds of others just like it. "No yoga today?"

"I'm taking a break," she said, wandering into the workshop. Of course, the break had been precipitated by the phone call from Kate, but she'd get to that.

Poking through his tools, she was amazed at the varied shapes and sizes of the awls and blades.

"Those're sharp," he warned, "be careful."

"Who's the table for?" she asked, wandering back toward him.

"No one in particular," he said, straightening up to narrow his gaze at her. "And it occurs to me that you've never been that interested in what I'm working on before."

"Of course I am," she protested. "I'm very proud of you, Cash. You do beautiful work and I've always said so. Ask anyone."

He tossed the blade he was holding onto the workbench, folded his arms across his chest and looked down at her with suspicion. "Okay, Grace, there's a reason you're here, full of compliments so early in the morning, so spill it."

She winced.

Instantly, his attitude changed. "Are you okay? Is there something—"

"I'm fine," she said quickly, wanting to reassure him at least on that score. But blast it, if she had Kate here in front of her right now, she'd slap her silly.

"Then what?" More wary than suspicious now and that tore at Grace.

The man shouldn't have to live his life on guard. He should let go of the past and move on. Enjoy his life.

She'd seen how he and Jo were together, and the romantic in her wished that something would come of it. Wished he would let himself love Jo and be loved by her. Have a family so she could entertain honorary grandchildren before she got too old to recognize them.

And she was still stalling.

"It's your mother," she said flatly, keeping her gaze locked with his.

"What's wrong with her?"

"Such a good question," she murmured, but then rushed on. "She called me this morning. Said she didn't get an answer at your house—"

"I've been out here most of the night."

"Yes, well, she's not coming this summer and she wanted me to tell you."

The words tasted bitter, since Grace knew very well how much this news would hurt him. Kate and her friends traveled the country year round, never staying in any one place too long. Yet every summer, she'd come here, to Grace's house. And it was the one time of the year that Cash could count on seeing his mother.

She waited to see reaction flash in his dark eyes, but it didn't happen. "Did you hear me?"

"Yeah," he said, and picked up the blade again. "Doesn't matter."

"What do you mean it doesn't matter? You built that darling little cottage for her. You wanted her to come and now she's not."

"The cottage is gone, remember?" Another curl of wood dropped to the floor.

Grace moved to the radio, flicked it off, and instantly, silence dropped between them.

"You could build it again," she said, though she knew she wasn't really helping.

"She wouldn't want it. I know that. You know that."

"Yes, but—"

"Grace." A note of defeat sounded in his voice. "She won't stay if I build her a dozen cottages. People just don't stay."

She almost argued with the tone of weary acceptance in his voice, but then thought better of it. Hadn't she just been telling herself that he had to get past wanting to rewrite his family history? Stop hoping that Kate would become the mother he'd always wanted her to be?

"You're right. She wouldn't."

He gave her a quick smile. "So, why keep beating my head against that stone wall? It's better this way anyway."

"Which way is that?"

He smoothed his big hand up and down the table leg, checking for flaws, feeling the wood grain, and she knew he was giving himself time to think. To put the words together. Finally, he glanced at her again. "It's better alone, Grace. It's not easy, but it's better."

"You're wrong," she said, walking closer to him. Staring up into his eyes, she said, "Being alone *is* the easy way. It means you don't have to connect. You don't have to be there for anyone but yourself. It means hiding out."

He laughed shortly. "Great. Thanks. Glad you could stop by."

He was shutting her out, and by heaven, she wouldn't allow that. "For the first time in your life, Cash Hunter, I'm ashamed of you."

His gaze snapped to hers. "What the hell for?"

"Do you think I don't have eyes? Do you think I don't *know* that you have feelings for Jo Marconi?"

"Doesn't matter," he said, digging his blade into the wing of a butterfly and making it deeper.

"It's all that does matter," she said shortly, grabbing his arm, forcing him to look at her. "And you're turning your back on it."

Cash fought down a rising tide of fury and reminded himself that this tiny woman was the closest thing he'd ever really known to a real mother. But even all the love he had for her wouldn't let him take that one lying down. "Hell, Grace, that's a family tradition!"

"What?"

"Closing people out. It's what we *do*. My father did it, my mother did it, even *you*, Grace."

The sting of hurt feelings shone in her eyes. "I don't know what you're talking about."

"Yeah?" he countered, letting his irritation guide his words. "Well, if you're so much better at loving someone than I am, why did you never remarry?"

She took a step back, stunned to her shoes. "I—"

"You've been mourning a husband you didn't love for thirty years, Grace." Shaking his head, he gave her a sad smile. "You never once admitted that he died in a car wreck the night you threw him out."

Her hand flew to her throat. "How did you—"

"Mom told me."

Her lips thinned into a grim slash that he couldn't ever remember seeing on her face before. He'd hurt her, and he felt bad about that, but damn it. "I'm sorry, Grace. But for God's sake, if anyone should understand how I feel about this, it should be *you*."

"Is that right?"

"Damn straight. You're nuts about Hank Marconi, but I don't see you saying yes to any of his proposals." He picked up a honing stone and wiped it carefully over the edge of his carving tool. When he was finished, he looked at her again. "I don't see you willing to take a chance. Willing to risk the pain again. How are you so different from me?"

Grace staggered back a step or two and her eyes were wide with hurt and just the faintest shimmer of tears. Cash felt as if he'd kicked a puppy. Just like that, all the anger left him and he knew that if she let those tears fall, he'd be on his knees in front of her, begging her to forgive him. God, he couldn't lose *Grace*.

Her hand at her mouth, she only stared at him in shocked silence. In the quiet, he heard the wind coursing through the trees outside. Out on the lake, a duck called to its mate, and from a distance, he heard Grace's goats and sheep waking up and making a racket.

Cash scrubbed one hand over his face, then pushed it through his hair with enough strength to rip it all out, strand by strand. His life was suddenly in the toilet, so he attacked the only woman in his life who'd ever been a constant? Great. Nice job.

"Pay no attention to me, Grace," he said, "haven't had any sleep and shouldn't be around people. It's no excuse, but I'm sorry. I shouldn't have said any of that to you."

"No." She held up one small hand to hush him up. "No, you were right."

"Grace—"

"You just wait a minute now," she said, and some of her fire was back, though those tears were still sparkling in her big eyes. "You had your say, and now it's my shot for a rebuttal. Everything you said is completely true."

"Ah, damn it . . ." He reached for her and pulled her into a hard, tight hug.

She patted his back, then stepped away. "Don't go all soft on me now, Cash. You made your point. And it was something, I'm ashamed to say, that I never admitted to myself. Your uncle, my late husband, was a dreadful man." She frowned in memory. "He was loud and rude and overbearing and I knew almost from our honeymoon that I'd made a huge mistake. I stuck it out another year, though, before throwing him out, and then when he died, it seemed . . . *easier,* somehow, to rewrite history."

She blew out a breath and shook her head until the gold hoops at her ears swung in a wild rhythm. "Foolish. Even cowardly. But sometime over the years, even I began to believe the lies I'd built up. As for not remarrying, you're right about that, too. I was too afraid to trust anyone again. Too scared to let myself love completely again. Too used to being alone to even *try.*"

"I didn't mean to hurt you," he blurted.

She smiled. "Oh, honey, I *know* that. The truth isn't always easy, but sooner or later, you've got to look at it." She came closer, reached up and cupped his face between her hands. "And now, I've got a truth for you."

He braced himself, because despite her love for him, Grace had never held back from telling him just what she was thinking. "Yes, ma'am?"

She smiled again. "Don't look so worried—it's nothing dire. I just want you to think about something for me, Cash."

"What's that?"

"If I'm willing to admit that I've been dead wrong about way too many things in my life—I want you to consider the possibility that *you're* wrong, too."

"Grace—"

"And I want you to think about it *now*. Don't wait too long, Cash. Love—*real* love—doesn't come around every day."

"You two ready?" Jo looked at Melanie, then shifted her gaze to Linda Sandoval, Steve's assistant.

Melanie swallowed hard, inhaled sharply, then nodded. "As I'll ever be."

"That'll do," Jo said, and gave her a quick smile. As for herself, she was *more* than ready. The first time she'd come to the city to see this pond scum, she'd dressed to impress. Today, she'd dressed to impress *herself*.

To remind herself of who she was, who she'd become, she wore her neatly pressed jeans, a red, starched MARCONI CONSTRUCTION T-shirt, and boots polished to a mirror shine. All symbols of the life she'd built. Of the life she was *proud* of.

Linda threw open the double doors, and the three women marched into Steve Smith's office as a united front. The city sprawled out behind him, but the tinted windows prevented sunlight from staking its claim on the room. His desk lamp was on, casting his face in shadow.

Jo felt the tension ratchet up in the room and reminded herself that today was Melanie's show. She
only hoped the other woman's nerves wouldn't desert
her when she needed them most.

Steve stood up behind his desk, his gaze flicking
disinterestedly between his wife, his assistant, and the
woman he'd raped so long ago.

"What's going on here?" he demanded, and kept his
voice at the low growl that usually had people hopping
to fulfill his every request. "Melanie? What're you doing here? I told you to stay at the house."

Here we go, Jo thought, and stiffened her spine as if
she could *will* extra strength into the fragile blonde beside her. She needn't have worried.

"I'm finished doing what you tell me," the woman
said, and though her voice was a little shaky, she lifted
her chin and stood her ground.

Jo wanted to applaud.

Steve wanted to hit her. He'd taken as much of this
crap from women as he was going to. Ever since the
Marconi bitch had shown up in his office, he'd been
waiting for the other shoe to drop. The one thing he
hadn't expected was for his mewling bitch of a wife to
suddenly find a spine.

But he could take care of this.

"Linda." His voice snapped with the cadence of a
man used to having his orders followed. "Call Security. Tell them this woman"—he pointed at Jo—
"forced my wife to bring her into my office. See that
they—"

"No."

His gaze swiveled to the woman who had *never,* in

six years of working for him, said no to him. "I beg your pardon?"

"I said I won't be calling Security. And frankly, if I were you, I wouldn't want them to hear any of this."

His blood roared in his ears. He couldn't hear. Couldn't think. His mouth went dry, then suddenly filled with saliva so fast, he spat on his desk as he shouted, "What the hell is wrong with you? Do what you're told!"

"I don't work for you anymore, Mr. Smith," Linda said, "I quit this morning. My resignation is there. On your desk."

He looked for it briefly, then dismissed the whole idea. "Ridiculous. You can't quit."

"Looks like she can." The Marconi bitch was *laughing* at him.

"Steve," Melanie said, drawing his attention back to her. "I want a divorce."

"Like hell." He came around the edge of his desk and stalked toward her, hands itching to connect with her soft, pale flesh. He could almost taste the satisfaction. "There's no divorce and you know it. I'm going to be in the state senate—" He raised one hand.

Jo stepped in front of Melanie and Steve smiled. The only thing better than hitting his wife would be belting this bitch from his past. His eye was still bruised and shadowed from the lucky punch she'd gotten in on her last visit. But this time it would be different, he told himself, feeding the fury within, *this* time . . .

Melanie—meek, pitiful little *Melanie*—pushed Jo out of the way and glared at him. "You're not going to hit her. Or me. You're not in charge here. Not anymore."

Like a bull bedeviled by flies, he shook his head and snarled.

"Atta girl," Jo whispered, but the sound barely reached him through the pounding in his head.

Melanie looked straight into his eyes and said, "If you don't agree to a fast divorce, I'm going to the police. I'll tell them everything."

"They won't believe you."

"Maybe not," she acknowledged with a short nod. "But the charges will still be there. On the record. Where any newspaper reporter can find them. What kind of headlines do you think they'd make?"

This couldn't be happening. Not to *him*. Melanie *never* fought back. It was all that Marconi bitch's fault. He spared her a quick, vicious look before shifting his gaze back to his wife. "If you think—"

"Listen to me," she said, interrupting him so neatly that he was stunned into silence. "I'm going to divorce you. You are going to sign a paper relinquishing all rights to our child—"

He staggered. "*What* child?"

"And then you're going to leave me alone. Forever. Because if you don't, I will make you sorry."

"You're out of your mind. *All* of you are, if you think for one minute that I'm going along with any of this."

"Oh," Jo said, stepping up alongside Melanie as if they were soldiers standing for review. "There's more. You're going to resign from the senate race."

"You *are* insane!"

She smiled, but the curve of her mouth had nothing

to do with humor and everything to do with the deadly gleam in her eyes. "You're going to do just what we say. You'll quit the race and you'll give Melanie her divorce *and* you'll stay away from her child. You'll go along with all of it, or—" She stepped in closer to him, glaring at him as if he were an especially disgusting bug. "Or . . . I will personally take out a full-page ad in the Sunday paper exposing you as the rapist and professional prick that you are."

"You can't do that, you bitch," he argued, even though he felt the land beneath his feet starting to shift and tremble. "I'll sue you for every dime you've got."

"Go ahead," she taunted. "I can always build another business. But you'll still be a prick. And you *still* won't get elected."

"And," Linda spoke up, and Steve's gaze shifted to her. "Just in case you're trying to think of a way to ooze out of this, you should know. I've contacted three or four of your former . . . 'dates.' They're all willing to testify about the bruises you gave *them*."

This could not be happening.

He'd worked his whole life for this chance at greatness. He'd worked, plotted, schemed, and now at last, he was finally poised to take the place he'd been born to have. State senator. And after that . . . who knew? Maybe even the *presidency*.

"In fact," Jo said, taking a manila envelope from Linda and pulling out a sheaf of typed papers. "We've already got a couple of the notarized statements." Her gaze drilled into his. "They make fascinating reading."

That shift in the earth became a gaping chasm that swallowed Steve Smith's career in one noisy gulp. He glared at them, each in turn, and knew, even as he thought about fighting them just a little longer, that they'd already *won.*

He was finished.

Everything was gone.

"You can all go to hell," he croaked, throat tight with futile rage.

Melanie looked him up and down. "Been there," she said. "Done that. Expect to hear from my lawyer tomorrow."

Then she left, followed quickly by Linda, the "loyal" assistant who'd turned on him like a rabid dog. And he was alone with the woman who had started this mess. The woman who'd come back out of the past just in time to squash his future. She stared at him now with a disinterested sort of pity.

"What do you want? What's left?" he demanded, reaching into his jacket pocket for his wallet. "Money? Credit cards? What's the going rate for ruining a man's life?"

She shook her head at him. "I seem to remember that ten years ago, you had something quite illuminating to say to me when you left me lying on that stinking floor." She tapped one finger against her chin. "Let's see, what was it again?" Then, glaring at him, she said, "Oh right. I remember. *'Life is hard. Get over it.'*"

"Get out," he said, fists at his sides, fury spitting through his blood.

"You know," Jo mused, turning slowly for the door,

"when I imagined this little meeting, I was so *sure* that I would enjoy seeing you get yours . . ."

"Yeah?" he goaded.

She stopped in the doorway, and looking back, she smiled, a wide, happy smile filled with the sweet taste of victory. "And I was right."

Nineteen

"I am proud of you, Josefina. What you did was very good."

She took the morning paper from her father's hand and smiled down at the headline: SMITH WITHDRAWS FROM RACE. A swell of something a lot like pride filled her. Quickly, she scanned the article, picking out the highlights to quietly crow over . . . *'retires from politics for personal reasons . . . Mrs. Smith unavailable for comment, having left the city for a long rest . . . '* Jo chuckled. The weasel. Long rest is right. Without him in her life, Melanie would probably sleep better at night than she ever had.

"Very good." Papa took back the paper and laid one big, work-worn hand on her shoulder.

Looking into those pale blue eyes so much like her own, Jo said, "Thanks, Papa. And you know what, I'm pretty proud of me, too."

"Issa good day," Nana said, stirring chopped fresh oregano into the eggs she had scrambling in the cast-iron skillet.

"And Melanie? She's all right?"

"Took her to the airport myself last night," Jo said,

snitching a piece of bacon and taking a bite. "And with all we've got on him, that slime ball will leave her alone."

"Good." Papa poured himself a cup of coffee and walked to the kitchen table. Sitting down, he gave Bear a scratch behind the ears, then asked Jo, "So, now you've finished with the other business, you're ready to start the Stevenson job this morning?"

No. Now that Steve Smith had been handled, she had another piece of business to take care of. "I've got something to do first, but I'll meet you there. In an hour or so, okay?"

"Sure, sure. This something," Papa asked. "It's important?"

Nana slanted her a sidelong glance and Jo wondered if the old woman was somehow trying to read her mind. Wouldn't surprise her. "Yeah, it is. But I'll be there later."

"Sure, sure." Papa opened the paper while Nana shouted up the stairs, "Jack! Mangia!" Then she turned to Jo. "You shoulda eat before the important thing, Josefina. Cash can wait."

Jo gaped at her, but Nana was already turning toward the table. Heading for the front door, Jo wondered if the mind-reading thing came with the ability to give the evil eye, or was it the other way around?

Something classical was playing on the radio. Filled with violins and cellos and harps, the music soared out the double doors of the workshop and lifted into the clear morning sky like a prayer.

Jo jumped out of the truck and slammed the door.

Before she could take another step, though, Cash was there. As if he'd been waiting for her.

"Saw the morning paper."

"Pretty good, huh?"

"Retiring for personal reasons?"

"Not as good as having the lying slug arrested," Jo admitted, "but I'll take what I can get on this one."

"Melanie?"

"In Michigan by now and happy, I think."

"Good." He stared at her and she wished that she could read the emotions churning in those dark eyes of his. But today, they were closed to her. Physically, he was right in front of her, but she knew that emotionally, he was sliding further away from her with every passing second.

She ached, just knowing that. And a part of her wondered if she was already fighting a losing battle. But another, more stubborn part of her dug in her heels and resolved to settle whatever was between them once and for all.

"Cash, I've got something to say to you and I want you to stay quiet until I'm finished."

He pulled a white shop towel out of the back pocket of his jeans and wiped both hands on it. "All right."

"Good, good." She swallowed hard and rubbed her suddenly damp palms on her jeans. Her stomach jumped and her heartbeat felt like a jackhammer. *Oh God.* This was the most important moment of her life, and she was about to faint.

He took a step toward her, concern flashing across his face. "You okay?"

"Probably not," she admitted, with a weak smile.

"But I will be. Once I get this said." But where to start? Anxious now, she started pacing. She always thought better when she was moving and, right now, she needed all the help she could get. "I wanted to thank you—for all the moral support when I needed it."

"You're welcome."

She stopped. "No talking, remember?"

"Right."

"Okay." She sucked in air as if she were going down for the third time. Why was it easier to face down a scumbag than it was to tell the most important man in your life that you loved him? Why was she so afraid of what she'd always dreamed of feeling?

She lifted her gaze to his. A soft wind ruffled the dark hair lying across his forehead. There were shadows under his dark eyes and she wondered if it was thoughts of *her* that were keeping him up at night. God, she hoped so.

"There's no easy way to say this so I'm just going to say it." She walked up close to him, reached out and took both of his hands in hers. She held on tight while she looked directly into his eyes and blurted out the words before they could get strangled up inside her. "I love you."

He opened his mouth, but she tightened her grip on his hands and spoke up quickly. "Not finished. Let me say it all, okay?"

He nodded and she kept going. Funny, it was easier to talk to him when she was touching him. When she could hold on to him and draw on his strength as she had before.

"It surprised me, too," she said. "How I feel. I didn't expect it. Wasn't looking for it. But maybe that's when you find the important stuff, you know?" She shrugged, released his hands and reached up to take his face between her palms. "I *do* love you, Cash. And I think you love me."

"Jo—" He covered her hands with his and looked at her through eyes that shone with a soul-deep regret that Jo simply didn't want to see.

So she kept talking. Faster now, almost desperate to say it all. "I want us to be together, Cash. A family. I want the life we could build together."

He sighed, turned his face and kissed her palm before pulling her hands away and letting her go. Though she still felt the near electrical hum of his touch on her skin, he was backing up. Backing away.

And she could feel her heart breaking.

"I'm sorry," he said, shaking his head sadly.

"Don't be sorry, Cash," Jo whispered, and wondered how she was drawing breath into lungs that felt frozen solid with a cold that went down to her bones. "Be in love with me."

"I wish I could be the man you want," he said, and scrubbed one hand across his mouth, as if even he were trying to keep the words from escaping. "But I'm not."

"Yes you are." Jo heard the tremor in her voice and swallowed back the disappointment crowding her. She'd somehow thought that this would go better.

She'd thought that once he heard that she loved him, he'd be able to see what they could have together. To see that this was where he belonged. That *she* was the one woman meant for him.

And now . . .

His features were grim, his body as stiff as if he

himself had been carved out of the wood he created such beauty from.

"I told you before, Jo," he said, and she suddenly wished he would call her "Josefina" again. But he hadn't. Not since she'd told him not to. "I'm not looking for permanent. Permanent doesn't exist. Not for me."

"I used to feel that way," she said, hating that her voice sounded as tremulous as she felt. "I always figured that I'd stay single. After what happened with—" She stopped, shrugged, and let it go. "Doesn't matter. I just never wanted what other women wanted. I had my job. My family. That was enough." She lifted her face into a soft kiss of wind and welcomed the warm air. "But it's not anymore. Now I want more. Now, I want it all."

"I can't give you that." He folded his arms over his chest as if holding himself in place.

"Why the hell not?" Jo swallowed past the knot of emotion jammed in her throat.

"Because I don't do relationships. They're too damn painful and I'm not trying it again."

"What's this 'again' you keep talking about?" God, how was she still standing?

He threw the shop towel onto the ground and stuffed his hands into his jeans pockets. "Remember, once, you asked me if I'd ever been in love?"

"Yeah."

"I proposed to her. Bought her a ring."

Jo winced, realizing that the one thing he wouldn't do for her, he'd done for someone else. Someone who hadn't wanted him as much as she did.

"I loved her kid, too," he said, and his eyes softened

in memory. "A boy, about four. She was the widow of my best friend. He was military, killed on a mission."

"I'm sorry, but—"

"It started just as me looking out for her and Davey. Told myself I was doing it for Dave—my friend." He smiled grimly. "But things changed. I loved her. Loved that kid. And when I asked her to marry me, she said yes. A month before the wedding, my friend came back. Alive." Cash sighed. "He was in black ops. Military. Went on a covert mission, was listed as dead. Turns out, he was just being held in some sinkhole. He escaped and now he wanted his life back." His gaze locked on Jo. "She threw the ring at me, said, 'See ya,' and left without looking back."

Jo's heart ached for him. She knew how he must have felt. Knew what family meant to him. And for him to come so close to having what he'd always wanted only to lose it again must have been awful for him. "Okay, you were hurt. And I'm sorry. But for God's sake, Cash. She loved her husband and she got a miracle."

"I know that." Cash looked at Jo and read sympathy and understanding in her pale blue eyes. The same eyes that had haunted him for days. The eyes that kept him awake at night. The soft jasmine scent of her shampoo drifted to him on the wind and he dragged it into his lungs, trapping it there, holding her close the only way he could now.

Every instinct he possessed urged him to grab her, to bury his face in the curve of her neck and feel the warmth of her steal through him. But he couldn't. It was already too hard. Harder than it should have been. On both of them.

He focused instead on old pain to keep him from causing new. "I knew it then, too. Didn't seem to help much. She'd said she loved *me*, too. Still she left. Ripped my heart out to lose her and that boy, Jo." He steeled himself to meet her gaze. To not look away. "I thought I'd found a family. I hadn't. No way in hell am I going through that again."

Jo stepped up to him, laid both hands on his chest, and he swore he could feel her pulse beat right through the palms of her hands. "I'm not asking you to go through that again, Cash." Shaking her head, she stared up at him and said, "I'm not talking about *leaving* you. I'm talking about *staying*."

"For now." He wouldn't believe. Not again. He'd spent most of his life waiting for people he loved to stay—yet they always left. *Always*. No reason to believe anything had changed.

"You know," Jo said, taking a step back, lowering her hands. "I just realized something. This whole time, I thought *I* was the one stuck in the past. But it was never really me, Cash. It was *you*."

He rubbed his chest, still feeling the imprint of her hands. "I'm not *stuck* anywhere," he said, not sure anymore if he was trying to convince her—or himself.

"Sure you are," she said on a choked-off laugh that sounded as if it had scraped her throat in its escape. "I tell you I *love* you and you tell me no thanks, because you don't want to be hurt if I leave you?"

It sounded stupid said out loud like that, but damn it, Cash had the scars to prove that the pain was real. And what he felt for Jo Marconi was so much more than he'd ever felt before—the devastation when he lost her would be that much more, too. And just like that, his resolve strengthened and his heart iced over, despite how much he wanted her. "I don't have to explain myself to you, Jo."

"No, you really don't," she said, sniffing just a little and blinking back what he feared was a sheen of tears in her eyes. When a strong woman cried, she could break a man—and Cash felt his insides shake.

"I actually think I'm starting to understand something about you." She tipped her head to one side and that ponytail swung behind her head, rippling in the wind. "All those women you've been with. They all left and you think that proves something, don't you? That no one will stay."

"You think it doesn't?" He kept his gaze off that fall of hair that he wanted to touch so badly.

"I think you spend the night with lonely, unhappy women. I think you *deliberately* choose to sleep with women who would *never* stay with you. That way when they do leave, you're safe." She looked up at him, forcing his gaze to meet hers. Forcing him to see what this was doing to her.

"I think they leave because you give them nothing to stay for," Jo said softly. "They weren't women to you, they were *causes.*"

"You're wrong." *But she's not,* his brain whispered. The women he'd slept with in the past had all been unhappy. He'd told himself that he'd lived the way he had to protect his own heart. But *had* he been sabotaging himself all along? Making sure that he'd *never* stumble on happiness?

"See," Jo said, tapping the toe of her boot against

the dirt, sending up tiny dust clouds. "I don't think so. I think you set yourself up to fail. I think you *like* being alone. Because that way, you never have to *try*. Even the woman you loved was still in love with someone else and you can't forgive her for that."

"Bullshit." His chest was tight, his breath coming in strangled gasps. Her words pushed through his mind and added to the chorus of everything Grace had said to him just the day before. Truth? *No.*

Shaking her head, she gave him a smile filled with regret. "You have one-night stands with women you'd never be interested in for the long haul. Then you hold up their leaving as proof that relationships don't last."

"Really?" he reminded her. "Well, I slept with *you,* too."

"The exception that proves the rule," Jo said. "And even then, you kept expecting me to get up and walk away. When I didn't play the game as expected, you practically *threw* me out, with all that talk about 'healing' me, just so you could stay in charge." The toe of her boot stopped tapping and she swung her head to the other side, the ponytail keeping time. "You're cut off, Cash. You won't let *anyone* in."

"I'm not cut off from everything. I'm a part of this town," he said, trying hard now to show them both that he wasn't as cold and distant as he was suddenly feeling.

"No you're not." She drilled an index finger into his chest. "You stay out here, away from everyone. Even when you're trying to help—with stunts like the Money Fairy—you do it anonymously. You don't want to step in and have people count on you. You think they'll all let you down, so you make sure they never get the chance to actually do it."

The music from the workroom soared around them. The ducks on the lake squabbled and squawked and the wind pushed through the trees, rattling new leaves like silken wind chimes.

"You don't know what you're talking about." Cash sighed, stepped around her and stalked toward the workshop. He couldn't stand there looking at her and *not* touch her. He couldn't listen to her and not want to defend himself. And damned if he could think of a way to defend his position at the moment.

Naturally, Jo stayed just a step or two behind him.

"I know *exactly* what I'm talking about and we both know it." She grabbed his arm, her strong fingers digging into his flesh as she jerked him around to face her. "You're hiding, Cash."

"Then I'm not doing much of a job," he pointed out. "*You* keep finding me."

"You know what I mean."

Yeah, he did. And a part of him knew she was right. Fine. He had kept himself separate from the town. From the people who might have been his friends. And the women in his life had never meant anything more to him than a few hours of shared pleasure.

But he had reasons for living as he did.

"And what about Jack?"

"Huh?" He blinked down at her.

"He's just a little boy, Cash," she said softly, her voice strained. "You became his friend. He *cares* about you. And now you're shutting him out, too. Why?"

"God, Jo, I could have killed him." Guilt swamped

Maureen Child

him, pushing aside everything else. "I was careless. He was curious and he could have *died.* It's better to just—"

"Leave?" she asked, her voice even softer now.

"I didn't mean to hurt him," he said, shifting his gaze to hers, hoping to read understanding there.

He didn't. And that fact jabbed at him. Had he done to Jack exactly what adults had done to *him* when he was a kid? God. When had life gotten so damn complicated?

"See, Cash? You leave, too."

Reaching out for her, he took her by the shoulders and let himself relish, just for a moment, the feel of her beneath his hands again. Then he let her go. "This is *my* choice, Jo. *Mine.* I've never had a relationship that worked out and I'm not going to experiment with you." That was true enough, though except for Diane, he'd never really *tried* to have a real relationship. "I thought we could be friends. Fine. We can't. So this is where it ends. I don't want to hurt you."

"You really are an idiot, Cash."

"Thanks very much."

"So *what* if things go wrong?" she asked, and her impatience fired a spark of temper in her eyes. "You work through it. You shout, you fight, you make up. That's *life.* It's messy. It's dangerous and it's *painful.* Nobody's happy all the time, Cash. If you were, you'd get locked up in a rubber room and shot full of Thorazine. For God's sake, I was *raped.* My father had an affair while my mother was *dying.* Jack's a little boy and his mother *died.* Shit happens.

"The way you survive is leaning on the people you

love. Don't you get it, Cash? Love's a risk, but it's the only one worth taking."

Taking a chance, she held out one hand to him, hoping he'd take it. Hoping he'd believe in them—believe in *her* enough to risk his heart.

He stared at her for so long and so hard, Jo thought that maybe she'd gotten through. Maybe her words had battered away at the wall he'd erected around his heart, his soul.

She understood the fear of pain. Understood wanting to avoid it. But damn it, she was Italian. She could *never* understand turning down a chance at *love*.

"I can't do it."

All the air left her as her empty hand fell back to her side. "Can't or won't?"

"Doesn't matter." A shutter dropped over his eyes, and instead of the pain she'd felt in him a moment ago, now there was just cool detachment. "See, I'd rather lose you now, than later."

She reached up and snatched her hat off, wanting to throw it to the ground and jump up and down on it in frustration. Her emotions were raw, chafed, and sore. In just a few minutes' worth of talk, he'd battered a tender heart and ruined a perfectly good daydream of happily ever after. Finally, though, she welcomed a slow burn of anger, warming the chill inside. "Why are you so damn sure you're going to lose me?"

"Because I've lost everyone I've ever loved—except Grace. I want you, Jo, but I won't risk it. Not even for you. Because if I did and lost you anyway, the p... would kill me."

"You're an idiot."

A sad smile curved his mouth briefly. "You've said that before."

Tears made him blurry, but she fought them back, refusing to let him see her cry. Her mouth worked as she battled for control and she didn't speak again until she was sure her voice wouldn't break as neatly as her heart had.

"Yeah, but this is the first time I've really meant it." Sadly, she turned for her truck and paused with one hand on the door handle. Turning to look back at him one last time, she whispered, "I guess Mike was right after all. You *don't* deserve me."

At the Stevenson job, Hank Marconi stood back to take a long look at the cement slab being poured. His subcontractor, Reilly Concrete, didn't need any help, but Hank preferred keeping an eye on things.

Maybe, he thought, if he'd been paying closer attention over the years, he might have been able to find a way to help Josefina earlier. If he'd opened his eyes, he might have noticed that there was something going on between Cash and Jo without having to be told by a ten-year-old boy.

But, he thought, folding his hands atop a shovel handle and resting his chin on them, like Grace always said, things happen when they're supposed to. He wasn't sure he believed that entirely, but it was more comforting than sorting over your mistakes.

"Henry?"

Surprise jolted him, but he straightened up and turned around, already smiling as he watched Grace approach. Amazing that just hearing her voice could him feel like a teenager again. His palms went damp, his heartbeat quickened, and his stomach jumped with excitement.

He walked to meet her, holding out one hand to help her make her way across a minefield of construction tools. She was small and perfect. From her neatly styled hair to the designer shoes on her tiny feet. He was a lucky man and he knew it. He'd found *real* love, twice in a single lifetime.

When his wife, Sylvia, died so long ago, she'd taken most of his heart with her. He'd been lost in his own misery—until Grace. She'd helped him to live again. She'd shown him that love wasn't only for the young.

"What brings you out here?" he asked, guiding her to a chair in the far corner of the Stevenson yard.

The roar of the cement truck moaned on as the workers scooped the wet stuff out with shovels.

"I called Mike," Grace said, pitching her voice to be heard over that roar. "She told me where I could find you. I had to see you, Henry."

"Grace." He went down on one knee in front of her and took both of her hands in his. "What's wrong?"

"Nothing," she said, and squeezed his hands. "And everything."

For the first time, he noticed that her hair wasn't entirely perfect today. A strand or two was out of place and the makeup she never left the house without had been slapped on hurriedly. "You're starting to worry me."

"No, no. It's not like that. Oh, Henry." She pulled her hands free to cup his bearded face. "I'm such a fool."

"Says who?"

"Me, you wonderful man. But thank you for automatically leaping to my defense. Though I don't deserve it." She laughed and he felt better, but things were still pretty strange.

"You want to tell me what's going on, Grace?"

"I've come to my senses, Henry. Finally and at long last, I've come to my senses."

"Still not making things clear, honey."

"I know, but I will. You've asked me to marry you three times, haven't you?"

"Yes." He said it gruffly, remembering how she'd turned him down every time. It was the only flaw he'd ever found in her. This refusal to share his name. "And you said no all three times. What's your point, Grace?"

"My point is that *I* want to ask you this time, Henry. I want you to forgive me for being so stubborn and prideful and foolish. For not having the strength of heart that *you* have."

"Grace—"

"I'm asking you to marry me, Henry. Soon."

Pleasure swelled in his chest and his heart felt full enough to burst, but he had to know. "You've always said you preferred living in sin with me. What changed your mind?"

She leaned into him, kissed him hard and fast and then smiled wistfully. "I realized, Henry, that the only sin between us was the one I kept making. The sin of not appreciating your love. The sin of cowardice. I was too afraid to try again. Too afraid of my past to see a future."

He smiled. "And now?"

"Now, the future is *all* I see. And my future is *you*. I *love* you, Henry Marconi, and I would be so proud to be your wife."

Emotion clogged his throat and filled his eyes. Carefully, as if she were made of spun sugar, he pulled her into his arms and held her close, next to his heart.

"Marry me, Gracie, *amore mio,* my love."

She pulled back, looked him in the eye, and crying, said, "Yes, please."

"Well, that's perfect, isn't it?"

"You should be happy for Papa," Sam told Jo as she marched in familiar circles around Mike's sofa.

"I am happy for him," Jo said, thinking about the look on her father's face that evening when he'd broken the news. Heck, even Nana had bent far enough to wish him luck now that he would no longer be sinning.

"But don't you think it's a little pathetic? On the same day I crash and burn with Cash, my *father* gets engaged? What kind of universe is this?" *Oh God, oh God.* She wanted to cry, but there just weren't any more tears. She wanted to scream, but it wouldn't help. She wanted to go see Cash.

And knew she couldn't.

"What'd Cash say?" Mike asked the question they'd all been dancing around.

Jo stopped walking, and looked out at Jack, playing catch in the front yard with Lucas. The boy would heal, she thought. And so would she. Eventually. "Doesn't really matter how he said no, does it?"

She turned back around to look at her sisters as outside, the baseball slammed into the house with a thud.

"The point is, Cash loves me but he's too damn stubborn to admit it. And short of torture, I can't think of a way to make him say the words." Amazingly enough, there *were* a few tears left. She wiped them away. "Besides, I don't *want* a man I have to force to love me. So. It's over."

"Doesn't sound over to me," Sam muttered.

"It will be, as soon as I stop thinking about him," Jo told her. "Shouldn't take more than a year or two. Or a dozen."

"He's a jerk."

"Thank you, Sam. He is."

"He doesn't deserve you."

She smiled at Mike. "I told him you said that."

A second passed, then two, then another. And finally, Jo erupted, breaking the silence with a heartfelt question. "Who wants him, anyway?"

"Uh, *you*?" Mike asked.

She flopped onto the couch. "I hate when you're right."

Twenty

Cash's eyes felt gritty. Like marbles stuck in a bucket of sand. He reached up and rubbed them with his thumb and forefinger, but it didn't help. What he *needed* was sleep. But every time he shut his eyes, he saw Josefina. Saying good-bye to him.

For two days—or was it three?—he'd been in a fog. He heard Jo's voice, saw the disappointment etched onto her features, heard the rumble of the truck engine as she drove out of his life.

Blowing out a heavy breath, Cash ripped a slice of bread into bits and tossed them out onto the surface of the lake. The ducks came close, zeroing in on the free food like missiles on a guidance system. He smiled in spite of the thoughts crashing through his mind like bumper cars with crazed kids at the wheel.

Absently, he continued feeding the ducks while at the same time he sorted through those careening thoughts, trying to find his way again. His road had always been clear to him. He'd known what to do, how to act, what to think.

Now, it seemed as though the more time he put into trying to figure things out, the fuzzier everything got. He tossed a chunk of bread at the male duck, who, instead of eating it, used his bill to push it at his mate. "Even ol' Donald there's got his priorities straighter than you do," he muttered.

But then Donald Duck, sitting in his little lake, didn't have to worry about his mate flying off and leaving him. "Or do you?" he asked, tossing the last of the bread at the pair of squawkers. "Do you worry and love her anyway?"

Man, you are in deep trouble when you start having meaningful dialogues with ducks.

Dropping to the dewy grass at the edge of the lake, he drew his knees up, braced his forearms atop them, and let his empty hands dangle. Cash stared past the reeds, dipping and swaying in front of him, to the center of the lake. He stared blindly at the wind-driven ripples on the cool surface. The morning sunlight glanced off the lake and shot into his already aching eyes, but Cash figured he had the extra pain coming. Christ knew, he'd caused Jo plenty.

But she didn't understand—nobody did. Not even Grace. And now that she was *engaged,* for God's sake, to Hank Marconi, she was further from siding with him than ever.

But Grace didn't matter. It was Jo who had to see what he meant. How he felt. And he didn't know how in the hell to *make* her see. He remembered exactly why he'd avoided getting close to anyone since losing Diane and her son in college. He'd loved them both with everything he had in him, and when she left him, when she took her child and walked away, Cash had felt as if he'd lost a limb. As if his body, his soul, had been hollowed out.

It had taken months and months to recover, and at

times, he'd doubted he ever would. Everything he'd wanted his whole life, he'd finally found with Diane. And then suddenly, it was all gone again.

When he'd at last reclaimed his life, he'd made a vow to never care that deeply for anyone again. To never again risk that kind of loss. That kind of pain.

Now, those feelings were back and deeper, stronger, than they'd been so long ago. What he felt for Josefina was so much bigger than what he'd been capable of back then, that he knew the pain of losing her would be commensurate. Bigger. Harder. Enough to kill him. Losing her now was hard. Losing her later was unthinkable.

What kind of idiot was he that he hadn't noticed what had been happening? How had Josefina and her brother become such an integral part of his life? And what the hell could he do about it now?

The rest of his life stretched out in front of him, emptier than he wanted to think about. There would be no Marconis making him nuts. No more Josefina, spitting fire one minute and kissing him brainless the next. No more Jack, laughing and driving him nuts in the workshop.

"You ruined *everything!*"

Startled, Cash turned and watched a furious little boy rushing at him. God, he'd been so wrapped up in his own misery, he hadn't even heard the kid coming. Pushing to his feet, he was standing when Jack charged him. The cast on his left arm, covered now with names and drawings and fraying at the edge, caught Cash in the center of his chest and the air left him in a whoosh.

"Jack." He grabbed the boy and held him still,

though the kid was such a mass of fury and emotion, it was like trying to keep hold of a handful of Jell-O.

"Lemme go," he shouted, kicking out and nailing Cash's shin with unerring accuracy.

"Hey!" He released him instantly, then reached down to rub his leg. "What's going on?"

The boy was neat and clean. His hair had been cut, his jeans actually *fit* him, he was wearing a blue shirt with a collar, and it looked as if he'd finally gotten a new pair of sneakers. But his pale blue eyes, so much like his older sister's, were filled with hot, angry tears and a flush of temper stained his cheeks.

"What's *wrong* with you?" Jack demanded. "You messed up everything."

Confusion rattled in Cash's mind, but dealing with a Marconi always produced that reaction. "You want to tell me what I did?"

"You made Jo *cry*."

Ah God. "Jack . . ."

"No!" The boy gave him a one-armed push that didn't budge him an inch. "It was all gonna be great. Me'n Jo were gonna live here with you and you guys would get married and I could work on the furniture with you and we'd go to my ball games and—"

Cash's heart took a nosedive. While the adults had been dancing around each other, a little boy had been building dreams. And God, he remembered all too clearly how precious a little boy's dreams were. How easily shattered. How devastating when grown-ups paid no attention to their destruction.

Jo'd been right about this, too, he thought grimly. He'd become friends with a lonely little boy, then when things got complicated, he'd bailed. He'd done exactly what had been done to him as a kid. He'd turned his back on affection in favor of clinging to fear. He'd let Jo walk away when everything in him had wanted to beg her to stay.

He'd let pain become his anchor instead of hope.

"Jack," he said, going down on one knee in the still-damp grass. "I'm really sorry."

"Sorry doesn't matter." His voice broke and Cash wasn't sure which of them was more shattered by the sound.

"I heard Jo talking to Mike and Sam the other night at Mike's house." Jack was talking again, one word tumbling after the other, in a torrent that seemed to be pouring directly from his bruised heart. "She said that you didn't say you *love* her. Why didn't you *say* it?"

Cash dipped his head, avoiding the hurt in those eyes, and viciously rubbed the back of his neck. The kid had hit it right on the nose. He *had* ruined everything. He'd had a shot at something great. Something real. And he'd let it slip through his fingers.

"I know you love her. I saw you kissing and stuff."

"Jack," he started, then stopped, not knowing what the hell to say next. How to explain to a kid that adults got scared, too? How to tell a little boy that the man he admired had less courage than he did himself?

"My mom used to tell me every day," Jack rushed on, not giving him a chance. "She said 'I love you' were the most important words in the *world*. She said *everybody* knows that. How can you be a grown-up and not know that?"

"It's not that easy, Jack," he said, wearily getting to

his feet as the boy stormed at him. Tears spilled over onto flushed cheeks and the kid's breath huffed like a steam engine.

"Sure it is," he said, wiping his nose with his forearm and frantically blinking away the tears. "Jo loves you, Cash. I heard her. She told Mike she loves you."

Something inside Cash shattered, splintered into thousands of jagged shards that tore at his soul, his heart, leaving him bleeding. *God*. She did love him. He'd seen it in her eyes. Heard it in her voice. And hadn't wanted to trust it. Hadn't wanted to let go of old pains long enough to grab a chance at joy.

I love you. He'd never said those words . . . to anyone. Not even to Diane. He'd held them back, waiting, always waiting for the rug to be pulled out from under his feet. He'd locked away his heart, then blamed everyone else for not wanting it.

"You ruined it, Cash," Jack said, his voice now a painful hush. "And you made Jo cry. A lot. She's graduating today and she should be happy, but she's not. 'Cause of *you*."

Graduation day?

"I'm a Marconi and Jo says Marconis stick together." Jack lifted his chin and glared up at the man who'd let him down so completely. "So I had to come here and do this."

He bunched his good right hand into a small, tight fist, then slammed it into Cash's stomach. It wasn't much of a blow, but pain shot through him anyway, right down to the soles of his feet.

"I *hate* you for making Jo cry." Jack turned and ran around to the front of the house.

Cash didn't move fast enough to stop him, but he

was in time to watch as the hurt little boy climbed onto his bike and rode off in a hurry, spraying up dirt in a rooster tail behind him.

The kid was right. He *had* ruined everything.

Which meant that it was up to *him* to fix it.

"Ohmigod!"

Lucas dropped to his wife's side. "What is it, are you okay? Is it the babies?"

"No, no." Mike waved him off irritably. "I just saw my *feet* for the first time in three weeks." My ankles look like *tree trunks*! And I'm talking *redwood* here, not aspen."

"Jeez, give me a heart attack," Lucas muttered, collapsing into the gunmetal-gray folding chair beside her. "You shouldn't have come today."

"Right." She snorted. "Like I'm not going to see Jo graduate." From her uncomfortable perch on the uncomfortable metal chair, Mike looked up at her family, all of them trying to spot Jo through the rampaging crowd. Thank God, everyone had been seated during the actual graduation ceremony, or Mike wouldn't have been able to see a thing. "She looked great, didn't she?"

"Yeah," he agreed, covering her hand with his. "She did good."

Mike grabbed hold of his hand and held on. "Damn right she did, and she didn't need that dumb SOB here, either."

"Give it a rest, Mike," Lucas sighed.

"Give it a rest?" She blinked at him, eyes wide, mouth hanging open in stunned shock. "Hello, have you met me? Mike Marconi?"

"Gallagher," he added with a smile.

"Okay, yeah, you've met me." She smiled back at him and wondered if falling in love had really mellowed her out. God, she hoped not. She really liked . . . "Ow."

"Ow?" He went pale. "Ow *what*?"

"Nothing. Just a backache. It's these crummy chairs . . ."

"You're sure."

"Course I'm sure." *Sort of*. A few pains. A couple of twinges. All normal when you're carrying around, like, a bazillion extra pounds of weight. Right? She was fine . . .

Changing the subject, she reached out and tugged on her father's shirt. "Do you see her, Papa?"

"Too many people," he grumbled, then helped Grace stand on one of the hideous chairs so she could see over the heads of the crowd.

"Issa no good for you, Michaela, so many people with the bambinos so close." Nana leaned over her, planting both aged hands on Mike's belly, as if communing with the children inside. "Issa too much."

"That's what I told her," Lucas complained.

"You're a gooda boy," Nana pronounced.

"I'm not going home," Mike said to no one in particular, then muffled another groan as a sharper pain shot from her backbone straight through the center of her. She was only surprised it didn't dart right out through her belly button like a bolt of lightning.

"What?" Nana's radar was on high alert.

"Nothing," Mike lied. "It's nothing."

"There she is," Grace shouted, and started waving both arms high in the air while screaming, *"Josefina! Over here!"*

"Gonna make a fine Marconi out of her," Mike said, approving of the near hysterical shouting, but no one was listening.

"Aunt Mike." Emma squeezed out from her father's grasp and plopped down on Lucas's lap. "Did you see my new puppy?"

"Sure did, kiddo."

"She's so soft, feel." Emma held the squirming golden retriever puppy out to receive a pet.

"I can't believe your mom let you bring the puppy."

"She couldn't stay home," Emma said, horrified at the idea. "I just got her yesterday, she woulda been scared without me."

Emma's face was wreathed with that ferocious fire of puppy love.

"What was I thinking?"

"Emma?" Sam's voice, worried, carried over the laughing, shouting, talking people. "Where's Emma?"

"She's here," Mike called back.

"Emma, don't you go anywhere. Stay right by Aunt Mike."

"I've got her," Lucas yelled, wrapping one arm around his niece's waist for good measure.

"Where's Jo?" Mike demanded, getting really tired of her view. All she could see were butts. Denim-covered, silk-covered, wide ones, narrow ones, fat ones, and toned ones. People talked, people moved around, and here she sat, trapped by her own humongous weight, unable to stand on her *tree trunks* to join the crowd. Stuck in this chair, she wouldn't be able to see Jo unless her sister were kneeling in front of her.

"Here she comes, here she comes!" Grace shouted louder, waved her arms, then wrapped one arm around

Papa's neck for balance. Still shouting, she called out a description. "Oh, Mike, she looks so *happy*! She's carrying the flowers you gave her, Henry. And— Oh dear."

"What?" Mike shouted.

"Did you *see* that?" Sam demanded. "Jeff, go hit him!"

"Hit *who*?" Mike slapped her father's back, trying for information.

"I'm not going to hit the poor guy," Jeff was saying. "I know what it's like dealing with Marconi women."

"Amen," Lucas shouted.

Mike glared at the man she loved. "Will somebody tell me what the hell's going on?"

"It's *Cash*," Jack yelled, and pushed through the crowd of family members to come to Mike's side. Leaning down, his grin was wide and excitement danced in his eyes. "Cash *came*. He went up to get Jo and started pulling her away, but she was pulling back and then she hit him with the flowers."

"She *did*?" *Damn*. And she'd missed it.

"Twice," Jack said, holding up two fingers just in case she missed his shout.

Mike loved it and wanted to know more. Quickly, she urged the kid up onto the chair next to her. "Get up there, little brother. Give me a blow-by-blow description."

"A what?"

"You know, like on *Monday Night Football*? A play-by-play. Pretend you're John Madden," Mike urged, ignoring her husband telling her to butt out. Like any Marconi was going to butt out of this. *Hah!*

"Okay—" Jack jumped a little and held on to his father for stability. "I see 'em."

"What're they doing?" Mike yelled, absently wiping puppy drool off her arm.

"Jo's yelling at him!"

"Way to go, Josefina!" Sam crowed from the front of the crowd.

"What'd Cash do?" Mike bit her lip as another, stronger pain hit her like a sledgehammer. Starting at the tips of her toes, it shot straight up her body until it funneled out the top of her head. *Wow.* Okay, that can't be good. She took an experimental breath and didn't pass out, so she figured she had a few minutes yet.

"I wanna see," Emma shouted, squirming on Lucas's lap. "If Jack gets to see, I get to!"

"Oh gross . . ." Jack groaned.

"What?" Mike shouted, pain forgotten in her frantic need to *know*. "What's happening?"

"He's kissin' her!"

"Fighting dirty," Sam said.

"Way to go, Cash," Lucas called.

"Now what?" Mike demanded, jamming an elbow into her beloved's ribs.

"He's talking to her," Jack said, a tone of hope in his voice.

"Is she talking back?"

"Nope," Jack said, sounding just a little disappointed. "She's shaking her head hard. Her dumb hat fell off."

"Mortarboards aren't really hats," Grace said.

"Not the point," Mike reminded her.

"Oh, hey, he's kissing her again," Jack yelled.

"That's nice," Emma sighed. "Like a fairy tale."

"Is she kissing him back?" Mike asked.

"How do I tell?"

She opened her mouth.

"Michaela . . ." Papa's warning voice rumbled out.

"Fine, fine . . . Is she hugging him?"

"Nope," Jack yelled. "Oh, she just kicked him!"

"Score one for our side," Sam said, and leaned through the crowd to slap Mike's upraised hand.

"I wanna see Aunt Jo, too." Emma crawled out of Lucas's lap, and climbed onto the folding chair beside Jack. The little girl's black patent-leather shoes were slippery, though, and when she fell, the puppy tumbled free and took off like a shot. The last anyone saw of her was a small white ball of fluff, darting between hundreds of pairs of legs.

"Missy!" Emma's squeal, pitched only slightly lower than a dog whistle, slammed through every head there. *"Daddy, catch her!"*

Everyone moved at once. Jack jumped off the chair, helped Emma up, and threaded his way through the sea of people crowding around the graduates. Even from Mike's vantage point, she saw people jump out of the way as the puppy careened past. A woman in a white sheath with violent purple pansies all over it stumbled back, crashing into a graduate, who then toppled onto an old man, knocking his walker into the fray. The walker caught another woman's skirt and lifted it high enough for her to get the mother of all gooses.

Then the rest of the family jumped into the fray. Jeff was already in pursuit of his daughter's puppy while Grace shouted directions to him and Sam was hanging on to Emma while the little girl sobbed her heart out.

Lucas patted Mike's hand and Mike tried to ignore the vise tightening around her middle.

"There she is!" Grace shouted. "Just past the statue of the ugly thing!"

Jeff took off at an angle, dodging people, keeping his gaze glued to the ground. He didn't see the flower cart in time and did a head-first somersault before popping back up again like a circus acrobat.

"Way to go, Jeff!" Grace yelled.

"Go help." Mike let go of Lucas's hand and smiled at him. After a moment's hesitation, he was off and running.

"Left, Lucas, go *left*," Grace called out, gesturing wildly with both arms now. "Head her off at the pass! Oh!" She winced. "That must have hurt, poor woman."

"Oh, Mommy, she's gone, *she's gone*!" Emma's wail was reaching heights Pavarotti would have envied.

Mike shifted on her chair and squeezed her eyes shut as one more pain soared through her body. When she got her breath back, she shouted, "What happened to Jo and Cash?"

"I'm right here," Jo answered, appearing out of nowhere, holding a bouquet of stems with a few battered petals still clinging to them. Her hair was a wreck, her mouth was all puffy from what must have been a heck of a kiss, and there was fire in her eyes—which to Mike's way of thinking was *way* better than the misery she'd seen there earlier this morning.

"Where'd everybody go?" Jo asked.

"Chasing the puppy," Sam said, still patting Emma's back.

"The puppy made a break for it," Mike said, and

rubbed her belly, as if trying to calm the kids down just a little.

"She could be *dying*," Emma screeched.

Everyone winced.

"Issa no good, all this excitement for Michaela," Nana said, and crossed herself to show them all she meant business.

"You okay, Mike?" Jo dropped into a chair next to her.

"Sure. Fine." She was breathing a little heavily but no way was she going to miss all of this.

"Jo, damn it, you have to listen to me," Cash said as he pushed through the crowd, stopping to apologize to the woman whose hat he'd knocked off.

"No I don't," she said.

"I'm sorry!" He threw both hands high. "How many times do I have to say it? I'm an idiot. Like you said."

"He is pretty convincing," Mike said.

"Mike, you're looking a little pale," Jo whispered.

"I'm feeling a little—"

"Its'a the bambinos!" Nana shouted. Then, drawing up to her full four feet nine inches, she stretched up her arms toward heaven and yelled, "The bambinos! They *come*!"

"Anybody miss that?" Mike asked, cringing a little as people started turning to stare.

"I told you not to deliver at the graduation!" She smiled, patted Mike's face, then jumped to her feet, demanding, "Where the hell's Lucas?"

"He's chasing the puppy," Papa said, sitting down to take Mike's hand in his.

"We'll find him!" Grace shouted, then bailed off her

chair and dived into the crowd, a white-haired tornado on a mission.

"Aunt Mike, are your babies coming now?" Emma asked, coming closer to stare at the hem of Mike's dress, as if expecting to see little heads pop out to say howdy.

"Oh, dear God," Mike moaned.

"Sorry, Mike," Cash said, "but I've got to get this said. Jo, you have to listen." He grabbed her, but she shook him off.

"I can't listen to you now, Mike's having her baby and we need to get her to the hospital."

"Issa no need to worry," Nana said, kneeling down in front of Mike. "I am here. I take care of the bambinos."

Horrified, Mike stared at the wizened little woman already getting into position. "Nana, I love you, but no way! Oh God, where's Lucas?" She grabbed her father's hand and squeezed hard enough to break bones.

"He's coming!" Sam said from her perch on one of the chairs. Then, to someone else, she snarled, "Mind your own business, haven't you ever seen someone give birth?"

"Oh God, not giving birth," Mike moaned. "I want a hospital. I want *drugs.*"

"It's okay, Mike, we'll get you there," Jo promised, trying not to look at Cash, trying not to read too much into his being here. She'd almost fainted when he came up out of the crowd, insisting that he'd had to be a part of her big day.

"Getting a little serious here, people!" Mike groaned and tried to lever herself to her feet. No way. Wasn't gonna happen. Not under her own power, anyway.

"No stand up, sit, sit, stay *quieta*," Nana said, still looking ready to play doctor.

"Mike? Michaela?"

"Lucas, oh, thank God." She waved a hand at her husband. "Get me to the hospital, will you?"

"Right. I'll get the car." Lucas stood up, turned in a fast circle, stared at Jo and shouted, *"Where's the car?"*

"Relax, Rocket Man," Mike laughed at her husband's panic, but ended up whimpering.

"Oh, my God. Get a car," the calm, logical, sensible scientist shouted. *"Anybody's* car!"

"We need hot water," Nana said.

"Nana, you're *not* a doctor," Jo reminded her.

"Emma baby, I found your puppy!" Jeff rushed into the family group, cradling a happy, thoroughly excited retriever.

"Missy!"

Cash watched them all, on the outside again, and he knew without a single doubt in his mind that he wanted to be *inside*. He wanted, needed, these crazy, warm, wonderful people in his life.

He wanted to be a part of the Marconi family circus. He wanted to be one of the lucky men who were loved by a Marconi woman. And he damn well wasn't leaving until Jo heard him out.

"Jo, I was so wrong. I can't believe how wrong I was. You were right," he added, tossing that in, hoping she'd appreciate it. "I've been hiding all my life."

She just stared at him.

But at least she was still looking at him.

"I'm tired of it. I want more. I *need* more," Cash

said, his voice throbbing with the ache inside. "I *need* you. I need you in my life. Because without you, *Josefina,* there *is* no life."

She licked her lips, shot an uneasy glance at her family. Weakening? he wondered. God, he hoped so.

"You're everything," he said, letting all he felt pour from his gaze. "You're more than I ever dreamed. More than I deserve."

"Got that right," Mike muttered, and Jo frowned at her.

"Give me a chance," Cash said, taking one hesitant step toward her. "Let me prove to you how important you are to me. Give me a lifetime to prove it."

She stared at him, then slowly shook her head, and Cash saw his future slipping away before his eyes.

"Did you bother to tell her that you're in love with her?" Jeff asked, handing the puppy to his daughter.

"No," Cash admitted with a choked laugh. "I didn't."

"Might be a good place to start," Jeff said, moving to stand next to Cash.

"I *do* love you, Josefina," Cash said, gaze locked on her again. "More than I've ever loved anything in my life."

Lucas shifted a look from his wife to Cash and Jeff, then slowly stood up and aligned himself with the men. Looking at Jo, he said, "Give the guy a break. I know how scary it is to fall in love with a Marconi. Makes you say and do some pretty dumb things."

"Hey," Mike said, clearly offended.

Jack pushed through his sisters to stand in front of Cash. Facing Jo, he said, "He does too love you, Jo.

And you should listen to him. 'Cause then you could marry him and we could all live in the big house."

Jo scowled at them. The Marconi men banding together. Then Cash gave her a smile that warmed her through despite her hesitation. He was here, standing in the middle of Marconi central, asking her to let him in. Asking her to stay.

To let *him* stay.

The sunshine spread out over the interested crowd and dazzled her eyes until she was pretty sure Cash was highlighted by a golden light beaming directly at her.

"You're all nuts," Mike managed to say between panting breaths. "I'm in *labor,* here—*remember*?"

"You'll be fine, honey." Sam gave Mike's hand a sympathetic pat, then walked over to stand next to her husband.

"Sam!" Shocked, Jo glared at her.

"Men are idiots, true," Sam said, kissing Jeff's cheek. "No offense, honey. But at least Cash is here, trying to say the right thing."

Papa took Grace's hand and led her over to stand with the others at Cash's side.

"You, too, Papa?"

"It's time, Josefina. Let go of the past. Grab your future." He slapped one beefy hand against Cash's back with enough force to send him staggering. "He loves you, Josefina. Don't hold the hurt so tightly you can hold nothing else."

Jo's conviction wavered as her gaze slid from one member of her family to another until finally settling on Cash. His gaze locked with hers and she *felt* the power of his love surround her and lift her higher than she ever thought she could fly.

Behind her, Mike was panting, Nana had her rosary out, and Emma wanted to see the babies. But otherwise, her entire family had sided with Cash. She was standing alone, but staring into Cash's eyes, she knew she would never have to stand alone again—if she could forgive him for doubting, and trust in him now.

"I love you so much, Josefina," Cash whispered, heart in his eyes.

And suddenly, the answer was so clear. So wonderfully, miraculously *clear.*

Slowly, her mouth curved, wider, wider, until she was grinning like a loon.

"Fine!" She shouted it, laughing, then threw up her hands in surrender. Her royal-blue graduation gown slapped in the wind and she'd never felt better. "I *love you*! We'll get married! Everybody happy now?"

Applause and shouts of approval rose up from the crowd, but Cash had heard enough. Grinning like a crazy man, he ran at her, scooped her up and swung her in a tight circle, kissing her as if her lips meant life.

And maybe they did.

"Hey!" Mike's shriek brought them all back to earth. Eyes wide, looking just a little panicked, she said, "I *told* you guys I was in labor. My water just broke. *Now* can we go to the hospital?"

In moments, the Marconi family, *all* of them, had Mike bundled into a car, and they formed a small but determined convoy on the Coast Road toward Chandler Community Hospital. Together, they waited in the pale green lobby that had seen both misery and joy over the years. Together, they waited for the news that all was well. That Mike and her children were safe.

And three hours later, when a tired Lucas staggered out to join them, a dazed grin on his face, the Marconi family welcomed Justine and Sylvia Gallagher into the world.

Epilogue

Three and a half months later . . .

Jo Marconi went to six o'clock mass on the morning of her wedding.

She sat in the back pew of St. Joseph's church and let the familiar rituals wash over her in comforting waves. The sounds, the words, the smells, all took her back to a childhood that had led her here. To this one moment.

And as mass ended and the other early worshippers slipped from the quiet church, Jo kept her seat, waiting for the privacy she needed. Her gaze swept over the old church. She'd spent every Sunday of her childhood here. Her gaze shifted around the inside of the church. Gray stone walls, stained-glass windows allowing rainbows of sunlight to stream down on pews polished by years of devoted Catholics sliding across them. She'd made her first Communion here, her Confirmation, and today, she'd be married in front of that altar.

When she was alone in the quiet that somehow always seemed more profound in a church, she looked up at the crucifix behind the altar. A year ago, she'd come to shout at God. To tell Him she didn't need Him anymore.

And now she was back.

To thank Him for not giving up on her.

She slid out of her pew and walked up the center aisle, her boot heels clicking noisily against the stone. A sense of peace rose up in her and she smiled as she knelt on the cold marble kneeler before a gleaming mahogany altar rail.

"I'm back," she said, her voice echoing weirdly in the quiet. "And I missed You. I missed being here and I wanted You to know that I won't be staying away again."

Her hands curled over the cool slick wood in front of her as she stared up at the beautifully carved crucifix. "Before, I blamed You for everything that was going so wrong, but I guess You know that." She dipped her head in apology, then said what she'd come to say.

"I finally figured it out. You're not supposed to make everything right. Not Your job. That's *our* job." She took a breath, smiled, and released it again slowly as a whisper. "I'm going to be all right. I wanted You to know that, too. The family's good. Happy. And so am I. At last."

She pushed up from the kneeler, stepped back and genuflected, crossing herself in the age-old symbol of faith. Then she winked up at the man on the cross. "I'll see You this afternoon."

And as she left, still smiling, Monsignor Gable stepped out of the shadows. Lifting his gaze to heaven, he whispered, "Nice job."

At three o'clock in the afternoon, the old church was crowded. Seemed as though everyone in Chandler had turned out for Josefina Marconi's wedding.

The organ in the choir loft groaned and sighed and people shifted impatiently in their seats. The Donovan family took up one whole pew, with Trish shushing her five older brothers as if they were ten-year-olds.

Mama Candellano bounced Carla's baby girl on her knee while hooking her free arm around her grandson Jonas's shoulders. Carla and her husband, Jackson Wyatt, leaned into each other. Nick Candellano and his wife, Tasha, shared a secret smile over the coming baby no one knew about yet, while Nick cradled the child they'd already made together. Paul Candellano and his wife, Stevie, tried to shush their baby girl, but her wail bounced off the walls of the old church, picking up steam as it went. Beth and Tony Candellano tried to corral their kids, but they were determined to march up and down the polished pews, their shoes clip-clopping like quickened heartbeats.

In the front row, looking very self-satisfied, Jack grinned, as if he'd planned the wedding himself. Nana Coletti sat between Mike and Lucas, shifting her gaze from one great-granddaughter to the other, as if she couldn't get enough of them. Sam and Jeff tried to assure Emma that her puppy would be fine waiting for her at home, but she wasn't convinced. Sam rubbed one hand over her belly and worried.

Grace, newly married, her face still flush with freshly realized love, sat in the front pew, looking back, waiting for a glimpse of her new husband and stepdaughter. When Jo and Cash got back from their honeymoon, Papa and Grace would be leaving on their cruise to Europe. But today was for family.

And Jo stood in the back of the church where all of her life's most important moments had happened and smiled at all of them. She had the life she'd always dreamed of. She had the love she'd secretly yearned for. She had more blessings in her life than anyone had a right to. And she was more grateful than she could say.

In just a few minutes, she'd have a new husband and a surrogate son. Jack would be living with her and Cash and neither of them would have it any other way.

Organ music swelled, filling the old church with soaring notes that felt like a blessing. Jo swallowed hard, took a deep breath, and tightened her grip on the ivory-ribbon-covered stems of her bouquet of blue and green hydrangeas.

She wore a sleeveless ivory gown, with a trail of pale crystal beads that edged the bodice and hem of the floor-length dress. Her veil billowed around her in a cloud of lace and tulle, held in place by a crystal tiara tucked into her hair, pulled up and away from her face. And for the first time in her life, she felt truly *beautiful*.

The ancient hymn being played slowly drifted into the "wedding march." Papa stepped up beside her, lifted her veil and looked at her through eyes blurry with tears.

"You are a vision, Josefina," he whispered, bending to give her a kiss. "I wish your mother were here to see you."

Just for a minute, Jo's eyes filled, too, but she blinked the tears back and smiled at the man who had been her first great love. "She *is*, Papa. She's here. Can't you feel her?"

His mouth worked and he cleared his throat before nodding gruffly. "Yes. I can. And she is as proud of you as I am."

"I love you, Papa," Jo said softly, reaching up to smooth his beard.

"And I you. Now, it's time to be married. To move into your future."

She nodded, took a step, then stopped. "You're sure you're okay with Jack's coming to live with Cash and me?"

"It's better. For him," Papa said, threading her arm through his. "And for Grace and me. My new wife, she likes to take trips, and I like to spend time with my new wife."

Jo inhaled sharply, nodded, then grinned despite a sudden flurry of nerves. "It's a little scary. I'm about to be a *wife*."

"Ah, but Cash is going to be a *husband*. And this is just as scary. Trust me on this, Josefina."

"I do trust you, Papa." Impulsively, she reached out and gave him a hard hug. "Thank you. For everything."

The organist hit a note a little harder than the others and started up the "Wedding March" from the beginning again. Impatient.

Patting her hand, Papa set off down the aisle with her and Jo smiled into the faces of those she loved. The people of Chandler. The people who had been a part of her life, always. She saw friends, family, and then she looked to the head of the aisle and she saw only Cash.

Handsome in an impeccably cut tuxedo, he stood alone at the altar. They'd agreed to have no attendants, wanting the ceremony to be only about *them*. And as Papa let her go and Cash took her hand in his, then lifted it to kiss her knuckles, she knew it was the right choice.

"I love you, Josefina," he whispered. "More than I ever thought possible."

"I love you, Cash," she said softly. "Forever."

She felt so sure of him—of *them*—she wanted to sing with it. Instead, she bent her head and listened as Monsignor Gable blessed their union and made them one.

A half hour later, the organist played the recessional as the happy couple kissed each other thoroughly to the sound of applause filling the old church. As Jo and Cash left the altar, laughing while they headed for the reception already set up in the meadow, Sam leaned in close to Jeff.

"Okay, wedding's over," she said, muffling a groan. "Your son's ready to be born. Let's rock and roll."